THE QUIET WAR
CANADIAN FRONT

MICHAEL J. LALONDE

THE QUIET WAR

CANADIAN FRONT

MICHAEL J. LALONDE

Published by North Vanguard Press™, an imprint of Vanguard Leaders Incorporated.
North Vanguard Press™ is a trademark of Vanguard Leaders Inc.
ISBNs
EBook: 978-1-0691114-0-1
Paperback: 978-1-0691114-2-5
Hardcover: 978-1-0691114-1-8
Audiobook: 978-1-0691114-4-9

The Quiet War: Canadian Front is a work of fiction. Names and incidents are either products of the author's imagination or are used fictitiously. Any resemblance to actual events or persons, living or dead, is entirely coincidental.

North Vanguard Press™
Toronto, ON
www.northvanguardpress.com

Cover background image licensed from Shutterstock (Image ID: 1329927230) by PRESSLAB.
Cover Design: Adam Hay Studio, UK
Editor: Amanda Clarke
Narrator: Justin Hay
Author: Michael J. Lalonde
Printed in Canada, the United States of America, the United Kingdom, and Australia.
Library and Archives Canada Cataloguing in Publication

Title: *The Quiet War*, Book 1: *Canadian Front* / Michael J. Lalonde.
Other titles: *Canadian Front*
Names: Lalonde, Michael J., author.
Identifiers: Canadiana (print) 2025031617X | Canadiana (ebook) 20250321939 | ISBN 9781069111418 (hardcover) | ISBN 9781069111425 (softcover) | ISBN 9781069111401 (Kindle)
Subjects: LCGFT: War fiction. | LCGFT: Political fiction. | LCGFT: Novels.
Classification: LCC PS8623.A4574 Q54 2025 | DDC C813/.6—dc23

"This book nails the mindset of Canadian special operations—calm under pressure, ruthless when it counts, and often carrying the weight afterward. It's as close to real as fiction gets."

- Randy Turner, retired JTF2 Assaulter and founder of Direct Action Combat Performance

"A superb opener to the Quiet War series – razor-sharp military action, masterful espionage, and a geopolitical premise that feels ripped from tomorrow's headlines. A thrill ride you won't want to put down."

- R.A. Flannagan, author of *The CANZUK at War Series*

"With steady pacing and grounded heroes this thriller feels too real and stands apart from other geopolitical stories by showing what Canada can do when it is force to act. The narrative is active and passionate, a cinematic glimpse into the high-stakes world of The Quiet War."

- NetGalley

The Quiet War Series

Canadian Front (2025)

Alpha One (2026)

Ready Aye Ready (2027)

Stories from The Quiet War

The First Lie (2025)

Vanguard Ranger (2027)

This book is dedicated to the men and women who keep Canada safe. To the unsung heroes whose efforts often go unnoticed. From Canada's first expeditionary force in the Boer War through the First and Second World Wars, the Korean War, peacekeeping operations, Afghanistan, Libya, Iraq, and the dozens of smaller conflicts we never hear about, Canadian soldiers have lain it all on the line so that people like you and me can sleep peacefully, without fear or worry about what the next day might bring.

We know all too well that not everyone in the world enjoys that sense of security. To those who never came home, and to those who did but were never the same, I thank you with the fullness of my heart. Your efforts and your sacrifices will never be forgotten.

"I did it not because I was superhuman, not because I wasn't scared, but because that's what we do. We stand between evil and the innocent... no matter the cost."

- Private Jess Randall Larochelle, Star of Military Valour, 1st Battalion, Royal Canadian Regiment

In September 2006, during a Taliban attack on his outpost in Afghanistan, Private Jess Larochelle volunteered to man an exposed machine-gun position—the last line between a few dozen enemy fighters and the Canadians behind him. When an RPG hit his position, the blast hurled him several metres, killing and wounding comrades and leaving him with a broken back, broken neck, and a detached retina.

When he regained consciousness and saw the position about to be overrun, Larochelle dragged himself back to the gun, fought on, and single-handedly broke the assault. After exhausting his machine-gun ammunition, he exposed himself to hostile fire to launch roughly fifteen M72 rockets, finally forcing the Taliban to withdraw.

Were it not for his actions, many Canadian soldiers could have been killed or captured by the Taliban. Private Larochelle single-handedly prevented a horrific national tragedy.

Larochelle was awarded the Star of Military Valour, Canada's second-highest honour. Many, including former Chief of the Defence Staff Rick Hillier, argue he should have received the Victoria Cross, and a growing movement is fighting to see that honour granted to him posthumously. I fully support this initiative and encourage Canadians to contact their Member of Parliament and the press for action.

LIST OF ABBREVIATIONS

Acronyms and abbreviations appearing in this book are drawn from actual Canadian, British, and American military and intelligence usage. They are presented here for reader clarity and authenticity.

CANADA

1 CAD – 1st Canadian Air Division
427 SOAS – 427 Special Operations Aviation Squadron
AAR – After-Action Review
C8 SFW – Special Forces Weapon
CAF – Canadian Armed Forces
CANSOFCOM – Canadian Special Operations Forces Command

CFB – Canadian Forces Base
CFSMI – Canadian Forces School of Military Intelligence
CJIRU – Canadian Joint Incident Response Unit
CJOC – Canadian Joint Operations Command
CSIS – Canadian Security Intelligence Service
CSOR – Canadian Special Operations
J2 – Senior Intelligence Officer within a joint headquarters
JTF2 – Joint Task Force Two
JTFX – Joint Task Force X
MRR – Modular Rail Rifle
RCAF – Royal Canadian Air Force
Recce – Reconnaissance
SH OP/SHOP – Source Handler Operator
SOATF – Special Operations Air Task Force

BRITISH
GCHQ – Government Communications Headquarters
NOC – Non-Official Cover
SAS – 22nd Special Air Service Regiment
SIS (MI6) – Secret Intelligence Service

AMERICAN
JSOC – Joint Special Operations Command

GENERAL/MULTINATIONAL
CQB – Close Quarters Battle
HUMINT – Human Intelligence
ISR – Intelligence, Surveillance, and Reconnaissance
NCO – Non-Commissioned Officer
NVGs – Night Vision Goggles
OP – Observation Post
OPFOR – Opposition Force

OSINT – Open Source Intelligence
POS – Position
QRF – Quick Reaction Force
SDR – Surveillance Detection Route
SITREP – Situation Report
SLLS – Stop, look, listen, and smell
SOF – Special Operations Force
SOP – Standard Operating Procedure
TOC – Tactical Operations Centre
UAV – Unmanned Aerial Vehicle

AUTHOR'S NOTE

Military, espionage, and political thrillers have long been dominated by the familiar pantheon of American and British special operations units and intelligence agencies—SEAL Team 6, Delta Force, the SAS, the SBS, the CIA, and MI6—with good reason: they are elite, battle-tested organizations that lend themselves to compelling fiction. But Canadian military fiction is notably absent from literature, Canadian special operations in particular. Even here at home, few Canadians know the capabilities of our own Tier-1 and Tier-2 units, Joint Task Force 2 (JTF2), and the Canadian Special Operations Regiment (CSOR). These men and women are among the best special operators in the world, yet fiction has largely left them behind.

With *The Quiet War* series, I wanted to change that. I set out to create a body of work that properly situates Canada's special operations and intelligence services within the broader allied community to show what our elite can do when push comes to shove and when our political leaders finally find the will to use them.

At the same time, I wanted to explore the human cost behind the heroism and the toll that war takes on those who fight it, the culture that drives them, and the often unrealistic demands placed on modern special operators. I wanted to confront the consequences of that culture and the price paid not only by those who serve, but by the families and nations that depend on them. Later instalments will also showcase Canada's conventional forces and the capabilities that they can bring to bear when properly resourced.

This series also examines another uncomfortable truth: the wilful blindness of Canada's political class across all parties when it comes to national defence. For too long, our leaders have assumed Canada would never be targeted. But what if that complacency were exploited? What if an adversary decided to test the limits of our readiness and our resolve?

As I began drawing up the premise behind *The Quiet War* and the antagonist's decision to topple Canada first, I started to brainstorm what it would take to bring our country to its knees. What I discovered chilled me to my core.

With a little creativity, it would be all too easy.

I found myself deleting several attack arcs out of fear of unintentionally delivering blueprints to potential adversaries. What remains is the backbone of the series.

The Quiet War is a fusion of high-tempo special operations, conventional warfare, espionage, and geopolitical intrigue set against the backdrop of modern hybrid warfare, where the most devastating battles are not always fought on distant battlefields. Some are being fought at home, in our own societies, against enemies we cannot see.

Misinformation, propaganda, and subversion can be as dangerous as bullets and bombs. What most don't realize is that a good portion of misinformation and propaganda originates outside our borders, sometimes coopting parts of our civil society into unwitting or even willing participants.

The series brings together deep, intimate character exploration with external conflicts where the stakes couldn't be higher: the preservation of the Western way of life. Defending a nation is a complex business, requiring contributions from several institutions and a myriad of personnel. Therefore, most of the formal installments in the series avoid the typical lone-wolf operative going rogue to save the day. They can certainly be fun stories to read, but my aim is to demonstrate how all the moving pieces of the puzzle come together, the frictions it can cause, and the challenges that need to be overcome. Through these stories, you'll get to see what works and what doesn't work.

The first novel, *Canadian Front*, serves as a brief introduction to JTF2 as the men of Alpha Team grapple with loss and a high-stakes mission. Although in recent years the Canadian Armed Forces (CAF) have been more forthcoming about their Tier-1 special operations unit, much about them remains shrouded in secrecy for good reason. Nothing in this book betrays that secrecy. The ranks of the characters, their positions, the teams, the unit's organizational structure, and tactics as depicted in the pages that follow should not be taken as gospel. I have never been a member of JTF2, nor am I privy to any special insider knowledge about the unit. What I do have is 23 years of military experience in the CAF, much of it as an intelligence officer, and a strong research ability—a necessary tool in the intelligence business. The narrative that follows is based on information readily available to the public, filtered through my creative process.

Since Canada is a nation with a rich history of multilateralism in all things, including military operations, the series will expand to include old allies like the United Kingdom and the United States as each nation struggles to counter Al-Najm al-Saghir and his global conspiracy. To our dear friends to the south and across the pond: you may notice some spelling choices that look a little off. That's because the book was written in Canadian English—a style of English some have described as sitting neatly between the American and British versions, which, when you think about it, is fitting given our geography.

This series is meant as much to entertain as to warn. If we continue down the path of complacency, it may not be long before a real Al-Najm appears and fiction gives way to a far colder reality. I hope you enjoy reading this first installment as much as I enjoyed writing it.

– Michael J. Lalonde
Toronto, Ontario

PROLOGUE

AL-NAJM AL-SAGHIR'S HEADQUARTERS
MOROCCO, UNKNOWN LOCATION
MONDAY, JUNE 3
15:00 LOCAL TIME

Control was an illusion. Al-Najm al-Saghir had long accepted this. Yet, in surrendering to that truth, he had learned to shape illusion into something more enduring. Every deception was an instrument, every detail a blade honed to a singular purpose. Nowhere was that philosophy more evident than where he now stood. Concealed behind jagged mountain rocks, the entrance was invisible unless one knew exactly where to look. Inside, the stone chamber felt ancient and untouched by time, the air cool and heavy with oppressive silence. At its centre stood a large steel table surrounded by metallic chairs. Al-Najm stood motionless, his dark eyes fixed calmly on the space soon to be occupied by his co-conspirators. Patience, after all, was a virtue he possessed in abundance.

Malik, one of Al-Najm's top lieutenants, waited nearby, shifting his weight restlessly as his fingers tapped silently against his thigh. Tall and broad-shouldered, with close-cropped blond hair and a jagged scar running along his jaw, he had the posture of a man accustomed to action, never truly at rest.

"Do you think they will go for it?"

Al-Najm did not answer at first. He let the silence settle, heavy as the stone around them. When he finally spoke, his words carried the faint precision of a manufactured Arabic accent. Each syllable deliberate, his tone calm and detached, the cadence almost too perfect to be native.

"They will."

Malik hesitated. "How can you be so sure?"

Al-Najm's gaze didn't shift. "Because they have failed. Repeatedly. They are men who imagine themselves architects yet build nothing. They will understand soon enough."

Malik nodded slowly.

Al-Najm watched him from the corner of his eye. Malik was a rare breed. He carried the quiet menace of a true believer, unwavering in purpose, yet he was more than a fanatic. He was competent, something most ideologues weren't. More importantly, he could grasp the shape of the larger design once it was revealed to him, which earned him a place at Al-Najm's side in this warren where every shadow seemed to watch.

The walls held their silence like a secret passed down through centuries. There were no cameras, no screens. Nothing electronic that could betray the conversation about to take place. Though it was unlikely any signal could pierce the depths of the mountain, Al-Najm had ensured the walls were embedded with Faraday shielding. Even if one of his visitors foolishly brought an electronic device, no signals would escape this room. As a final precaution, he had positioned his elite guards along the edges of the chamber, partially hidden by the shadows. Everything was in place.

This gathering, 20 years in the making, was the culmination of meticulous planning, manipulation, misinformation, alliance building, and a series of attacks across the globe that had left governments and economies in disarray without a trace of who was responsible. Unless Al-Najm wanted someone to take credit for his actions.

He combined strength and reason and forged himself into a weapon that could strike but could never be struck back. He worked hard to build a legitimate and productive life in the heart of Western society. Those who knew him as Al-Najm al-Saghir didn't know his real name, and those who knew him by his real name had no reason to suspect that he had risen to become one of the most powerful masterminds of subversion, manipulation, and violence in the world.

The few aware of Al-Najm's existence considered him a terrorist. They couldn't have been more wrong. Mere terrorism was sloppy, ineffectual, and outdated. Besides, most practitioners of terrorism used such practices to effect political change. A child's tactic for a child's goal. What he had in mind was far more ambitious. The acts of barbarism that terrorists were known for had a role to play. But absent a grand strategy to make them matter, such attacks accomplished little besides galvanizing a military response.

Long-term, these tactics could erode Western nations' resolve to wage war, but as far as Al-Najm was concerned, if it reached that point, he'd already lost. He cared little about who controlled Afghanistan, Iraq, or Syria. Nothing short of the destruction of the Western way of life would suffice. Influencing politics mattered not.

He was intent on reshaping entire societies.

His co-conspirators began to arrive and took their places around the table. When Al-Najm took his seat, a subtle tension filled the room. He always hid his face behind a dark keffiyeh, leaving only his calculating eyes exposed, though even those were hidden behind contact lenses that disguised their natural colour.

Assembled before him were senior generals from Russia, China, Iran, North Korea, and Venezuela, along with a few corporate magnates. Al-Najm scanned the room. Each of them was used to shaping events that altered nations. Though their backgrounds and cultures were vastly different, they all had two things in common: a desire to rid the globe of American influence and bitter impatience with the lack of progress on their respective national priorities. This made them vulnerable, which Al-Najm had leveraged with subtlety. Their presence wasn't sanctioned by their respective governments. Simply by gathering here, they had handed Al-Najm a weapon against them; exposure would bring dire consequences back home, making his grip on them all the stronger.

Al-Najm remained silent. He listened patiently to the discussion unfolding around him. It started cordially enough. Each of the generals vented their frustrations with American hegemony, but that was where their unity ended.

Ali Khorasani, a Brigadier General in Iran's Quds Force, leaned forward, his neatly trimmed beard flecked lightly with grey, framing a mouth drawn into a bitter scowl. "The Quds Force has disrupted American operations from Baghdad to

Beirut. We have paid in blood while you all debate and posture. When will the rest of you finally act?"

Colonel General Ivan Pavlovich Reznikov, head of the GRU, straightened in his chair, the cold intensity of his pale-blue eyes fixed squarely on Khorasani. "You speak of sacrifice and bloodshed as if Iranian soldiers were dying by the thousands," he said with barely concealed contempt. "Your Quds Force hides behind terrorists and proxies. Annoyances, nothing more." He waved his right hand dismissively. "If Iran's military dared to take direct action as we have in Ukraine, perhaps you might achieve more than headlines and petty sabotage."

General Wei Zhou of the People's Liberation Army turned slowly toward Reznikov. The lean Chinese officer adjusted his posture with minimal movement, radiating quiet disdain. "And what has your bold invasion achieved, General Reznikov? Your armies were driven from Kyiv by a vastly smaller nation. You have become trapped in a war of attrition. You have inflicted nowhere near enough damage to distract the Americans sufficiently. Until you manage that, China cannot move decisively on Taiwan."

Jin-Seong Park, Major General and Director of North Korea's Reconnaissance General Bureau (RGB), was about to speak until Al-Najm raised his hand.

A heavy silence blanketed the room. When Al-Najm finally spoke, his voice was deliberate. "Your frustrations are understandable. None of your nations have achieved any measure of success. That is why you are here," he said, leaving the implication to stand on its own. They needed him, and they knew it. "Thus far, your efforts have lacked unity of purpose. That changes now."

Al-Najm let his words linger. He watched the men absorb the gravity of their failures and the pact that lay before them.

Their eyes, full of suspicion, were now fixed on him. They knew only fragments of what Al-Najm had built: a global network that controlled some of the world's most powerful mercenaries, terror groups, and transnational criminal organizations, but his true power came from his mastery of information warfare. Al-Najm had turned entire populations against their governments using propaganda to twist narratives and sow discord. He manipulated the media, planted false stories, and fuelled anger across Western societies, though he couldn't take sole credit. The "new media," as he referred to it, had unwittingly helped a great deal.

His influence had infiltrated universities, social movements, and protests. He had weaponized the disillusionment of the West's youth. The irony of the situation was not lost on him. They were so quick to embrace Al-Najm's invisible hand, encouraging them to silence their opponents, that they could not see how they, too, would be silenced in the end.

Reznikov was the first to break the silence. "Let's get on with it. The Americans are weak and have a lame-duck president. We should devise a plan to attack quickly."

The others nodded in agreement.

"We attack them by not attacking them," Al-Najm said.

He stood and paced around the room, the eyes of the gathering following his every movement.

"Strike them directly, and you give the Americans a reason to unite. After the Soviet Union fell, the Americans turned inward. Divisions over race reignited. There were riots, domestic terrorism, cults, and armed militias. But 9/11 provided them a rallying point, and they fought back. They need a villain. Without one, they are once again devouring themselves."

Al-Najm stopped for a moment, focusing his gaze on the men around the table. "You would all rush to be that villain, but America's villains have a way of becoming its saviours." He shook his head. "There shall be no saviours for the Americans this time."

Al-Najm's voice dropped, taking on a sharper edge. "We start with Canada."

"Canada?" Khorasani scoffed. "Why bother with Canada?"

"You underestimate the power of an easy victory." Al-Najm's tone was calm, almost mocking. He resumed his pacing. "Canada is divided politically and culturally. Separatism is a persistent undercurrent in Quebec and the Prairies. Their western region feels abandoned. This kind of discontent festers and, unlike the Americans, they are unlikely to unite against anything except the United States." His voice carried a tang of irony.

"He has a point," Reznikov said. "Their military is weak, their internal security is scattered, and their government is consumed with social justice and identity politics. Canada is vulnerable in ways other NATO countries are not."

"Precisely," Al-Najm said. His gaze zeroed in on Zhou, knowing his next point would resonate with the general. "Its government is obsessed with style over substance, more concerned with appearances than actions. And large swaths of their public now question their own history. They suffer from an incurable national identity crisis. This makes them blind to real threats."

Zhou nodded silently then glanced at Park, who returned the nod.

Al-Najm allowed himself a faint smile under his keffiyeh. "My lieutenants have already planted seeds among Canada's youth, turning many of them against their government, particularly over Israel. They don't realize they are aligning with my network, but they will serve our purpose."

He sat back down, his voice taking on a hint of menace. "If we destroy Canada, the Americans will be forced to focus their attention on North America. It will hit close to home but won't have the same effect as attacking them directly. They will waste time searching for an enemy they cannot find. That will give each of you the opening you need to advance your nations' agendas."

Al-Najm spent the next two hours detailing his plan and assigning tasks to everyone in the room, patiently addressing their questions along the way.

"Impressive," Reznikov said. "The only problem I foresee is time. It will be difficult for any of us to bring our resources to bear so quickly without causing suspicion. We are all being watched by Western intelligence and our own internal security."

Park leaned forward, his round face brightening with a playful grin beneath slicked-back hair. A devoted student of Western culture, he'd opted for an expensive, open-collared shirt under a casual designer blazer. "I like your plan. I do. You can count on North Korea to unwittingly do its part," he said. "But I have to side with Comrade Reznikov." He smiled and winked at the Russian. "Your timeline is like trying to hit a fastball with a chopstick. It can't be done."

General Zhou let out a slow, deliberate exhale as he closed his eyes, pressing fingertips firmly against his forehead in quiet embarrassment over his junior partner's comments. He recovered his composure a beat later and looked at Al-Najm. "I can implement my part of the plan immediately, but I agree with the others. Your opening act comes too soon."

Over the next few minutes, each man around the table shared similar sentiments.

Al-Najm had anticipated this. He shared their assessment of the timeline. He had no intention of using their resources for his opening move, but he allowed them to express their thoughts nevertheless. These men needed to feel like they were in control, and illusions were his specialty.

Alexander Volk, one of the corporate magnates, exchanged a nod with Al-Najm. Volk's bearing was relaxed, standing out starkly among the military generals. The youngest at the table, in his mid-thirties, Volk had an angular face framed by thin, stylish glasses. His dark, wavy hair accentuated his youthful confidence.

"I can assist by providing professional mercenaries and cyberwarfare," Volk said, a tint of arrogance in his tone.

Reznikov's eyes flicked dismissively toward Volk's designer suit and polished appearance. "You sell your services to the West as readily as you do to any of us. Trusting you with my operations is out of the question."

"Indeed, I do, General. Which is why I can guarantee that the West will not discover our plans until it is too late. I designed their cybersecurity. I can influence what they know and don't know. And my mercenaries can support the first phase of the operation in Africa. The risk will be mine to take. If it doesn't work, you simply walk away."

Reznikov glanced at Al-Najm and nodded his approval.

"And what role will you be playing," Khorasani said, pointing his finger at Al-Najm, "aside from giving us orders?"

Al-Najm crossed his arms across his chest. "I've taken steps to collapse Canada's national health-care system, destroying a key pillar of what national patriotism they have left. Their political leaders will be too busy pointing fingers and salvaging their own careers to see the larger plan."

Khorasani leaned back in his chair and mulled it over. A moment later, he leaned forward, palms flat on the table. "Very well. I will play my part in this."

Seeing no further objections, Al-Najm clapped his hands together. "It is settled then. Preparations will begin at once. We do not stop at Canada, but it is where we begin. A small victory, but one that could fracture the Western alliance and create openings for us all."

As the men around the table took their leave, Al-Najm felt a deep sense of satisfaction as he reflected on the inevitable outcome that would soon follow.

Canada would not only fall. It would vanish. Quietly, completely. And no one would know who to blame.

1

RIO GRANDE CAFÉ
BELIZE CITY, BELIZE
SATURDAY, OCTOBER 12
22:09 LOCAL TIME

Retired Warrant Officer Nathan Cutler was finally settling into his new reality. Gone were the days of back-channel source meets in Mosul safe houses, late-night surveillance, and long, sandy convoys into some of the most dangerous cities on earth. He wasn't running agents in war zones anymore, wasn't passing bribes folded into matchbooks or whispering into secure phones in makeshift operations centres. After two years of civilian life, he was still trying to disengage the warrior side of his mind.

Now, sitting beneath the swaying limbs of a bougainvillea covered trellis, the warm breeze carrying the scent of sea salt and grilled snapper, Nathan let the soldier inside him loosen his grip. The soft clink of silverware and low murmur of conversation filled the open-air dining courtyard, lit by hanging bulbs that cast a golden hue across sun-worn stone and linen-covered tables. This part of town, a ten-minute walk from the Canadian consulate, was remarkably peaceful. Almost idyllic. A world away from the tension-soaked deserts he used to know.

The Canadian military had always been the fixed point on his compass, the thing that told him who he was and where he fit in the world. His wife had also been an important part of his identity. He'd taken great pride in the fact that his marriage had survived where so many others had failed. The long periods of isolation, the kind that soldiers felt despite being surrounded by their brothers in arms, always felt lighter knowing she was waiting for him when he got home. But she'd left him shortly after he got out of the army. Without his uniform to put on in the morning and his wife to come home to, Nathan had learned what it felt like to be truly alone.

Worse still, he could no longer afford the Canada he had fought for, nor did he recognize the country that bore its name. To him, it had become a place that celebrated the very erosion of the freedoms he had risked his life to protect, embracing a culture that celebrated the silencing of diverse points of view rather than defending liberty. So he'd left. Belize offered an affordable, tropical climate, and while it too had political frictions, it wasn't his country, so he didn't really care. He'd hoped his sojourn would offer a chance to reinvent himself and quiet his mind.

A warm breeze curled in off the water as he settled back in his chair. His plate was empty save for a smear of tamarind glaze and a few charred ends of plantain. He reached for his beer, already lukewarm, without thinking. Across the courtyard, the ceiling fans spun half-heartedly beneath the open rafters, doing little more than shifting the weight of the evening heat. Through the slow drift of air and lantern glow, Nathan saw motion at the edge of his vision. Keira was crossing the courtyard toward him, bare shoulders catching the light, long dirty blond braids swaying with each step.

He tried and failed to avoid staring at her as she approached while balancing two drinks with effortless grace. Her build was slim and athletic, the kind that always drew notice. Tonight it was framed by a cropped halter top clinging to sun-bronzed skin and a short wrap skirt that swayed with each step. The outfit was casual enough to pass as beachwear in Belize City, yet practical enough to serve as her uniform at the café.

"Fancy another beer, Mr. Cutler?" she said brightly, her British accent making the words sound far more inviting than a simple question.

"Isn't this your night off?" he asked, raising an eyebrow.

"It is." She beamed, sliding into the seat beside him, and passing him a beer.

Nathan drew back slightly, surprise flickering across his face. "Do you always come into work on your night off?"

Keira leaned in slightly, locking eyes with him. "Never. Unless there's someone I want to see."

"Who's the lucky man?"

Keira's expression softened as she placed a hand on his. "Must you ask?"

Okay... Now this is odd.

They'd known each other for months now, having met on a scuba diving trip to the Great Blue Hole, a popular yet challenging dive 70 kilometres from the coast. They had developed a rapport of sorts. It was a little dance they played every time he dined here, which was just about every night since they'd met. He figured her flirting was simply part of the job.

But this? This was different—forward and bold. Nathan figured Keira could easily have her pick of the crop. She was young, attractive, intelligent, and charming in a way that disarmed him far too easily.

Alarm bells went off in his mind.

Tall, dark-haired, and muscular, Nathan held up well for 43. He prided himself on maintaining the same high level of fitness he'd held throughout his military career. But she was what, mid-twenties? That alone made him skeptical. He'd spent enough time in intelligence work to know that young women who seemed too good to be true often were. Charm was a tool. Attraction could be a tactic. He'd seen it used effectively more times than he could count and by women far less stunning than her.

But why target me? Nathan had been out of the intelligence world for two years. Before that, he was an instructor at Canadian Forces Base Kingston, where the military intelligence school was housed. He was just a nobody now, certainly not worth the effort of a honey trap.

He dismissed the thought of pursuing her, trusting the wrong smile had been the ruin of better men than him, but he was determined to find out what the fuck was going on.

"Well, Ms. Sterling," he said with a slight grin, holding her gaze, "maybe I just want to hear it."

Her smirk lingered as she tilted her head, voice dropping just enough. "Truth is, I fancy men who've seen a bit of life—proper soldiers, not lads playing at it. There's something about that... experience."

He had been suspicious before, but now he was downright unsettled; the intensity of her attention stirred instincts that told him something was off beneath the charm. He knew her, or at least he thought he did. If she was going to make a move, this wasn't how he'd thought it would play out, and certainly not in the café she worked at.

Nathan chuckled and shook his head slightly. "What makes you want to bare your soul all of a sudden?" He took a long sip of his beer.

Her smile turned wicked as she leaned closer. "If you really must know, I've been waiting for you to make the first move. But at this rate, I'll be your age before I get laid."

Laughter broke out of him before he could stop it; the mouthful of brew went the wrong way, fizzing up into his sinuses. The burn hit hard, beer spraying through his nose as he doubled over, coughing and sputtering. It stung like fire and tasted even worse. He swore under his breath, tears streaming from his eyes as he grabbed for a napkin. Keira was already laughing, eyes bright, clearly pleased with herself.

Whether it was her relentless charm, her striking figure, or the brutal cleansing his sinuses had just endured, he couldn't say, but as the night wore on, his guard began to slip. They lingered over a few more drinks, trading laughter and an endless volley of playful banter. It felt good to live in the moment instead of dissecting it, to let himself believe he was nothing more than a retired guy enjoying the company of a gorgeous young woman.

She leaned into him and stayed there, shoulder warm against his, eyes lifted to the black water across the horizon. The playfulness slipped, replaced by a thoughtful, faraway look, as if the night breeze were paging through thoughts she hadn't decided to share. When she spoke, her voice was softer. "This has been a lot more fun than logging AGRRA Benthos transects off Turneffe and uploading photoquadrats for UB-ERI," she said with a half laugh. "Don't get me wrong, I love the work. Really, I do. But counting parrotfish and coral lesions all afternoon then fighting dodgy Wi-Fi to push data to the lab isn't quite the same as a beer by the sea."

"I'm just gonna pretend I understand what all that means while I feign fascination with it."

"Sorry." Keira giggled. "Just a bunch of research I've been doing for my grad degree back home."

"Right. University of Essex," Nathan said. "How much longer are you here for?"

"A few more months. Maybe longer if I can drag it out."

They sat together in silence for a few minutes, finishing the last of their drinks. Keira took a deep breath, her body stiffening slightly as if she were steeling herself for something. She pulled away and turned to face him, mischief in her eyes.

"Can you keep a secret?" she asked, voice slightly elevated.

Nathan tipped his head slightly. "What kind of secret?"

Keira's voice rose a shade higher, her tone carrying the careless lilt of someone who'd had a few too many. "The deeply intimate, personal kind."

Before Nathan could react, she leaned into him, right arm draping lightly around his shoulders while her left hand settled on his thigh. Her lips hovered close to his ear, her breath warm against his skin. "There's something I've been wanting to tell you," she whispered, grazing his earlobe with a playful nip as she pressed closer.

Nathan felt a shiver run up his spine. Every muscle in his body tensed. *What the hell? Is this really happening? Ah, fuck it.* Whatever willpower he possessed collapsed, content to follow her advance wherever it took him.

"Listen carefully. I'll only say this once," Keira said, sliding her left hand slightly higher on his thigh.

"Warrant Officer Cutler," she breathed into his ear, "there's a package waiting for you in locker 214 at your hotel. It's urgent."

Nathan was about to say something, but Keira pressed a finger against his lips and began kissing his neck. "Sierra niner-four Uniform three-niner-one Tango three."

Keira swung her left leg over his right thigh. "You're surprised. Panicked even. Don't let it show." She ground against him. "Make a move on me. The one you've always wanted to and work through the problem while you do."

Instinct—whether from a surge of hormones or the understanding that he had to play along with Keira—overran any possible second-guessing. Nathan leaned into her with one decisive motion. His hand slid behind her neck, pulling her mouth to his. The kiss was unrestrained, the kind he'd thought about for months. He felt her body yield against his as he gripped her hip with his other hand. He lost himself in the act for a few moments before forcing his mind back to what she'd just said.

Sierra niner-four Uniform three-niner-one Tango three.

There was only one person on the face of the planet who knew that code phrase. The man who'd written it. An old contact named Sayyid, whom Nathan ran as a source in Mosul years ago. Sayyid had been Mukhabarat but not the kind that tortured dissidents or ran death squads. He'd been one of the few who'd seen the fall of Saddam as a blessing. When ISIS surged, he'd passed names, safe house locations, and cell phone intercepts from the new Iraqi National Intelligence

Service, or INIS, at great personal risk. Nathan had trusted him with his life more than once, and Sayyid had never let him down.

What the hell was Sayyid doing in Belize? What was his connection to Keira? Whatever it was, it had to be important. Sayyid was always several steps ahead of everyone else.

Keira broke the kiss barely long enough to let out a breathless moan before pressing her lips back against his, slowly undoing the top two buttons of his linen shirt.

His mind snapped back to the café. Keira was putting on quite a show, no doubt about that, but who was the audience? Certainly not him. By now, the courtyard had thinned to the late-night crowd with small clusters of couples and singles mingling over half-empty glasses, voices pitched low under the thrum of bassy island music spilling from the bar. The air was heavy with the scent of rum, sweat, and smoke, creating a light haze.

She must have felt his attention drifting because she caught his lower lip between her teeth, biting down just enough to make him flinch back to her. "Focus on me," she whispered, her tone a mix of tease and command. "Don't scan the room."

A waitress drifted over, tray tucked under one arm, hair pulled back from her face. "Last call." She gave Keira a quick grin. "So dis di one you tell me 'bout?"

"Oh, shush, you tattletale!" Keira said, blushing, as the waitress winked and moved to the next table.

"Talking about me, eh?" Nathan teased.

She bit down on his lip again. "Be a gentleman will you and walk me back to my flat." She moved her lips back to his ear, her voice barely audible over the Caribbean music. "And not a word about what I said until we get there."

***

The walk back to Keira's flat was uneventful. They followed Princess Margaret Drive to the waterfront where it became the Newtown Barracks. The sea lay to their left, a dark sheet broken by the glow of lamps along the promenade. Salt from the sea and diesel from a taxi idling near the Ramada hung in the air, and a soft onshore breeze pressed at their clothes. They held hands and took in the scenery as Keira stumbled into him occasionally. He couldn't tell if it was the alcohol or a continuation of her performance. In either case, he knew better than to say anything. Whoever she was, she was working with Sayyid, and that meant she had to be an ally. At least that's what he hoped.

Nathan didn't think Sayyid would ever willingly give up the code phrase, but torture and other forms of coercion could be persuasive. And there wasn't a man or woman alive who didn't have their limits. His mind raced with possibilities. The last time he'd been in contact with his old friend was 2017, nearly a decade ago, when Nathan's deployment was coming to an end. He'd tried to set up handover procedures so that another source handler from JTFX could take over where Nathan had left off, but Sayyid had declined. By then it was clear that Western countries wanted out of the Middle East, and Sayyid wasn't willing to continue tying his fate to a lame-duck force.

They kept a steady pace south toward Fort George. On their right, side streets led inland past low concrete homes and older wooden houses with deep verandas and louvred shutters. Some were freshly painted, others slumped with age, a mix that matched Belize City's habit of setting a modern office beside sagging colonial era architecture.

"Relax," Keira murmured, leaning into him again with

a sly grin. "You're a lucky bastard, walking a gorgeous young thing back to her flat without a care in the world. No scanning shadows, no brooding soldier act. Just one thought in your head: What you're gonna do with me once we get there. Got it?"

"Aren't you worried about being followed?" Nathan said.

"Not unless you carry on glaring over your shoulder like someone who's got something to hide."

They cut inland and stopped at a two-storey colonial house set behind a low metal fence. The sun had bleached the clapboards to a tired sea-green that still carried a hint of dignity. An external wooden staircase climbed to the second floor. It bent once at a small landing, then rose to a wraparound veranda shaded by a deep overhang. Two cane chairs and a small table waited by the rail. Jalousie windows lined the walls, slats angled to breathe in the night while keeping prying eyes out. From the veranda, Nathan could see down to Eyre Street and along the strip toward the creek. A good perch. A quick way out if needed.

Keira unlocked the door and waved him inside.

The flat wore the uniform of a grad student scraping by. A threadbare sofa slouched under a jalousie window. Stacks of books and dive manuals spilled across a chipped coffee table. A fan ticked overhead, blades stirring humid air that smelled faintly of salt, old wood, and—he took a subtle breath—*What was that*? Then it hit him: the stale tang of garlic from a pan left out too long. A plate sat in the sink, pasta welded to porcelain. On a line by the bathroom, a rash guard and wetsuit hung to dry, still carrying the chalky scent of seawater. Sand had settled in a small crescent by the door where she clearly kicked off her flip-flops without thinking. Posters of reef ecosystems and laminated dive maps clung to the walls, pinned with curling corners. But underneath the student vibes, Nathan caught something else.

Beside the sofa, a corkboard took up the only clear stretch of wall. It was a small, improvised atlas of people and places. Coloured tacks clustered across its pinboard like a sprawling constellation, threads bowing between them in tidy arcs. Red pins carried single-letter initials; blue pins marked cafés, guesthouses, and night venues; yellow pins annotated bus stops, local schools, and the pier. Handwritten yellow stickies darted across the board. Nathan followed the threads. He noticed the patterns, and it sent a chill down his spine. It was a makeshift link analysis.

"Don't mind the state of it," Keira said with a crooked grin. "I never get much time to play house."

Nathan frowned. "I'll find a way to get over the state of it once you tell me who you really are and where you got that code phrase from," he said, a hint of frustration in his tone.

"Have a seat, Warrant." Keira motioned toward the sofa as she pulled out her laptop, sitting next to him, opening the display, and pulling up a photo. "This is Sayyid al-Mazari, INIS, and a former source of yours from your time in Mosul. He gave me the code phrase."

Nathan's stomach churned, a cold unease crawling through him. So *they're working together or she extracted it from him.* His jaw tightened. If the information was extracted, that meant Sayyid was most likely dead; if he had given it to her freely, something serious must be about to happen.

She gave a half smile, the easy lilt back in her voice. "He's fine if that's what you're fretting about. I clocked him in Belize a few weeks ago and I've been working him ever since. At least trying to anyway. But he doesn't trust anyone and, believe it or not, has proven quite immune to my charms. I need your help, Nathan. He knows you're in Belize and you're the only one he'll talk to. He told me to give you the code phrase and the instructions."

Nathan's posture relaxed, leaning back into the sofa. "You still haven't told me who you are or why I should trust you. You've been deceiving me since the day we met."

Keira's shoulders dipped, the grin fading. "Surely you can see why I couldn't exactly waltz up and say, 'Sterling, Keira Sterling, MI6.' It's not a bloody Bond film, is it? You know how it is."

He nodded slowly. "And how do I know you're telling me the truth?"

She turned to face him. "Warrant Officer Nathan Charles Cutler, born October 12, 1981, happy belated birthday by the way. You were enrolled in a business degree at the University of Toronto. You dropped out after 9/11 and joined the Canadian Army as an enlisted man. Service number B87 045 644."

He shifted away from her slightly, creating distance between them. "How did you..."

"You were an infantryman with Third Battalion, Royal Canadian Regiment, and spent the first ten years of your career at Pet. You did three combat tours in Afghanistan, served as a section commander on your last tour, and were approached by JTFX shortly after your return."

Nathan swallowed hard and felt the colour draining from his face.

"You rebadged to Source Handler Operator and spent the rest of your career in Kingston, serving two HUMINT deployments in Iraq running sources. You were noted as having, and I quote, 'an uncanny ability to empathize with your targets, building trust quickly, allowing you to collect actionable intelligence that saved lives on a number of occasions,' for which you were awarded the Meritorious Service Medal."

His hands started to shake but she continued, "You were medically released in 2022 and were invited by CSIS to apply to be an intelligence officer in the service. You declined. Need I go on?"

"Ordinarily, I'd say I'm flattered," Nathan said, trying to regain his composure. "I'm afraid to ask what else you know."

"Much more than I need to," Keira said. "The point is, the only way I could have gotten that information, and in short order I might add, is through official channels between SIS and CSIS."

Neither spoke for the next few minutes. Nathan, still trying to process the multiple bombshells she'd dropped on him, felt exposed in a way he wasn't accustomed to. Normally, he was in control of the interaction between handler and source. And that's when it dawned on him. Keira wanted to run him as a source. She'd executed flawlessly, save for the sudden revelations. He knew from experience that a source handler wouldn't resort to such sudden measures unless there was a severe, time-sensitive threat.

He felt like he was going to be sick.

Keira sat with him but didn't press him. *She's good, no doubt about that.* She hadn't provided a smoking gun proving she was MI6, but he also knew that would never happen. It was conceivable she could have gotten his information through espionage rather than through cooperation, but even then it added more credence to her claims. Unless she was working for a belligerent foreign power, but he figured that was unlikely.

"I'm sorry for not being honest with you. Truly I am. I hadn't started trying to recruit you as a source until a few weeks ago. And I'm sorry for putting on that display back at the café. It was the safest way to convey the information to you and get you back here."

She'd apologized. *Now that's interesting.* In Nathan's experience, seasoned spooks tended not to apologize for doing their jobs. That meant Keira was likely still trying to come to terms with constantly putting on a disguise, not getting close to anyone, and worse still, not being able to trust anyone. The grad program, the research placement in Belize, the scuba diving, even the waitressing... It all had to be part of her cover—non-official cover. So, she's an NOC. And a new one at that.

He decided to test that theory.

Nathan took her right hand between both of his, locking his gaze with hers. "I understand. I'm sorry too."

Keira's lips parted as if to brush it off with another quip, but the look in his eyes held her. The sharpness drained from her expression, replaced by something raw and unguarded. For the briefest moment her eyes shimmered, tears welling. She blinked hard, drew in a quick breath, and forced the mask back into place, swallowing down whatever had almost broken through.

Nathan nodded slowly and gave her hand another squeeze. "All right, Agent Sterling, how can I be of service to his Majesty?"

She took a moment to compose herself, briefly wiping at her left eye, sniffling slightly. A long, shuddering breath escaped her, the rigid tension in her shoulders dissipating.

"As you know, Sayyid doesn't trust Western intelligence. As far as we can tell, you're the only one who's been able to run him. He surfaced in Belize about a month ago and, before you ask, we're just as surprised as you are. We have no idea why he's here. The SIS read all the reports you wrote back in the day. I'm sure you'll agree, if he's here, he's here for a reason."

That checked out. As far as Nathan was aware, Sayyid had never been outside the Middle East, so Belize did seem like an odd destination for him.

"I assume he's not vacationing."

Keira shook her head. "He's not here alone. He's got three associates with him. They've been carrying out surveillance. I don't have the resources here to track him properly, so I don't even know who they're watching. Except for me, that is."

"Watching you?"

"Since I made contact with him I've spotted one of his men following me a few times. I let him track me. I wanted to signal that they could trust me. He followed me to the café, and he saw me carrying on with you. After that, Sayyid approached me."

His gaze remained on her, but it was distant now, as if he were looking past her and into the dusty streets of Mosul. He gave a slow, almost imperceptible nod. Nathan had learned years ago never to offer anything that a fellow human intelligence professional could use to bolster their own story.

"He said he'd only talk to you, and that it was your call on whether to read me in. He gave me the code phrase and the information about the locker."

Nathan waited for her to continue.

"Said to tell you the access code is the same as Tango Five. I assume you know what that means?"

"Are you working a counterterrorism angle?" he asked, purposely ignoring the question for now.

"No. Up until now we had no reason to believe there was any terror-related nexus in Belize," she said. "I'm supporting Operation Dignity."

Nathan gave her a hard look, the muscles in his jaw tensing. "Don't tell me you're trying to get yourself kidnapped to infiltrate them."

Her expression brightened slightly. "Protective over me already, love? My hero."

"I'm not kidding, Keira. Artemis Circle is dangerous. You don't want to—"

"Thanks, Dad," she cut him off, smirking. "but I can look after myself."

Artemis Circle was infamous for sex trafficking across the globe. The thought of her getting tied up with them turned his stomach into knots. *Stay focused, Cutler. She's not your girlfriend; she's a spy. Don't get attached.*

"I'm doing far worse than that. I'm posing as a facilitator," she said, the amused look on her face dropping.

He nodded. Playing the role of a facilitator would certainly weigh on the soul.

"So I can identify targets for Hereford to prosecute," she said, as if wanting to justify her actions.

Hereford was the quiet shorthand for the SAS—the godfathers of Tier-1 special operations and the very unit that Canada's JTF2 had been modelled after. For years, JTF2 had been prosecuting Artemis Circle targets with lethality.

"Got it," he said. "Can we count on any muscle if the need arises?"

"Afraid not. They aren't due in country for another week."

"You're trusting me with an awful lot of information, Keira."

"Trust works both ways, doesn't it?" she said. "I'm asking you to trust me, too."

"True enough. Ok, what's next?"

"Go to the locker, find out what's in there. Then dine at the café like you normally do. When I give you the bill, hit on me. Make it clear you want another round. Then we'll come back here and you tell me what you know."

Nathan chuckled. "Another round? What about the first round?"

"Don't get cute," she said, but there was a lightness in her tone. "Now get going. And don't run an SDR. Remember, you're playing the part of a middle-aged man who just won the lottery."

"What if I'm followed?"

"If you stay in character you shouldn't be, but we'll be keeping an eye on you just the same. Leave the counter-surveillance to us."

"You weren't kidding when you said you were asking me to trust you," Nathan said.

2

CH-146 GRIFFON
UNDISCLOSED LOCATION
SUNDAY, OCTOBER 13
01:21 LOCAL TIME

The familiar whine of the CH-146 Griffon's engines did little to settle the churn in Sergeant Sebastien Ray's gut. Nicknamed Rocky for his uncanny resemblance to a bald, rough-edged version of Sylvester Stallone, he couldn't shake the memories that had haunted him for the past several months. Eight years ago, Matthew Lion, newly minted leader of JTF2's Alpha Team, had said that combat leadership was the art of managing chaos. But in the high-stakes world of Tier-1 special operations, it wasn't enough to manage chaos; one had to conquer it. To do this, a leader had to impose his will on the objective and the surrounding area, tame the untameable. There were few phenomena on earth less tameable than combat. Only a true master of war had a chance—and even then, never more than a fragile one.

Rocky had rolled his eyes the first time he'd heard Lion's sermon. At the time, Alpha Team had been completely reconstituted since the original crew had aged out.

"We have tall boots to fill," Lion had said, though Rocky couldn't remember what came afterwards, having tuned the arrogant bastard out. Alpha was one of the unit's original teams and the most storied. Lion had taken the reins from Alpha's first and only team leader, the venerated Marc Tremblay. The team was handpicked from squadrons across the unit. Though they came from diverse backgrounds, all of them considered themselves the best of the best.

Rocky smiled wryly at the irony. *If only youth lasted.* Nearly a decade of non-stop operations could change a man's perspective. He wondered what the next decade might look like.

He glanced at his men as the two CH-146 Griffons' rotors thumped their teeth-rattling rhythm through the night. Now a collection of seasoned veterans, Alpha was about to hit a multibuilding compound where three hostages were being held in a small one-story building. It was a complex op by any standard, requiring a stealth insertion, coordinated movement, two detachments, and minimal communication. Just another day at the office, except this time, there was no Matt Lion leading the team. The guilt started to resurface as it had for the past nine months. Holding himself together was proving to be much more difficult than Tier-1 culture led one to believe. Rocky found himself wishing he could hear one more sermon from Lion. He closed his eyes, trying to will the memories aside, but it never worked. Sadly, Lion had never delivered a sermon on how to manage the chaos within.

Rocky had disliked Lion at the time. Who was he to be appointed command of Alpha Team? Rocky, two years Lion's senior, had been gunning for team leadership for a while, and the sergeant major had assured him he was next in line until Tremblay, who had been grooming Lion, stepped in and made his preference clear.

Tremblay, now a commissioned officer, was a gruff soldier's soldier. The troops loved him. Lion was more of an academic than a warrior, or so it seemed. He was soft-spoken, mild-mannered, and infuriatingly polite. The last thing Alpha needed, as far as Rocky had been concerned, was a warrior philosopher. The sting of having been appointed Alpha Two, Lion's second in command, gnawed at him. Rocky was constantly at odds with him during the team's initial workup training. Things deteriorated quickly. Alpha failed all of its pre-deployment certifications. Things got so bad that there were rumours the CO was considering disbanding the new team as a failed experiment.

Following a late-night after-action report, or AAR, in the team cage, Guy Deschamps, Alpha Three and known to everyone as Champs, had had enough. Of average height with dark hair and a full beard, he stood squarely in front of Rocky, eyes hard.

"If you don't sort your shit out, people are going to come home in body bags," Champs said, his voice low but cutting. "Figure it out, or I'll go above both your heads and tell command what a shit show this is."

He turned sharply and stormed out of the team cage, the metal door slamming behind him.

Rocky turned to face Lion, who was leaning over the equipment table at the centre of the team cage, studying a map. Even hunched forward, Lion cut an imposing figure at six-foot-four with a muscular, athletic build, his clean-shaven face setting him apart from the rest of the lads. The arrogant prick was even too good for a beard. By contrast, Rocky stood shorter but thick with power, a bald slab of muscle that gave him the look of a bruiser cast in steel, more street fighter than the poster boy before him.

"He's right, Rocky. This can't continue," Lion said calmly. "I've tolerated the chip on your shoulder long enough. Whatever your issue is with me—"

"Fuck you!" Rocky barked. "Tolerated? Who the fuck do you think you are?"

Lion didn't flinch. "Who I *think* I am is irrelevant," Lion said calmly, raising his gaze to Rocky. "I *am* Alpha One."

He stepped away from the table, walking toward Rocky. "Now, out with it. What is your issue?"

"You have no fucking business leading a team," Rocky spat. "I've been busting my ass preparing for command for the past two years. I've deployed twice and run dozens of missions in between. What have you been doing? Oh, right, getting a master's degree in bullshitology while the rest of us have been fighting a war."

Rocky stepped into Lion's personal space. "You're not a fucking warrior; you've got your eyes on a commission. Everyone knows it."

"Seriously? This is all jealousy?" Lion shook his head in confusion.

Rocky didn't think. Consumed with rage, face red with fury, he charged at his commander who deftly dodged the attack, using Rocky's forward momentum to hurl him into the table, which came crashing down along with Rocky.

"Alright," Lion said. "You want to take a run at me? Show me what kind of warrior you are? I'll indulge."

Rocky, furious with Lion but more so with himself for being so easily upended, threw the broken table clear and sprang to his feet. The altercation was violent but brief. He managed to get two solid hits off before Lion put him down like the rabid dog Rocky had become.

He barely registered the pain, too stunned by the shock of having his ass handed to him so thoroughly.

"Are we good now?" Lion extended his hand.

Rocky nodded. What else could he say? He felt humiliated and had no ground to stand on. The man he'd insisted wasn't a warrior had just wiped the floor with him. Rocky was prideful, always had been, but he was honest, too, and there was no disputing that he was in the wrong. He grasped Lion's hand, who helped him to his feet.

The next morning, Rocky and Lion were summoned to the Squadron Commander's office, each looking like they had been in a bar fight: Lion sporting a black eye and Rocky with gauze stuffed in his nose. Captain Tremblay stood behind his desk, tall and fit with a full head of dark brown hair streaked faintly with grey. His voice rolled through the room. It was deep and gravelly, thick with a French Canadian accent.

"What in the holy fuck! Esti tabarnak! I called you idiots in here to ream you out about Alpha's performance. Clearly, there's more going on here than sucking at your jobs."

Rocky saw Lion wince from the corner of his eye and felt a pang of guilt.

Tremblay, now eye to eye with Lion, dropped his voice to a menacing tone. "What happened?"

Rocky watched Lion, his expression tightening as he seemed to weigh his words before speaking.

"Sir, my hand-to-hand has been lacking. As you know, Master Corporal Ray is an MMA instructor. I asked him to help me with my technique. We got a little carried away."

Tremblay, known for his flamboyant outbursts, looked like he was about to burst at the seams. He paused for a moment, then looked Lion square in the eye. "I never thought I'd see the day when Matt Lion lied to my face."

He turned to Rocky. "Why don't you elaborate for me?"

"Sir," Rocky began, "it happened just like Matt said. He managed to land a blow on my nose; I'm pretty sure it's busted, and... I was already mid-swing and couldn't see straight, and I think that's when I landed a fist on his eye. After that—"

"Alright, shut up," Tremblay said. "At least you idiots are on the same page for one goddamn thing."

He circled behind his desk, staring out the window at a group of candidates undergoing selection week. Tremblay stayed by the window for a while, watching the young men endure unspeakable hardships.

"Gentlemen, I'm only going to say this once," Tremblay said, looking at the candidates lying face-first in the mud, struggling to force one last push-up out of their exhausted bodies. "The needs of the country always come before the needs of the personality. Am I understood?"

"Yes, sir," both men responded in unison.

Tremblay nodded, still looking out the window. "Get out."

The two men walked from the headquarters building to the mess hall. Rocky broke the silence. "You didn't have to do that. It was my fault. You should have been straight with him."

Lion stopped, shaking his head. "No, it was my fault."

Rocky frowned. "How do you figure?"

"I'm the leader. Everything that goes wrong is my fault."

"You still should have told him."

Lion chuckled. "You obviously don't know Tremblay very well."

"Not really."

"Had I ratted you out over a problem that I failed to solve, he would have busted me down to private and sent me back to a battalion." Lion locked eyes with Rocky. "I'm serious about what I said. Everything that went down is on me. Set it aside and focus on the task at hand. We need to do the name Alpha justice."

A loud voice crackled in his headset, snapping Rocky's mind back to the present. "Five mikes until insertion."

Focus on the mission.

The CH-146 Griffons screamed through the night, engines howling as the birds ate the last few klicks to the target, skimming 50 feet above ground level on a nap-of-the-earth run, terrain masking to stay off radar. Night vision goggle–compatible cabin light washed hard shadows across the men's faces. Alpha Team was minutes from infil. Rocky rode the door, hips on the threshold, boots hanging over the skid, clipped in on a gunner's belt lanyard to the cabin anchor point, carbine canted outboard as he scanned for threats.

His primary weapon was the Colt Canada Modular Rail Rifle, or MRR, the modern successor to the C8 carbine. The platform came in several barrel lengths. For this operation, he carried an 11.6-inch configuration that balanced compact handling with enough reach for open patches between tree lines. The rifle's monolithic upper and slim M-LOK handguard provided a continuous top rail and modular mounting points without the bulky weight of older systems. Its free-floating, cold hammer forged, chrome-lined barrel was designed to stay consistent under hard use and brutal weather.

The lighter front end made the weapon easier to handle in close quarters, an advantage they would need once they pushed through the treeline and into the compound. A suppressor capped the muzzle. Contrary to Hollywood portrayals, it didn't make the weapon quiet, but it dulled the sound enough that it could blend into the background chaos, making it harder for the enemy to track where death was coming from based on sound alone.

A laser module sat on the rail just behind the muzzle, projecting a red dot in low light and a green dot in daylight directly onto the target, especially useful in close quarters battle (CQB) the bread and butter of all Tier-1 operators, for instant point-and-shoot. Unlike a conventional sight, the laser allowed the operator to aim without aligning his eye to optic or iron sights, a critical advantage when a full cheek weld would put his head in the enemy's line of fire. The downside was that a visible laser could reveal an operator's position, which is why there was a pressure support thumb switch located near where the offhand gripped the rail to turn it on or off as required. Sitting next to the laser module on the left side of the rail was an Inforce light, giving Rocky the option to switch from an infrared to a visual white light to identify targets or blind them.

Further back on the rail was an Aimpoint Micro T-2, a small optic sight mounted on an elevated platform, allowing Rocky to keep his head up and his eyes downrange instead of craning his neck tight to the stock. The heads-up posture made it far faster to pick up threats while moving. Directly behind the T-2, on a quick-flip Unity-style mount, rested a 3× magnifier, allowing him to flip it into line with the T-2, transforming the red aiming dot into a telescoped aiming point for midrange shots. When longer shots weren't needed, he could flip it down against the rail, keeping it out of the way so it didn't get snagged on anything.

Rounding out the rig, Rocky wore a low-profile, two-point, padded sling with a quick-adjust tab, keeping the weapon tight to his chest for fast movement, allowing him to transition instantly to a sidearm or perform one-handed manipulations, and locking down the carbine for a stable, controlled shot.

Alpha was seconds away from the target now, and the vibration of the CH-146 Griffon hammered through Rocky's frame, but it was nothing compared to the gnawing emptiness inside. With the objective looming, it threatened to pull him under entirely.

The birds touched down; the operators unfastened themselves and disembarked immediately. The CH-146 Griffons sat on the ground for no more than a few seconds before lifting off and departing. Rocky organized his twelve-man team into two dets of six. In his det he had five assaulters and a sniper. Champs, leading the second det, had four assaulters, a light machine gunner, and a sniper.

Both dets went to prone, waiting and listening, ensuring there were no nearby patrols or unanticipated badgers. "Jupiter, Alpha Two. In position," Rocky whispered into his headset.

"Alpha Two, Jupiter. No contacts on thermal. Charlie Mike, how copy?"

"Good copy," Rocky responded. *Infiltration, check—only a dozen more objectives to go. Stay focused.*

He gave a sharp hand signal, and both dets slowly began their silent trek to the compound roughly 500 metres away. Rocky's det approached from the north while Champs' det flanked from the west. It was bitterly cold and moonless, the night washed only by starlight that gave shape but little depth. Manoeuvring two elements at night onto the same objective was extremely dangerous. In near-zero light conditions, operators could become disoriented, and the risk of blue-on-blue engagements was high. Technology mitigated this to some extent. The night vision goggles the men wore picked up the infrared strobes on each other's helmets, which helped, but it wasn't a perfect solution.

The manoeuvre sounded simple enough on paper, but it wasn't something you'd want to try with a bunch of guys who weren't familiar with each other. Communicating while moving was paramount. That you couldn't afford to communicate verbally so close to an objective at night changed nothing. Subtle movements and body language from one operator conveyed to the next what the first was about to do. Building that chemistry within one det was hard enough; accomplishing the same thing between two dets was a whole other level of difficulty.

Neither Rocky nor Champs could see each other or their respective dets. There was no subtle body language to work from. The synchronization came from training and repeating similar approaches hundreds of times. Both teams were advancing through lightly wooded terrain with small patches of dense trees. Rocky knew exactly how long Champs and his det would take to get to their next objective, assuming nothing went wrong. Unfortunately, things often did go wrong, especially at night. That the enemy had a vote, and could and would do something either unpredicted or incredibly stupid, was well understood. Rocky had to know how the other det would deal with any number of situations that could pop up and how long it would take. Should their technology fail, as it was known to do from time to time, each man needed to know exactly where the other's det would be at any given time.

Rocky heard two clicks in his headset. He immediately motioned for his men to halt and take cover. Two clicks over the comms meant one or more unknowns heading his way. Someone in Champs' det must have seen the movement. That Jupiter hadn't alerted Rocky to the movement told him everything he needed to know. If the CE-145C Vigilance, CANSOFCOM's new ISR aircraft providing overwatch for the mission, hadn't seen this element approaching, it meant they were likely using some kind of multispectral camouflage over their garments, significantly reducing their heat signatures. If they spaced themselves out enough and stayed under the cover of thicker wooded areas, it was possible to defeat ISR platforms. That told Rocky three things: They were professionals, they were prepared, and they could only approach from one of two locations where the trees were thick enough to provide cover.

He listened as another six clicks came through his headset. *Okay, I have six unknowns employing IR-defeating tactics heading my way.* Given the context, Rocky assessed that these unknowns were hostile and acted accordingly.

Rocky nodded to Ethan Miles, Alpha Five, a tall, slim sniper, who read him instantly and understood what he wanted. Miles would cover the further grouping of trees, roughly 300 metres away. The rest of the team knew their roles in this situation without being told. One assaulter would remain with Miles and cover him, ensuring that no unpleasant surprises crept up on the sniper while his field of view was limited to what he saw through his scope; the other four quietly moved into an ambush position near the closer grouping of trees, roughly 50 metres away. Their night vision goggles were useless now, so the three assaulters who were wearing them moved them to an upright position over their helmets. Since they had already allowed their eyes to become fully dark-adapted before donning the NVGs, their night vision would be fully restored in two to five minutes. The other two assaulters already had their NVGs in the upward position as a precaution to avoid situations where the entire team could be blinded for a few minutes.

The det flipped their Unity magnifiers into the upward position, allowing them to take aimed shots at any figure moving within their arcs of fire. Rocky clicked the mic twice in quick succession, signalling to Champs an acknowledgement. He would report the new development to Jupiter on Rocky's behalf.

Rocky had a decision to make. Once he got eyes on the six hostiles approaching, he could either take them out or let them pass. He would open fire only as a last resort. They were 200 metres away from the compound; any gunfire, suppressed or otherwise, would likely give them away. Noise travelled farther at night. The only background sounds to cover the supersonic cracks of bullets flying were crickets and the occasional owl. Not enough to mask gunfire. And that was assuming the enemy fighters didn't get any shots off themselves. If they weren't using suppressors and managed to take even one shot, it was game over. Their stealth approach would be compromised, and Alpha would have to either fight its way through the enemy force or do the unthinkable: abort, leaving the hostages to their fate, which was unacceptable.

The int team—short for intelligence in Canadian parlance—had assessed the presence of roughly three dozen fighters. *Assessed* being the operative word. Rocky knew better than to take any intelligence estimate as absolute fact. Such assessments were built on fragments of information pieced together by intelligence analysts, and it was rare that anyone had the whole picture.

Three dozen or more. If a firefight broke out and he decided to storm the compound anyway, there was no guarantee that the hostages wouldn't be executed by the time they fought their way through. If his men couldn't get eyes on the hostiles Champs had spotted Rocky's det would have to hunt and stalk them to make sure they couldn't disrupt the mission, but that would take time, possibly a lot of time, and it would tie up assaulters that he desperately needed for the assault.

Click-Click... Click-Click. Miles signalled he had eyes on two targets. *Four more to go, probably in the closer grouping of trees.* Rocky waited. A few moments later, he heard another burst of clicks indicating that the other four were in the near treeline. Rocky did the math in his head. Champs had spotted them roughly twelve minutes ago, about 150 metres away from where they were now. That rate of advance was consistent with a tactical march.

He caught a glimpse of them through his T-2, enhanced by the Unity magnifier. They were spaced out, as he'd predicted; all carried assault rifles and tactical vests, likely body armour plates too. Rocky motioned to the assaulter nearest him who pulled his NVGs down over his eyes. A brief moment later, the assaulter gave Rocky the thumbs-up. *NVGs are still working, and no strobes detected. No risk of blue-on-blue fire.*

He nodded in return and continued to observe. Rocky was sure they hadn't been spotted. There was nothing in the gunmen's demeanour that indicated they were on alert; besides, they'd likely have opened fire by now if he'd been spotted.

"Patience is a funny thing," Lion had stressed a few years ago. "Sometimes it's a virtue, and other times it's certain death. The trick is being able to identify which reality you're in."

Rocky decided that patience would be a virtue, at least for the time being.

"Alpha Two, Jupiter. All Star."

Ok, Champs and his det are in position, ready to assault. Rocky double-clicked, signalling his acknowledgement, followed by a short pause and another click. *Hold.* He knew that Champs and Jupiter would understand that meant he was still dealing with an obstacle to the mission.

Another ten minutes passed, and the hostiles hadn't moved. Clearly, they were unwilling to wander away from the camouflage afforded by the wooded areas. Rocky motioned to Master Corporal Lucien Leneaux, Alpha Four, the team's tactical intelligence operator, nicknamed Spooky. He hated that name, but it was either Spooky or Lucy. Rocky figured he'd chosen the lesser of two evils.

Spooky, shorter than most of the other operators but lean and wiry, pulled a tablet out of his satchel and got to work. Once again, the benefit of hundreds of training evolutions, countless missions, and chemistry paid off. He began assessing the terrain for Rocky. He had access to overhead imagery that had been taken earlier in the day, the live night feed courtesy of the Vigilance flying overhead, and a digital map. Spooky pinpointed the locations of the two groups of hostiles, and the software autogenerated likely fields of view from the hostiles' perspective, marking light green areas for spots their adversaries could see and red areas for places where they would be blind. When he finished his work, he passed the screen to Rocky.

It's not a patrol; it's a goddamn observation post. The screen was almost entirely green. Rocky examined the terrain features for another few minutes and concluded that the two clumps of trees where the six fighters were stationed gave them the best possible field of view without risk of exposure.

Best, but not perfect. The map showed just enough patches of red to offer an avenue of advance, though it meant approaching the compound from a direction Rocky hadn't planned. He handed the tablet back to Spooky with a curt hand signal. Spooky nodded, gave a quick thumbs-up, and crawled forward to Master Corporal Ron Dykstraw, Alpha Six, a former pathfinder with Third Battalion, Princess Patricia's Canadian Light Infantry. The team called him Hangman, earned for his less-than-stellar habit of getting tangled in trees during airborne insertions. He was lean and athletic with short, sandy-blond hair and a patchy beard.

Hangman studied the tablet for a few minutes then nodded. Rocky took that as confirmation and weighed the map again. The terrain showed little chance of other tree clusters that could mask observers along their new approach. He raised a thumbs-up, and the team began moving, crawling forward, prone, until the ground allowed them to rise and continue upright.

Moving unseen and unheard at such close range to the two groups of fighters was a grinding test of nerve. Every shift of a knee, every slow drag of an elbow felt like it might give them away. Time stretched, broken into long pauses where the only sound was their own breathing and the faint rustle of leaves. Forty-five minutes bled past before they finally slipped beyond the observation post. Relief came sharp but brief as they reached the new breach point without incident.

"All stations, Alpha Two. In position. Audible incoming," Rocky whispered into the comms.

3

FORT GEORGE
BELIZE CITY
SUNDAY, OCTOBER 13
00:49 LOCAL TIME

Nathan made his way toward his hotel, roughly a forty-five-minute walk from Keira's flat. He walked north along Barrack Road, then cut inland across Calle Al Mar, and walked up Joseph Street before pushing north again on Princess Margaret Drive, trying his best to look the part. It took every iota of discipline within him to maintain a steady, leisurely pace. The thought of what might be waiting in the locker pulled at him like gravity, countered only by Keira's voice echoing in his head. *I'm a middle-aged man who just won the proverbial lottery.* But it was an act he couldn't relate to. He'd had short-term girlfriends before

Julie—girls his age. *How the fuck does a man in his 40s act after sleeping with a woman nearly half his age? Should I have a spring in my step or should I be spent?* Fortunately, the double mystery—what Sayyid had left for him and what part of Keira was real, what part fabricated—so occupied his mind that he didn't have the mental bandwidth to run any SDR routines.

He walked up University Drive, bringing him between the University of Belize and Saint John's College campus. The street narrowed into a corridor of contrasts. To his left, low concrete buildings and shop fronts broke the line of student apartments with a handful of bars closing for the night. The smell of fried chicken and stale beer lingered in the warm air, mixing with damp earth from the thick treeline across the road. A handful of students drifted past in loose packs, laughter too loud, one of them singing something Nathan couldn't make out, before the group dissolved into giggles. He walked past them, and the street fell quiet. That's when he caught the motion in the reflection of a dark window—a figure crossing under a lamp, matching his pace, 20 metres back. Not close enough to crowd him, but close enough to keep him in sight. Another shape flickered near the tree line, something low and quick, the shuffle of feet on gravel.

Every old instinct in him snapped awake.

The only people nearby were the person walking behind him and another in the treeline to his right. Soon, he would have to turn off University Drive and move north along Bachelor Avenue to reach his hotel, but if he did that, and these people were following him, he'd be leading them straight to the place he lived. On the other hand, Keira's warning flashed in his mind. *Don't run an SDR*. That made sense. Only an agent, operator, or someone with something to hide would conduct a surveillance detection route—a series of turns and misdirection designed to spot a tail and lose one. Operators routinely used them to make sure they weren't being followed, which could compromise a mission or a safe house. If he started doing that now, and someone was following him, Nathan would be telling his follower that he was someone who ought to be followed.

Leave the counter-surveillance to us.

He gritted his teeth. It was too late to second-guess Keira now. If she were deceiving him, he was already screwed. He had no choice but to trust her, so he continued walking toward his hotel. The tail began to close on him, footsteps quickening. He felt the muscles in his body tense as he instinctively prepared himself for a confrontation. Then, two more figures emerged from Chancellor Avenue on his left, university-aged males, clearly drunk by the way they stumbled. They slammed directly into the person behind Nathan, seemingly by accident, and began shouting profanities at the man. As Nathan continued walking, he heard a grunt. He looked over his shoulder briefly. It looked like the two drunks had shoved the other man, who had fallen to the ground. One of the drunk students began shouting something unintelligible at the figure in the treeline, apparently goading him into a fight.

Nathan turned left on Graduate Crescent then north onto Bachelor Avenue, reaching his hotel a few minutes later without incident. The Stoic Inn sat back from the road behind a low wire fence, its paint faded to a chalky blue that looked almost white in the sodium glow. Three storeys of poured concrete and square geometry. Functional and no frills, it was the kind of building that belonged to a city more practical than pretty. A cracked sign above the front steps hummed faintly, half its bulbs dead. The front office was dark, except for the glow of a small television behind the counter where the night clerk dozed in his chair. Nathan went up the stairwell to the third floor and entered his room. He wanted some time to calm down before he went back downstairs to check the locker. Whatever was in there could wait for a bit, and on the off chance that someone had managed to follow him to his hotel, all they'd find was a man who went straight to his room.

His suite was nothing special, but the price was right. It had tiled floors, a ceiling fan, and a kitchenette wedged beside a window unit that groaned in protest when switched on. The furniture was a mismatched collection of varnished plywood and wicker: a table, a single chair, and a narrow bed made up with sheets that had gone thin from too many washings.

He moved to the balcony where he caught the faint glint of the northern waterfront. Off to the east, the airport lights shimmered against the dark horizon. A dog barked somewhere in the neighbourhood. Beyond that, silence. He set his palms on the rust-flecked but solid metal railing, leaned his weight into it, and closed his eyes.

Sayyid's name replayed in his thoughts, a ghost from another life. If the old man had surfaced in Istanbul, Amman, or even Ottawa, it might have made sense. Belize was something else entirely. And in Nathan's experience, anything that far out of pattern meant the stakes were higher than anyone wanted to admit. *What did you stumble onto, old friend?* But even as he turned the question over, it wasn't Sayyid's face that lingered. It was Keira's. He was convinced the man he'd spotted behind him and the other in the treeline were trailing him. The intervention from the drunken students was too convenient to be a coincidence. They were likely the counter-surveillance Keira had spoken of. Then again, the entire episode could have been staged to give him a false sense of security, to ease any suspicion he might have about her. He cursed to himself and decided that he preferred being the handler rather than the handled and wondered how torn his previous sources had been when he was handling them.

***

About an hour later, Nathan changed into a green T-shirt and black gym shorts, then made his way down the stairs. He took a moment to scan the main floor, careful to avoid the field of view of the security cameras he had made note of months ago when he checked in. The only other soul on the floor was the front desk clerk, still dozing. Satisfied, Nathan went to the locker room. The locker itself was puzzling, his having refused the clerk's offer upon check-in, not wanting to pay the extra $5 per month. He remembered the clerk's spiel: The lockers had a six-digit alphanumeric combination set by the guest.

He said to tell you the access code is the same as Tango Five.

Nathan recognized the old field cipher they'd used in Mosul. It was a six-digit passcode—429613—but every second digit represented a letter. The first of those letters corresponded to the middle character associated with its number on a phone keypad, the second to the first, and the third again to the middle. The result was 4B9M1E. He keyed in the code, and the door popped open, revealing a USB stick. He retrieved it, made his way back up the stairs, into his room, and sat at the small table where his laptop was. He disconnected the Wi-Fi, a makeshift air gapping solution, before plugging the stick into his computer. He opened the file explorer. There was one folder containing one unnamed MP4 file with no metadata beyond a timestamp from two days ago. Nathan's thumb hovered over the trackpad for a heartbeat, then he double-clicked. The video player opened full screen. For a moment, there was only the static hiss and the faint click of a ceiling fan. Then the image steadied.

Sayyid al-Mazari's face filled the frame. The years had caught up to him in a way that had not been kind. Deep lines cut from his nose to the corners of his mouth, and the skin around his eyes had darkened into permanent shadows. His beard was silver-threaded through black, trimmed but uneven, and his hair had thinned to a grey fringe combed straight back. He had the look of a man who carried the weight of a thousand calculations and regrets. When he spoke, his voice carried the clipped vowels and softened consonants of an Iraqi who'd learned English at a young age.

"Nathan..." A pause. "I regret to come to you like this, my friend. I would rather be sitting across a table, drinking tea, as we once did. But that time is gone."

Sayyid exhaled, eyes closing briefly, then continued.

"I have been on Khalid al-Rashid for years. I chased him across the Middle East. Now he is here, in Belize. He arrived a month ago and I followed. He is not alone."

The video flickered, then cut to a shaky handheld shot. Khalid al-Rashid himself, one of the most wanted terrorists in the world, stepped out of a dark SUV on a Belize City backstreet, flanked by men carrying suppressed rifles. Another clip followed: a warehouse interior, with crates stacked against a wall, and a dozen fighters in mismatched fatigues, fitting magazines into their rifles. A third shot: a glimpse of what looked like a jungle canopy through drone footage, men moving through undergrowth, before disappearing.

"My team counts nearly fifty fighters. We have tracked them to an old compound deep within the Chiquibul rainforest. Nathan"—Sayyid's expression cracked, a flash of fatigue and dread breaking through—"I am sorry to tell you this. They are preparing to deliver a blow that will cripple Canada. Not some token attack. It is part of a larger existential threat against everything we hold dear."

Sayyid straightened, wiping sweat from his brow with the back of his hand. "I know everything. But I cannot risk it in this recording. We must meet in person. Only that way can I be sure this video has not fallen into the wrong hands."

The video flickered to a black screen with white writing. It was another cipher, much longer and more complicated than the earlier passcode.

"Do not underestimate them, my friend, and do not delay. If you are watching this, you are already a part of it."

Nathan's breathing went shallow. He pushed the laptop back as though distance might dull what he'd just seen, hands trembling against the tabletop. The cheap laminate under his palms was slick with sweat. For a long moment, he just stared at the cipher on the screen.

A blow that will cripple Canada... An existential threat to everything we hold dear. Nathan wasn't one to get spun up easily, but he'd worked closely with Sayyid for a long time. Every piece of intelligence his old source had passed to him had proven to be credible, and Sayyid himself wasn't prone to overexaggeration. The veteran intelligence professional preached the maxim of precision in language. His words were always direct with the meaning behind them unmistakable.

Nathan pulled out a pen and paper, wrote the cipher down, and began deciphering it. It took another hour to work through it. It was the time and place of his meeting with Sayyid, two days from now.

Nathan thought back to Keira's instructions. He'd need to meet up with her at the café again tomorrow night, but his obligations went beyond her. Retired or not, he had to report this up the chain of command. But how?

He pulled out a lighter and burned the paper he'd used to work through the cipher, then picked up his phone, toggled to an old friend who still worked at JTFX and dialled. The call went straight to voicemail, so he called it again, hoping the do-not-disturb setting might let his call through. He listened to the ring for what seemed like an eternity.

"Jesus, Nathan, it's two fucking thirty in the morning," Sam Noonan said. Nathan heard sheets shifting, followed by the soft whine of a woman in the background.

"I need the number for the CANSOFCOM duty officer. It's important. I don't have time to explain."

4

UNDISCLOSED LOCATION
SUNDAY, OCTOBER 13
02:01 LOCAL TIME

There was no light at the compound, not even the faint spark of a lighter or cigarette. *Definitely professionals.* From Rocky's vantage, the compound looked dead, but he knew differently. His det lay behind a low berm in an elevated position east of the compound, roughly 50 metres across in each direction, ringed by a six-foot concrete wall. At its centre sat the low one-storey building where the hostages were being held: a squat concrete block, paint flaked away in strips, with a single steel door on the north side and a small, barred window. Three other two-storey buildings stood inside the walls. Outside the compound, the ground dropped into scattered woods and low scrub, the maples, poplars, and occasional pine trees thinning into open pockets of grass and undergrowth.

The starlight did little to enhance visibility. Rocky lowered his NVGs over his eyes, and the world came alive in shades of green and shadow. The compound's edges sharpened, darkness giving way to depth and definition. The wall, buildings, and terrain stood out in contrast, as did the four machine gunners, one on each rooftop. He gave a thumbs-up to his det who followed his lead, moving their own NVGs into position.

"Gunner on each rooftop," Rocky whispered into his headset.

"Seen," Miles said. He was 50 metres behind the det on higher ground. "I've got eyes on everything except for the eastern corners and the western side of the buildings."

Master Sailor Logan Davis, the sniper attached to Champs' det, came over the net. "Alpha Ten. I've got it covered."

Each of the men studied the area carefully, making mental adjustments. The original plan called for Rocky's det to assault from the north. Now they were directly across from Champs' det, staged to the west of the square compound. Changing the initial breach location required a few adjustments. Instead of pushing through the northern gate, Rocky's team had to make it past the concrete wall. Breaching it was possible, but any cutting or demolition would generate noise that could alert the fighters inside and fatally compromise the stealth central to the concept of operations. But Lion had drilled into them that plans were fragile creations.

"Think it through, guys. What's the one thing that would completely upend us if it happened?" One of the men would offer up something, to which Lion would say "Good. Solve it. Now," pointing to another teammate. The men would put their heads together, usually coming up with more than one solution, but it took time to work through the problem. The first time Lion ran them through the exercise, it took nearly 30 minutes to hash out a fix. "We don't have 30 minutes to solve problems when we're downrange, folks," he'd say. "What else can screw us?"

Nearly every day when not on a mission Lion would sit the team down and run them through his now famous "work the problem" evolutions. Alpha Team spent hours a day inventing problems and then solving them. The next day, Lion would provide a stack of notes to the training cadre and tell them to find ways to trip Alpha up, a task the cadre took up with unbridled enthusiasm. There was no longer anything routine about training. The team, Lion included, had no idea what was coming their way. They would run through a training mission, solving one problem after another. It was relentless, but it worked. Each assaulter had spent so much time thinking about how to react to unforeseen circumstances that when it happened, they could act immediately. Every so often, they'd learn a lesson the hard way and endure unending ridicule for not carrying the right kit. It drove the men nuts, but proved effective. Alpha Team had never failed a mission or lost a man in combat.

Rocky flipped the switch on his laser module, setting it to infrared so the beam was invisible to anyone without NVGs, and aimed it at a section of the wall. "Bambam, assault ladder on my laser."

A six-foot concrete wall was climbable without a ladder but it was slower, and Rocky needed to get his assaulters over the wall quickly otherwise they'd be vulnerable to enemy fire.

Petty Officer Second Class Alain Gauthier, known as Bambam because of his thick, muscular bodybuilder frame, replied, "Seen."

"Jupiter, Alpha Two. Update."

"Alpha Two, Jupiter. We estimate eight times heat signatures in the target building. Three hostages and five hostiles."

During the mission brief a few hours earlier, the int shop had provided the team with a mock-up of the inside of the target building based on HUMINT reporting showing a large lobby-style room just past the main entrance with two more smaller rooms. Based on the report, Rocky figured there were at least two fighters in the lobby, probably a group of three more passed out in one room, and the three hostages passed out in the other. Unless they'd mixed them. If a hostage was in the same room as one of the fighters it would complicate the assault. The rooms would likely be dark, making a positive ID more difficult, adding a second or two to the time it would take to down the hostiles. The room by the door was another matter. The guys in there were likely awake and probably weren't just sitting in the pitch-black. There would be light in that room, making NVGs a no go.

"Tracking five times heat signatures in each of the other three buildings. No indication that the six contacts you spotted on the way in have moved."

That left six more fighters unaccounted for if the int estimate was accurate. Rocky figured there would be at least two by the gate and two more posted near the front door to the target building.

"All stations, Alpha Two. Does anyone have eyes on any fighters inside the ring?"

No response.

"Alpha Three, Alpha Two. SITREP."

"Ready in all respects," Champs said.

"All stations, Alpha Two. Approach."

Rocky and his det crept toward the eastern wall. Rocky, Hangman, Spooky, and Whiskey, Master Corporal Jake Reynolds, the team's medic famous for his thick, black, wavy hair, took up positions on the wall, weapons at the high ready position, two of them covering to the south, the other two to the north. Bambam dropped to one knee and unfastened the assault ladder from his kit, unfolded it, and placed it against the wall without a sound, then gave a thumbs-up. Hangman slung his MRR against his chest and climbed the first few steps of the ladder, then held, ensuring his head didn't protrude over the wall.

Two clicks in slow succession came through the comms, signalling that Champs' det was ready with a man on the ladder at the western wall.

"Execute."

Rocky heard four low, muffled pops followed almost instantaneously by thin, high snaps as bullets passed supersonic, then dull, heavy thuds.

"Rooftop gunners down," Miles said calmly over the comms.

Spooky squeezed Hangman's leg, who quickly pushed himself over the wall, dropping quietly, turning left, head up, gun up. Spooky landed immediately after, turning to the right, firing two rounds into the centre mass of a fighter in his arc. The man stumbled once, fell, and didn't move again. Rocky landed next, turning right, followed by Whiskey, who turned left, then Bambam, moving a step forward, covering the front.

Rocky heard two muffled pops from across the compound—the sound of suppressed MRRs. He turned, squeezing

Whiskey's shoulder, who did the same to Hangman's. Then Rocky turned back toward Spooky, squeezing his shoulder, and the five-man stack moved forward toward the eastern wall of the target building with Bambam covering the rear.

Less than 20 seconds had passed from the time Hangman cleared the wall until the stack reached the target building.

"In position," Champs whispered over the comms.

"I've got the door; you've got the gate. Go," Rocky said, squeezing Spooky's shoulder again. The stack moved along the side of the building, the first four pointing weapons forward, followed by Bambam, who moved backwards, covering the rear.

Spooky turned the corner left, firing two more rounds. Rocky was right behind him, firing two rounds of his own, each assaulter scoring two centre mass hits. The two fighters posted near the door never knew what hit them. Seconds later, Rocky and his det were stacked to the side of the main entrance. He heard a few more pops followed by Champs' voice. "Gate clear."

Hangman quickly assessed the steel door, then slung his MRR and drew the 12-gauge breaching shotgun designed to destroy locks, hinges, and strike plates with minimal ricochet and limited overpenetration. He nodded at Rocky, then placed the butt of the shotgun on his shoulder and pointed the muzzle at the locking mechanism. Bambam stood directly behind him, hand on his shoulder, followed by Rocky, Spooky, and Whiskey.

"NVGs off. Lights on," Rocky whispered. He glanced at the stack, making sure they were ready, then squeezed Bambam's shoulder who immediately squeezed Hangman's.

The shot rang out harder than suppressed rifle fire, a single hard report that cut through the night. There was a metallic rip as the locking mechanism cracked, followed by a brief metallic clatter; a little shower of paint and grit drifted like smoke.

Hangman shoved the door open and got clear of the frame.

Bambam burst through the doorway first, covering left and firing two rounds.

Rocky moved through the doorway so close behind Bambam that it seemed like the two entered at the same time. He covered right, saw a fighter standing from behind a desk, raising his pistol, but Rocky was faster. He fired two rounds into the man's chest.

Spooky pushed through half a second after Rocky and continued moving forward to the wooden door on the opposite side of the room with Whiskey directly behind him.

Tier-1 operators relied on violence of action to move against a numerically superior force: catch them off guard and destroy them before they had a chance to react. Initiative, speed, and violence were necessary ingredients. Nowhere was that truer than in a hostage rescue op.

Spooky didn't waste any time. He brought his left boot up, thrust forward with his hips, and smashed the interior wooden door open.

Whiskey moved through the door just as it blasted open. The crash and the bright white light from Whiskey's weapon caught the two groggy fighters off guard. He fired twice—one at each man, downing them both. "Clear," he said, as he ran toward a woman lying on the floor with her hands zip-tied behind her back.

Hangman, who entered the building last, moved left toward the other interior door. His boot collided with it a second after Spooky kicked the first door down.

Bambam burst through the second door, firing one shot. "Clear."

Rocky followed Bambam and saw the remaining hostages, two men, huddled in the far left corner with their hands bound behind them.

"Jupiter, Alpha Two. Gauntlet."

Before Rocky could issue his next command, the entire building lit up with bright light.

"End Ex. End Ex," the sergeant major said, leaning against a rail on the catwalk overhead.

Rocky let out a deep breath, took off his helmet, wiped the sweat off his forehead, and felt the sting of salt in his eyes for the first time.

The "dead" man lying in front of him rose to his feet, dusted himself off, and winked at Bambam.

"Thanks for not shooting me in the nuts this time. Glad your aim is finally improving," he said, chuckling as he walked toward the door.

"You'd have to have a set of nuts for me to be able to shoot them," Bambam shot back, chasing after him.

Rocky shook his head. Some things never changed.

***

Master Warrant Officer Elias Mercer, sergeant major of the training cell, stood in the doorway, all hard planes and quiet menace, a broad-shouldered veteran with a grey-streaked crewcut and eyes that missed nothing. The training cadre shepherded Alpha Team and the opposition force into the southern two-storey building, which had served as Jupiter's command post. The main room had a single heavy table at its centre with a three-dimensional model of the compound and its approaches pinned in plaster and resin. Along the walls, makeshift workstations had been set up with folding tables, military laptops, field notebooks, and cables snaking to portable routers. Voices filled the room as operators and mission support staff griped about the latest Sens game along with some customary good-natured ribbing. A burst of laughter broke out as Sergeant Natalia Maris shot down yet another one of Hangman's advances with the subtlety of a 2000-pound bomb.

Rocky glanced over at the grizzly sergeant major. Was that a smile or at least what passed for a smile from a sergeant major? He looked closer. Mercer's lips were pressed in a thin line that just barely curved at one edge. *I'll be damned.* He was pretty sure it was the first time the seasoned veteran had ever smiled, clearly content to watch Hangman get roasted a little more before calling things to order.

Maris, known to everyone as Talia, was no stranger to attention. It wasn't just her looks—though the dark hair that framed her face, the slight olive tint to her skin, and slender build didn't hurt—it was her confidence and professional competence that made her stand out. She was one of the most talented imagery analysts in the intelligence branch, and everyone in CANSOFCOM knew it.

"That baby face," Talia said, giving Hangman a once-over, "it's just not doing it for me."

"But what about the beard?" Hangman asked.

Talia squinted for a beat. "Hmm. Looks more like a failed recce mission. A few made it back, but the rest never showed up."

The room erupted into another roar, voices overlapping in a surge of laughter and applause, as Hangman brought both hands to his chest. "Oh no!" he cried, turning away, then dropping to his knees with both arms raised upwards, spread wide, as if waiting for some divine intervention to rescue him.

Grinning, Champs walked over to Hangman and placed a hand on his shoulder. "I don't think God's with you on this one, bud."

Mercer walked to the head of the table, palms flat on the wood, and looked up at the assembled men and women.

"Alright," he shouted, getting everyone's attention. "Let's get started."

The smiles and laughter vanished as everyone shifted back to the business of war and gathered around the table. Even Hangman, now back on his feet, had his game face on.

"For my new people," Mercer said, glancing toward the rookie support staff, "there's no rank here. No sirs or ma'ams. First names or nicknames unless you're in deep shit."

Mercer returned his gaze to the operators. "Now, for all you prima donnas. I'm not interested in your egos or personalities. No finger pointing. No blame. Keep your comments brief and to the point."

He turned to Rocky. "Assault lead. Tell us what your objective and constraints were."

"Our objective was to infiltrate the compound, rescue the three hostages, and exfil. Our constraints were the presence of hostages, avoiding collateral damage, and stealth," Rocky said.

Mercer nodded and turned toward Captain Michael Belanger, JTF2's newly appointed operations officer. "OPFOR lead, explain your disposition and intent."

Belanger wasn't your typical officer, or warrior for that matter. He had the look of an operator but the demeanour of a clown. He was tall and muscular, with light brown hair that was much longer than regulation and a matching bushy beard. More comfortable leaning against walls than standing upright with a military bearing, the NCOs of the conventional force couldn't stand his casual posture. He sauntered over to the map model on the table, pointing out the locations of the gate and door sentries and the rooftop gunners.

"My intent was to provide a professional, well-trained opposition force on a normal alert posture. The six guys Alpha Team ran into on their approach were meant to force an audible so we could see how they reacted." Belanger glanced toward Alpha Team. "You guys handled that well."

He adjusted the red ball cap, riddled with salt stains that he never bothered trying to clean, that sat backwards on his head. "I had the guys in the two-stories go to ground and actually sleep to see whether your insertion woke them. Same with the hostages and the fighters inside the target building except for the two in the main room."

Mercer nodded. "ISR."

Talia pointed to an image of a King Air 350ER airframe. "We're still testing the limits of the new Vigilance fleet. This evolution was as much a training eval for the aircraft, crew, and our analysts as it was for Alpha Team. We maintained positive tracking on the fighters outside the buildings and on the rooftops, but we couldn't see individual heat signatures inside the buildings."

Spooky raised a hand. "How were you able to tell us how many fighters were inside the building?"

Talia shifted her gaze to the sergeant major. "Can I geek out for a minute?"

Mercer nodded. "I'd like to hear the answer too."

"Ok, so, solid building materials like wood, concrete, drywall, or other roofing membranes block or absorb mid- to long-wave infrared. That means thermal imagers will show the outer surface temperature of the roof or walls, not the people inside, but you will see heat leaking to the exterior."

She motioned to the collators standing quietly behind the group. "I've had my team doing deep dive OSINT collection so we can build tables on how much heat you'd expect to see in different types of buildings across seasons and environments."

One of the collators brought up two images, side by side, of the same building.

"What you're looking at," she said, pointing to the screen, "is the southwest building of the compound. The image on the left shows the heat leakage from the building when it's empty. The one on the right shows the heat leakage with five people inside. See the difference?"

Rocky whistled. "Glad you guys are on our side."

"Agreed," Belanger said, making a point of fist pumping the three collators. "Good shit, all of you."

After a few more brief accolades, the sergeant major had the team run him through a short chronology of events, then shifted the after-action review to the debrief segment, which often felt more like an interrogation.

"You chose a stealth approach, so why did you breach with the 12-gauge instead of picking the lock?" Mercer asked.

Rocky nodded to Hangman, who stepped forward. "I checked the door and found thin steel with a weak lock. I could have picked it, but that would have taken longer. We'd already engaged the fighters outside, and there was no way to be sure that the shots hadn't woken up the baddies in the other buildings. Speed was the priority, and I was confident the gun would do the job."

Mercer nodded. "What about the fighters inside the target building?"

"There were two scenarios. Either they were already awake, in which case picking the lock would have given them more time, or they were still sleeping or unaware. In either case, violence of action was the way in."

"You agree with this approach?" Mercer asked Rocky.

"One hundred percent. Stealth got us to where we needed to be. The target building was small. Overwhelming violence was the way to go," Rocky said.

"Mike," the sergeant major said, nodding in the captain's direction.

"I checked with the OPFOR team. They didn't hear a thing, so you were still good to go on the stealth approach, but under the circumstances, you had no way of knowing that. I agree with your call," Belanger said.

"Any other points on that?" Mercer asked.

"I'd like to keep doing more runs with different teams, and different OPFOR guys to mix it up, and see if we get different results," Belanger said. "Start drawing up some tables like Talia's team did and try to establish a baseline."

Mercer scribbled down some notes, nodding. "I'll take that on as an action item."

The training cadre tossed out a few more questions, not necessarily to dispute the calls, but to test the thought process that went into the decisions. Every mission was different. No matter how similar some of them might seem there were always small nuances to adapt to. If the thinking behind a decision was sound, chances were the decision itself would be the right one.

Mercer moved through his agenda and invited everyone to bring forward things that had worked well that ought to be continued or built into standard operating procedures. That was the easy part. What came next often caused friction, especially for a gathering of type-A personalities.

"Now, let's talk about what didn't go so well. And remember what I said before: We're all tired, hungry, and ready to go home. No tantrums. Objective observations only," Mercer said.

Rocky listened intently as the mission's execution was dissected and critiqued, evoking distant memories of another sermon that remained undiminished even after all these years.

Lion had been pacing back and forth as he always did when he preached.

"AARs are all about courage."

The team looked at him like he'd truly gone mad this time.

"The courage," he continued, "to hear others tell us how bad we screwed up and why. This is by far one of the most important things we'll ever do. It's not fun, but it's how we improve. No one person has all the answers. The more people we hear from, the better the chances of someone spotting a fuck-up that we can fix."

The lesson had come during the early days, back when the members of the new Alpha Team were still learning to reconcile their egos with reality.

"You want to be the best? This is how we do it. We man up, we go in there, and we listen to what they have to say. We listen to each other. We don't make excuses. We find solutions."

Lion turned toward Rocky. "Oh, and, Alpha Two."

"Yeah, Matt?"

"No more throwing chairs at the training warrant."

"Got it," Rocky said, and decided then and there that Lion was right. It most certainly was not fun. Not one little bit.

Rocky's thoughts drifted back to the present.

"I didn't know exactly where each det was, but I had the benefit of knowing your plan," Sergeant Chris Booth, a CSOR operator, said. "So I led my six-man team directly between where I thought each of you would be. Couldn't see shit, but I heard the faint sound of twig snaps, so we turned in your direction, Rocky. We never did see you, even though we set up an OP barely 50 metres from your position, so good on that, but you gotta watch that noise."

Rocky nodded as each person spoke. The points were all minor, but fair. He took notes, as he'd done for years, to make sure lessons were followed up on and not forgotten. It was a simple concept, yet one that the Canadian military continued to struggle with.

"I think that about does it," Mercer said. "Let's start tearing down and—"

"I've got one more point that needs to be raised," said Bob Green, the ops warrant. He wasn't known for his tact or diplomacy. Stocky and broad-shouldered with close-cropped salt-and-pepper hair and a face lined from years of hard service, Green carried himself like the hardcore pipe hitter Rocky knew him to be. "I'm sorry, Elias, but someone's gotta say it."

Mercer sighed, nodding reluctantly. "Make it quick."

Green locked eyes with Rocky.

"Ah, fuck's sake," Rocky heard Champs mutter under his breath.

"Look, I get that you're struggling," Green began.

"Struggling?" Rocky countered.

"But you need to pull your head out of your ass."

"Watch yourself," Mercer warned, but Green continued, undeterred.

"You aren't Alpha Two. You need to accept reality. Alpha is your team to lead now. You've gotta start using Alpha One. It's confusing to those on the net."

Rocky's blood went hot in an instant, a rush straight to his face. "Was anyone confused?" Rocky asked, glancing around the room.

The room went quiet; the only sound Rocky heard was

his own breathing, growing heavier. "Looks like we're good then," he said.

Green took a few steps toward Rocky. "Alright, let's cut straight to it then. You're the team leader now. The fact that you refuse to use the call sign raises questions about your leadership. You did well tonight, but this was a training op. When you're downrange, you need to be fully dialled in, and I don't think you are."

Champs stepped forward, placing himself between Green and Rocky. "I think it's time for you to shut the fuck up, Bob."

"Bob, you're out of line," Mercer snapped. "We're done here."

Green shifted his gaze toward Mercer. "No, I'm not, Elias. You know I'm right. You're all thinking it; you just don't want to say anything. Since when do we approach things with kid gloves?"

He turned back toward Rocky. "What's your deal, man? It's your team now, you have—"

"It's not my team," Rocky shouted, bordering on screaming, voice cracking slightly. "It's Matt's team. You fucking hear me? It's Matt's team. He's Alpha One."

The room fell silent once more. Time seemed to stand still for a moment before Green spoke again, his voice softer now. "He's gone, man. You gotta move on."

Rocky bolted forward. "He's not fucking gone!" He screamed this time.

Champs spun quickly, putting himself in Rocky's path. The force of the impact would have knocked Champs to the floor had it not been for Hangman and Spooky, who converged on him.

"Whoa, easy, boss," Hangman said.

Rocky struggled against his teammates, who were barely able to contain him.

"I'm not taking Matt's call sign. Not until I hear from him, and neither is anyone else," Rocky barked.

Green didn't flinch, but his shoulders sagged slightly. "I'm sorry, Rocky," he said, barely above a whisper.

"You son of a bitch!" Rocky yelled.

Green turned toward Mercer. "Something's gotta be done."

The old warrior's face turned beet red as he slammed his fist down on the map model hard enough that it cracked, then started moving toward Green. "Goddammit, Bob—"

"That's enough," Belanger said, stepping between the two NCOs, then turning toward Green. "Take a walk."

"You can't ignore what just—"

"That," Belanger interrupted, "was a fucking order, Warrant Officer." The calm, easygoing officer was nowhere to be found. In its place was something else entirely. He locked eyes with Green. "Move."

"Yes, sir," Green muttered, then left the building.

Belanger moved toward the sergeant major, whose face looked like it had turned to stone. He placed a hand on his shoulder. "Elias, let's tear down and go home, yeah?"

"On it," Mercer said quietly, before turning to the grim-faced operators and supporters who were staring at the floor.

5

UNDISCLOSED TRAINING LOCATION
SUNDAY, OCTOBER 13
02:50 LOCAL TIME

Rocky pushed his cleaning rod through the breech until the end protruded through the muzzle of his MRR. He grabbed it with his other hand, pulling it all the way through, then inspected the swab at the opposite end. Satisfied, he slammed the upper receiver down against the lower receiver and pushed the rear takedown pin through the lug, locking them together. He glanced at his men, who were all sitting on the floor, leaning against the wall, weapons in their laps, each one absorbed in the same weapon cleaning routine. Talia and her three corporals were there too, sitting on their kit bags, fiddling with their laptops.

He heard the steel door they'd breached earlier crank open and turned. Mike Belanger stepped inside. He crouched in front of the group. "How's everyone doing?"

He received a few polite nods, but nobody responded.

"Mind if I pull up a piece of concrete?" Belanger asked.

Rocky motioned to the floor in front of them. "Make yourself at home."

Belanger sat in front of them, cross-legged, shifting his gaze between them. "What's everyone thinking about?"

More silence.

Every gaze stayed down. The black hole in Rocky's gut seemed to widen by the second. Not only could he not keep himself together, but his outburst had clearly gutted everyone's morale. He wanted to say something to pull them back somehow, but the words wouldn't come.

Belanger glanced down, nodding, then glanced back up again. "The CH-146 Griffons will be here soon, and none of you are leaving until someone starts talking to me."

Talia was the first to break the silence. "I'm thinking about beating the shit out of Bob."

A few of the men nodded in agreement. Belanger chuckled. "He's my ops warrant, don't hurt him too bad or I'll end up having to do some work." He shot the sideways smile he was known for. That earned him a few quiet laughs, but the mood quickly retreated toward darkness again.

Belanger didn't prod any further. He sat there, looking at the group, waiting.

"I'm thinking about Matt," Hangman said without looking up, pulling a swab through his barrel.

"Me too," Belanger said, eyes welling slightly. "Me too."

Rocky glanced at the group again. Champs ran his forearm across his eyes, trying to make it look like he was scratching them. Talia had tears running down her cheeks. Whiskey fumbled with his med kit, failing to fasten it back on his gear and throwing it across the room before burying his face in his hands.

Spooky, usually the calmest of the bunch, slammed his helmet against the concrete. "It makes no sense. He wouldn't just disappear."

"And what's HQ doing about it?" Bambam chimed in. "Fuck all. That's what."

"It's a fucking disgrace," Miles added. "You're all acting like he never existed."

Belanger swallowed hard but didn't say anything. He sat there and took it while everyone lambasted him. It was guilt by association. Lion and he were commissioned a little over a year ago. Now Lion was gone, and Belanger, formerly Bravo One, was a staff officer in the head shed with the rest of the warriors turned bureaucrats.

The team skewered Belanger for another fifteen minutes while Rocky sat in silence. He wished he had the same discipline and self-control that Belanger was showing. He'd improved leaps and bounds over the years, but he was still a hothead at heart. Rocky couldn't listen any longer, not when it was his conduct that had caused this mess in the first place. The training op had been a resounding success. All he'd had to do was keep his cool and shut his mouth, like Lion had taught him, while Green said his piece and he had failed.

"Knock it off, guys. It's not Mike's fault. And enough with the HQ garbage. He's still one of us," Rocky said.

"It's fine, man. Let them speak," Belanger said.

"No, it's not fine. I'm the one that fucked up back there, and turning on one of our own isn't helping." Rocky glared at the team.

"The only thing you're guilty of is being loyal," Talia said.

"Agreed," Champs said. "But he's right. Mike's not the enemy here." He rose to his feet and extended a hand to Belanger. "I'm sorry for what I said."

Rocky watched as, one by one, the team rose to their feet, following Champs' lead. *He should be the next Alpha One. Not me.*

The steel door creaked open again, and the sergeant major popped his head in. "Helos will be here in ten mikes. Get your gear over to the assembly area."

Champs started marshalling the group. Belanger caught Rocky's eye, gave a short nod, and led him outside. The two walked toward the main gate.

"Thanks for the save back there," Belanger said.

"Something tells me you were exactly where you wanted to be," Rocky said, before blowing into his hands, trying to keep them warm.

Belanger shrugged. "The team obviously had a lot they needed to say. Now it's your turn."

Rocky stopped walking, looked up at the stars, and shook his head. "What do you want me to say?"

"Look. Bob's a dick, but he's not wrong. Now I need you to be straight with me, man. Tell me what's going on."

"What the fuck do you think's going on? My team leader vanished into thin air right after our last op without a word. Not even a text. There's no way Matt would just take off without saying anything. And it's been radio silence from HQ for the past nine months." Rocky locked eyes with Belanger. "So why don't *you* tell *me* what's going on?"

Belanger turned away and exhaled. "Rocky, I can't say more than I already have."

"More than you have? You haven't said shit. If you want me to be straight with you, then you need to be straight with me."

Now it was Belanger who fell silent. Rocky took a few steps forward, stepping in front of him. "Is it national security related? If it is, say so or blink or something, and I'll drop it."

Belanger shook his head slowly.

"Is he..." The words caught in Rocky's throat. "Is he dead?"

Belanger's eyes squeezed shut. "I don't know."

Rocky felt his knees give out and crumpled to the ground, landing on his ass. He made no effort to pick himself back up.

"All I know is that something wasn't right with him when you guys came back from your last op."

"What? How? That doesn't make any sense."

"I can't tell you that," Belanger said, sitting down next to him.

Rocky felt like he was going to be sick. The look on Belanger's face when he'd said he didn't know if Matt was dead unsettled him in a way he'd never experienced before. The thought had crossed his mind several times in the past nine months, but he'd dismissed the possibility, reasoning that if Matt were dead, the unit would say so. There was no point in their keeping that a secret. But they didn't know.

He looked over at Belanger. Rocky could tell by the look on his face that he was scared out of his mind, yet he'd never let it show—until now.

"I don't think I can do this," Rocky said. "I can't lead like he did. Those are shoes I can never fill."

"Nobody can," Belanger agreed. "But you don't have to fill his shoes. You have to fill yours."

"I wish I could be like him."

Belanger laughed, though there was no humour in it. "No, you don't. Trust me."

"What do you mean?"

"I've known Matt since we were four years old."

"No shit? I had no idea."

Belanger stared up at the sky. "We don't advertise it. But we grew up together. He used to be so happy. His parents were absolute gems."

"Used to be?"

"His father started as a blue-collar guy, back when there wasn't much money in it. He busted his ass, became a lawyer, and got a job in the legal department of some brokerage house. His parents and his fifteen-year-old sister, Katie, moved to New York in late August 2001. Matt stayed with my family in Montreal while they got settled."

Rocky froze, the timeline clicking into place. "Jesus," he muttered. "Right before..."

"Tuesday, September 11, 2001, was Mitchell Lion's second day on the job. He brought April and Katie to the office with him that morning to show them the view."

Belanger wiped a tear from his eye. "After the first plane hit the North Tower, Mitchell called my dad so they could say goodbye to Matt. They were on the 103rd floor."

He paused for a moment before continuing. "I watched Matt listen to his family die. Katie screamed so loud that I could hear her voice, even though the phone was pressed to Matt's face. We were twelve at the time."

Rocky had no words. He was close to his family, especially his brother. Going through something like that would have killed him—he was sure of it. He felt an overwhelming rage building within him. It consumed him. His hands clenched into fists, and a burning fire replaced the black hole that had been eating away at him. "Those fucking bastards," he said; his tone was pure menace.

Belanger nodded. "Now you're starting to understand Matt's world. He was never the same after that. He didn't speak a word for five months."

"What got him talking again?"

"I'm sure you've seen the picture that surfaced in January 2002 of Alpha Team dragging Al Qaeda detainees off the back of a Herc."

"Who hasn't?" Rocky said. "We have it pinned up on the wall in the team cage."

"Matt saw it too, in January 2002. He was thirteen. I can still remember his first words: 'We're joining JTF2.' And you know who the guy in the middle of the picture is, right? The one dragging a terrorist by the hair?"

"Marc Tremblay," Rocky said, putting another piece of the puzzle together.

"Bingo. We had no idea who he was at the time, of course, but the image of Tremblay became a sort of childhood hero to Matt. We met him for the first time in our assaulter course, and, as you can imagine, we were blown away. The old man became a father figure for Matt in a way that nobody else could."

"Damn," Rocky said, thinking back to his initial jealousy of the Tremblay/Lion dynamic, now feeling like a complete idiot.

Belanger tossed a small rock he'd been fidgeting with, staring off in the distance. "Anyway, Matt became obsessed after he saw that picture. He spent every free minute in the school library, reading anything he could about war, combat, and leadership."

Belanger shifted his gaze back to Rocky. "He's been studying war and leadership since he was an adolescent. He dragged my lazy ass to every martial arts school he could convince my dad to pay for, and he excelled."

Rocky scoffed. "Fucking figures. I could have used that information nine years ago."

Belanger laughed out loud. "No doubt."

The laughter faded after a moment, and Belanger's expression turned grim again. "War created Matt. It's all he knows now, assuming he's still out there somewhere. He probably can't even remember anything that came before that day. It's like a burning fire inside him that never lets up. It drives him in ways that I still don't understand."

It was a lot to absorb. Rocky had known Lion for nearly a decade and considered him a good friend, despite their earlier clashes; however, there was clearly much about him he didn't know. Lion hadn't ever mentioned a sister. What Belanger said made sense, though. Lion was relentless. He pushed Alpha Team harder than any of the other team leaders, and that was saying something. Despite the ruthless tempo and the constant demand for excellence, the team loved him. Rocky mulled it over in his mind. Lion wasn't a tyrant. He was more of a gentle giant. On the other hand, there was no denying his mastery of violence even though he wasn't a violent man.

"I don't know," he said. "Maybe vengeance?"

"Nah," Belanger said, shaking his head. "Vengeance is so small, flat, and impotent compared to what's burning inside him. It's something far more dangerous than that. There isn't a word that exists that can describe it."

Rocky threw his hands up in frustration. "That doesn't jibe with the Matt that I know. He's so damn polite and kind it makes me want to barf sometimes."

"That's his parents," Belanger said. "And his sister," he added, voice cracking. He took a few minutes before continuing. "That's exactly who they were. They're still a big part of him; it's why that drive has such a hold over him."

Rocky had an epiphany. It felt like a flashbang cracking off in his mind, and it hurt. But everything made sense now, just in time for him to be unable to do anything about it.

"You're right," Rocky said. "It's not vengeance. He's on a desperate mission to save people who are already dead. It's a mission that can never end, so he tries to save everyone else, but that's not possible either. Fuck..."

Belanger, having regained his composure, raised an eyebrow. "Not bad for a blockhead. I never thought about it that way."

"I wish there were something I could do," Rocky said.

"There is, you dumb-ass! Lead the team. Keep it together until he comes back."

Rocky frowned. "What if it's too late, and he's already gone?"

"Look, even if he does come back, he can't keep leading Alpha Team. He's a captain now. That last op you guys ran was supposed to be his last as team leader. One way or another, you need to take up the mantle of Alpha One and honour his legacy."

Rocky wondered what that legacy was. There was no doubt that Lion had become a master of war. Rocky had seen him impose his will on chaos more than once. But had he been able to tame the chaos within? Probably not, though Rocky suspected he'd come very close. Still, close enough was never good enough, was it? Certainly not when it came to combat. And if Lion couldn't do it, what chance did he have? The thought sent a chill up his spine.

I should have listened to my mom and joined the goddamn Air Force.

Barely a second after the thought materialized, Rocky heard the low, rhythmic thump of the CH-146 Griffons' rotors building in the distance, the sound deepening into a steady chop that rolled across the compound.

Belanger sprang to his feet and smiled, extending a hand to Rocky, pulling him upright.

Rocky, now convinced that some cosmic being was trying to fuck with him, stared straight up at the sky. He tripped over himself and probably would have broken his fall with his nose had Belanger not caught him.

"Hey, cheer up," Belanger said, flashing a grin. "We're going home."

Rocky clung to Belanger's arm, still looking up at the sky. "Yeah. Home. That sounds good."

6

CH-146 GRIFFON
SOMEWHERE OVER ONTARIO
SUNDAY, OCTOBER 13
03:20 LOCAL TIME

Rocky's legs dangled into the night, the cold northern wind slapping at his face as the chopper banked east, rotors thundering above the endless dark. Below, multiple compounds of various sizes and designs were fully lit as clusters of contractors patched walls, replaced doors, and readied the sites for the next day's serial. As the CH-146 Griffon banked south, Rocky caught sight of several passenger aircraft scattered across additional training compounds—everything from sleek Gulfstream and Bombardier jets to narrow-bodied Airbus A320s and full-sized Boeing 777s. For units like JTF2, the SAS, and Delta, aircraft assaults were the pinnacle of special operations work and by far the most difficult. Rescuing passengers from a hijacked airliner wasn't just another mission; it was the ultimate test of precision, coordination, and nerve. JTF2 trained for it day in and day out, chasing perfection in a fight where even a second's hesitation could mean failure.

He smiled, feeling a sense of nostalgia as he remembered the hundreds of training serials Alpha Team had done on those aircraft. Their first attempts were absolute shit shows, but they were fun too. Lion brought the team alone for their first runs to avoid the added pressure of being observed by the unit. The demand on JTF2 members to constantly be at their best and demonstrate excellence in everything they did was a heavy burden to carry. It was a common philosophy among Tier-1 units. The results were difficult to argue against, but the cost was high. Rocky had seen the burnout it produced. Coupled with an assaulter's refusal to quit under any circumstances—an attribute that set them apart from the masses—good men went to early graves. The training routine back home was often more gruelling, demanding, and difficult than live operations. It left little downtime and even less time for families.

Without the typical pressure bearing down on them, Alpha Team's first attempt at aircraft takedowns felt like a breeze. It allowed them to try some unorthodox techniques; most were complete catastrophes, but a few of them worked. They also got to see a whole other side of their leader, who equipped a sense of humour to his gear, apparently for the first time.

"In the army," Lion said, mimicking the voice of the drill sergeant from *Full Metal Jacket*, "if you are doing something stupid and it starts to work, it is no longer classified as stupid."

The comment earned a few surprised laughs, and it served as the theme for the weekend. They experimented without pressure or fear of failure. On the Friday evening, after sixteen hours of evolution, the team sat on lawn chairs enjoying some well-earned beers. The alcohol and fatigue inevitably led to a heated debate, a common and usually harmless occurrence. Lion surprised the team again.

"While I find the discussion over the nuances between shit pumps and thud fucks to be utterly fascinating," he said, interrupting the debate over which category each officer fell under, "I'd like to shift the discussion to something of much greater importance."

Hangman rolled his eyes. "Ah fuck, here we go again."

Champs, ever the maintainer of order, wagged a finger at Hangman. "What's on your mind, boss?"

"A simple question," Lion said. "One that has burdened man since the beginning of time."

The team waited in silence during Lion's poetic pause.

"Tits or ass?" Lion said, with a serious expression. "That's what we need to determine. Right here. Right now."

The team erupted into laughter, and the debate shifted. Rocky found himself listening to each member's preference as they debated the merits of their position more fiercely than they had anything else.

"Come on, Rocky, quit holding out. You gotta choose a side," Whiskey insisted.

"No can do. I hit the jackpot. My wife has it all," Rocky said.

"Elaborate," Bambam said to a round of nods.

"Not a fucking chance," Rocky said. "Go perv somewhere else."

It went on forever—each man, apparently, deeply passionate about the topic.

At the end, Lion stood up, summarized each man's position, and amalgamated it into a holistic assessment in a way only he would think to do. Sadly, the pinnacle of his speech got interrupted.

"Wow. Nice, Matt. Nice," Talia said, approaching from behind. She'd volunteered to drive food and supplies to the men over the weekend, but she hadn't been expected until the next morning.

Lion's head snapped around, his face instantly turning beet red. He opened his mouth, but no words came out. It was the first time Rocky had seen him speechless. Lion stood there frozen, as did the rest of the team, until Rocky sprang into action. He got out of his chair and approached her.

"My fault," he said. "I put him up to it. He's always had such a stick up his ass, so I dared him to prove otherwise."

"And you chose the topic?" she asked, glaring at him.

"I did. It was inappropriate. I'm sorry, Talia."

"You're damn right it was inappropriate, Rocky. You're a married man. Shame on you!"

Rocky grimaced but didn't say anything.

Talia placed both her hands on her hips. "And the rest of you…" She paused. "I have no words."

The team, all red-faced now, lowered their gazes to the dirt beneath them, unable to look her in the eye. Silence stretched for a few minutes, then Rocky risked glancing upwards and saw Talia's face contorting, a flicker tightening the corners of her mouth, her eyes bright with strain.

"Oh my God—ahahaha! I had you guys *so* bad!" she gasped between fits of laughter, doubling over and clutching her stomach, crackling uncontrollably. "You should've seen your faces!"

For a moment, they just stared at her—wide-eyed, stunned, and utterly breathless with relief.

"Oh, relax," she teased. "Trust me, the ladies are far worse."

She turned toward Lion, one eyebrow arched, a teasing glint in her eye. As her weight slid to one side, her hip cocked subtly, the motion equal parts challenge and amusement. "So, Matt... Ass, huh?"

Rocky didn't think a man's face could get any redder than Lion's face already was, but once again, Alpha One found a way to surprise him.

"God help me," Lion said, trying his best to avoid Talia's gaze, and everyone burst out laughing.

The CH-146 Griffon jolted violently, tearing Rocky's mind back to the present. *What the...*

"Oops," the pilot said over the comms. "My bad."

Rocky tensed and exchanged a glance with his teammates.

"All good now. Settle in for the ride," the pilot said.

Rocky stared at the glow of the aircraft below until they blurred, then looked up at the stars, thinking of Lion and wondering if somewhere, under some other stretch of sky, his old team leader was still out there looking at the same stars. The thought steadied him, easing the tightening in his chest, and he drifted off to sleep.

7

EXCALIBUR INDUSTRIES
CANARY WHARF, LONDON
MONDAY, OCTOBER 14
08:30 LOCAL TIME

Alexander Volk had no desire to see the West destroyed, at least not in the way Al-Najm did. He thrived in Western society. It was his arena, his masterpiece of manipulation and profit, a system he depended on, no matter how much he despised it. Yet as he stood before the vast windows of his top-floor Canary Wharf office, watching the city pulse beneath the pale morning light, he saw not vitality but entropy. London's towers gleamed like monuments to efficiency, but he knew the truth. The institutions they housed were hollow, existing on complacency and self-congratulation rather than innovation. The West had become a culture of bureaucrats, activists, and moral accountants, each vying for superiority in a game that produced nothing of worth. Volk's empire, born from his own brilliant innovation and ruthlessness, suffocated under its endless red tape. The West, Britain in particular, needed to be made strong again, but it would have to be dismantled first. Stripped of its softness. Its illusions. And more importantly, its dependence on handouts and outrage.

His office reflected that philosophy: an elevated desk upon a black onyx dais, walls of brushed steel and veined stone—every line deliberate, every surface immaculate. It was not a place of comfort but command—a mirror of the order he intended to impose on the world beyond his tower. It was also a gallery of wealth refined. The vast room stretched beneath a soaring ceiling lined with recessed lighting that spilled across polished basalt floors. On one wall, an abstract oil painting—an original Richter—anchored the room in cultured authority, while a bronze timepiece the size of a shield ticked in perfect rhythm, its mechanical precision echoing Volk's own nature. A glass display case held artifacts of conquest: a decommissioned encryption module from the Cold War, a ceremonial dagger gifted by a Gulf prince, and an early prototype of his first cyberdefence terminal, polished to a mirror sheen. Everything in the office existed to remind visitors of where they stood and who owned it all.

Usually, his office was devoid of any chairs save for the one behind his desk. He preferred to make his visitors stand, keeping them in a perpetual state of discomfort, while he sat in his chair, slightly elevated. Only his most trusted people had the privilege of sitting in his presence.

But today wasn't a typical day. He was meeting with his psychologist, Dr. Margaret Ellison. Volk hated the old bat, her poised demeanour, especially the look on her face as she scribbled notes. When he'd first hired her five years ago he'd done his best to establish dominance, as he did in all his interactions, and failed. He'd tried to get a rise out of her, or get under her skin, but to no avail. Even his occasional tantrums had little effect. Had Volk believed in the supernatural, he would have sworn Ellison was an iron demon. Her words had certainly haunted his dreams more than once.

Volk hadn't hired her because he thought he needed counselling—he considered himself above such things—but his public relations advisor, a young woman whose ruthlessness nearly rivalled his own named Sienna Fairfax, insisted on it. The memory still gnawed at him.

"Everyone needs someone to talk to," she said. "It can't be one of us, and it can't be someone who would ever share the details. So hire a bloody psychologist for God's sake."

Volk had leaned back in his chair looking down at Fairfax who had taken the liberty of standing closer to his desk than he liked. Her long, dark hair framed a tailored suit—feminine yet unmistakably commanding. It lent her an aura of confidence far beyond her years. He waved her off. "I don't need a psychologist. I have—"

"I don't care," she cut in, drawing his ire, but also his attention. "You're an insufferable bastard, and it's starting to show in everything you do. Keep carrying on like this, and you'll lose the trust of all the snowflakes. And whether you like it or not, it's still their narrative to control. So, find someone to bitch to. Someone who can't share what you discuss."

Her rebuke both aroused and infuriated him. The mix was confusing. He wasn't one to bother with the opposite sex; women were an unnecessary distraction, a weakness.

He allowed himself to indulge rarely and never with someone from his organization. That would only exacerbate the distraction.

Volk considered firing her, but she knew too much. He'd had subordinates killed before and wasn't above doing it again. He dismissed the thought. She was the embodiment of excellence, and her loyalty had been proven more than once. People he could trust were in short supply, which made her valuable.

"Fine," he said at last. "Find someone suitable."

When she left, Volk took out a sheet of paper and wrote a contract with himself, stating in clear terms that he would never sleep with her or let her get too close. He signed it and locked it away in a safe that could only be opened by his biometrics in conjunction with a password that changed daily according to an algorithm he'd designed. If anyone other than him tried to access it, its contents would be immediately destroyed beyond recognition.

After he'd met with Dr. Ellison a few times, he'd signed another contract with himself promising not to have her killed no matter how much she pissed him off, which, as it turned out, happened several times per discussion.

Volk turned away from the window as two aides scurried about, setting up two chairs in front of his desk along with matching arm tables. Ellison had laughed in his face when he'd told her she would stand during their sessions. It was a small concession; the woman was in her sixties after all and would probably fall over before their talk ended. Still, it was one more reason to hate her. Yet, he'd come to rely on her. Not because he needed therapy. Volk knew for a fact that he didn't. But he'd realized she was the only person on earth who truly understood him. It was a vulnerability, to be sure—an excellent reason to have her killed but for that bloody contract.

The two aides withdrew. A moment later the glass doors to his office slid open, and the portly senior limped toward the chair, cane in hand and those fucking glasses that sat low on her nose. She plopped herself onto the chair, placing her hands in her lap.

"Good morning, Mr. Volk," she said, her tone measured and faintly amused. "You look as though you've already argued with half the world—and won, naturally."

His eyes narrowed. "You mock me."

"Oh, I wouldn't dare," she said, barely containing the sarcasm.

He took off his thin-framed glasses, pulled a cloth from the inside pocket of his suit jacket, and began wiping them, ensuring there wasn't a single speck of dust. "Why do you insist on pushing my buttons?" He kept his eyes focused on his glasses.

She shrugged. "I'm retired, you know, and my grandchildren have grown too hip for old granny. A woman needs something to amuse herself with."

Volk began considering a new contract that would promise not to enter into any further contracts with himself but relented. His judgment was absolute; thus it was only logical that he followed his own commitments. A slight smile formed on his face. The contract didn't say anything about having the wicked woman's tongue cut out.

The glass doors whispered open again, and one of the aides glided in, placing a mug of Panama Geisha espresso on each of the arm tables, sleek vessels of matte black porcelain trimmed with a thin band of platinum, the emblem of Excalibur Industries laser etched along the rim. The company name was Fairfax's brainchild. Naturally, he'd wanted to name the company Volk Industries, but she'd convinced him that using King Arthur's sword would help boost the company's brand as a defender of the United Kingdom.

It had worked.

"Are you going to join me for coffee, Mr. Volk, or keep brooding over your reflection in the glass like a disappointed god?"

He sighed. *Why do I pay her the salary of twenty therapists for this kind of abuse?* Volk slid his glasses back on with deliberate care then crossed the room to his chair opposite Ellison, settling into it, crossing one leg over the other.

"Thank you," Ellison said to the aide as he retreated once more.

They both took a sip of the espresso. "Exquisite as always," she said, looking over the mug. "I must say, I rather like the name. And the emblem of the sword. Pure genius."

Volk glared at her. She was well aware that he'd opposed the name and eagerly anticipated the day he could put his name on *his* company. "Are you going to ask me about my thoughts or continue irritating me?"

"Oh, come now, Mr. Volk. You've never needed a red carpet to offer your thoughts," she said, smiling curtly.

A muscle twitched in his jaw as he considered his next words, trying to develop a strategy to get the better of her. It never worked, but his persistence knew no bounds.

"Well, you do seem more agitated than usual. Is this about your new arrangement?"

He nodded slowly.

"Why?" she asked quietly. "Doubting your judgment?"

"Ridiculous," he said. "He's the only avenue that can help me achieve my objective. It was the right choice."

"What is it then?"

Volk took another sip of the espresso, his shoulders tensing. "I can't get a lock on him. I can't track him. I have no idea where he is or who else he might be plotting with. Had I not seen him with my own eyes, I'd swear he was a ghost."

"I understand."

"You do?"

"Of course. You can't control him, and it scares you," she said, looking through her glasses sitting on the edge of her nose as she scribbled some notes.

Volk jumped to his feet. "I'm not scared, damn you," he shouted as he began walking around his desk.

She simply nodded and listened as he bitched about his frustrations over Al-Najm for the next twenty minutes. When he was finally done, he collapsed back into his chair and began gulping down the last of his espresso.

"And you still can't tell me his name or this secret objective?"

"No."

"Very well. Let's change the subject then. How are things with Ms. Fairfax? Does she still... You know... Get under your skin?"

Volk's jaw tightened as he set the empty cup down with a sharp click. "She's competent." His gaze was fixed on the window. "That's all that matters."

"Do you think she suspects?"

Volk's eyes shot open, head turning sharply toward her. His fingers drummed once against the armrest before stilling. He'd never thought about that before. Was it possible that she knew? The idea of being read so easily made his stomach twist with equal parts anger and desire.

Ellison began giggling softly.

"I'm terribly sorry," she said after a beat, between giggles. "It's quite unprofessional of me," she managed before breaking into laughter.

Much to his surprise, he started laughing too. He had no idea why, but he was as incapable of controlling it as Ellison seemed to be.

A few minutes passed, and the office settled into silence. Volk fidgeted in his chair. "I don't understand it."

"Try not to worry about it. Not everything needs to be controlled. Besides, this tells me there is a tiny bit of hope that a small part of you might be normal."

"Ridiculous," he said, though there was no venom behind it this time.

They laughed again; then the glass doors slid open once more.

"I'm sorry to interrupt," Fairfax said, rushing forward. "This can't wait."

"Oh, speak of the devil," Ellison said.

Volk and Fairfax turned toward her—his expression a cold glare, hers one of startled confusion.

Ellison scribbled a few final notes, tore the page from her notepad, folded it neatly, and slipped it into an envelope. After sealing it, she handed it to Volk. "I'll leave you both to it. Good to see you again, Ms. Fairfax," she said as she departed.

"What was that about, then?" Fairfax asked, her tone light but edged with curiosity, one brow arched in that effortless, posh sort of way.

"Nothing," he said. "Why are you here?"

Fairfax glanced at the empty chair, a faint grin flickering across her lips as though she were turning over a thought. "May I?"

Volk's brow furrowed, irritation flashing in his eyes. He gave a terse nod.

"If you must."

She lowered herself into the chair with unhurried grace, crossing her legs. She leaned back, perfectly composed, as if the seat had always belonged to her. Volk realized he'd just made a mistake. This was turning into a terrible day.

"We've intercepted an encrypted transmission from the Canadian consulate in Belize," Fairfax said, her tone crisp but carrying a spark of intrigue. Clearly, she was enjoying her expanded role in his operation. Even bad news seemed to energize her. He admired that and appreciated the devotion.

He sat up straight in his chair. "I'm listening."

"A Canadian expat. A former soldier, apparently, just waltzed in and handed them a USB stick," Fairfax said, a trace of urgency colouring her tone. "They pushed it up to Special Operations Command through their so-called 'secret' network, said they don't have a top-secret capability over there. The engineers tore through it in minutes."

"That's not surprising," Volk said. "Go on."

"It was a video of Sayyid al-Mazari, INIS, sending a message to the veteran," Fairfax said, her voice quickening. "He claims he's spotted Khalid al-Rashid in Belize City plotting against Canada. Says it's part of a much bigger operation, that he knows everything—who's behind it, the lot—and he's proposing a face-to-face. The details of the meeting were written in gibberish. The engineers said it was a cipher of some sort. They cracked it."

Volk froze. For a moment, the colour drained from his face, the mask of control cracking. "For fuck's sake."

"What are your instructions?" Fairfax asked.

"When's our next communication window with The Little

Star's courier?"

The Little Star—the English translation of *Al-Najm al-Saghir*—was a codename only a handful of people on the planet knew.

"I'm told The Little Star himself is due in London in a day or two," Fairfax said.

Volk gulped. "We need to move quickly. Do we have any units in Central America?"

"None of ours. Just Khalid al-Rashid and his band, but we may not be able to reach them if they are already in the jungle."

"Bloody hell." Volk jumped to his feet, circling back to his desk. "We may have to rely on locals. Reach out to our Artemis Circle contact in Belize and summon the weasel over here immediately."

"You mean the Permanent Under-Secretary of State for Defence?"

"Yes. Sir Malcolm Havers. I want him here within the hour."

8

KEIRA STERLING'S FLAT
BELIZE CITY
MONDAY, OCTOBER 14
23:28 LOCAL TIME

Keira looked at Nathan, concern etched across her face. "So it's that bad then?" She placed a hand on his, giving it a squeeze. "Whatever it is, we'll figure it out."

Her words didn't register. Nathan couldn't get past his frustration. His attempt to pass what he considered actionable intelligence to CANSOFCOM on a matter of national security had gone nowhere. Before he could say much of substance, the duty officer had cut him off, citing operational security. She had urged him to pass his information along to the Canadian consulate, then terminated the call. He'd gone to the consulate first thing yesterday morning under the guise of losing his passport. They made him wait for three hours before he finally got a chance to speak with someone one-on-one. When he recounted the intelligence to the consulate officer, the young man looked at Nathan like he'd lost his mind. Canada, as far as the young officer had been concerned, didn't face national security threats, and that was simply that. Nathan supposed he shouldn't have been surprised. His fellow countrymen, having lived under the security umbrella provided by the United States for so long, didn't take national security seriously.

It was infuriating.

He threw a fit, provided the official with his service number, and challenged him to at least make a damn phone call to confirm Nathan's legitimacy, but the officer refused to budge.

"Mr. Cutler, we have a lot of important work to do here; we don't have the—"

"Yes, yes," Nathan cut him off. "I'm sure your paperwork is vital, but I'm telling you we're facing a real threat here. If you don't take me seriously and lives are lost, I'll go to every single media outlet that will talk to me and identify you by name, Mr. Bowes. The entire country will know that you could have acted but had 'better things to do.'"

Long ago, Nathan had learned that self-preservation was the most powerful tool one could use when trying to convince a bureaucrat to do anything outside of their daily routine. Bureaucracies weren't meant to move quickly. They were intentionally built to ensure that decisions were never made too quickly. He grasped the underlying logic on a macro scale, but Canada took the philosophy to the extreme. Caution gave way to risk aversion. The trick to getting things done was to convince the bureaucrat that the risk of inaction far exceeded the risk of action.

It still pissed him off.

An hour later, Nathan was given a secure laptop to write his report and upload the video which was then uploaded to Global Affairs Canada's headquarters, but he had no way of knowing if his message had reached the people who needed it.

Keira gave his hand a gentle shake. "Not long ago, I didn't have to try this hard to get a man's attention," she said, a mixture of annoyance and concern in her voice. "Maybe I'm losing my touch."

Nathan blinked, then shook his head slowly. "Sorry."

"I hate to sound like a heartless cow, but we don't have the luxury of sulking," Keira said. "Tell me what you found in the locker."

Nathan exhaled, the weight of it all pressing down on him. Frustration simmered beneath the fear—fear for his Canada. He felt more alienated from the country he'd once called home than he had when he left, but he still couldn't sit by and do nothing. He'd meet with Sayyid and learn whatever his old friend had to say, but what good would that do if nobody would listen? He felt small in that moment, like a single voice shouting into a storm no one else wanted to see. Nobody except the spy who had her hand on his arm. It should have felt comforting, but it didn't.

"Your hands are shaking, love," she said, as she placed each of her hands on his. "I can't help you if you don't start trusting me."

"Except it's not your job to help me, is it?" he snapped, pulling his hands away from hers.

She stared at him, taken aback. "Why are you acting like I've done something wrong?"

He glared at her before looking away, his gaze landing on the corkboard. The link analysis she relied on to pose as a facilitator for a sex trafficking ring. "You haven't done anything wrong. You're just doing your job. I get it. Don't worry."

She straightened a little, arms crossing loosely, her brow knitting in mild confusion. "Have I hurt your feelings somehow? Is that it?" The irritation in her tone was real, but her eyes held a flicker of something else that Nathan couldn't identify.

He couldn't think clearly; the conflicting emotions were too much, and he was well past his best-before date. He'd lost his nerve for this line of work. Even when he was in the zone, he had never faced something this big before. Nathan was no stranger to being surrounded by tactical threats to his life and to those of his comrades. That was something he could deal with, but the fate of a nation was something else entirely. Sayyid's words had been intentionally cryptic. He knew that, but the grave concern behind the words was obvious. Whatever this was, it was big, and his own country had slapped him down and treated him like a nuisance. Nathan was starting to understand how it felt to be truly alone. It wasn't something he'd had to contend with as a soldier.

Then there was Keira. The beautiful woman nearly half his age. The spy. The only one who had bothered with him. A girl whose survival depended on her ability to lie. And the one he'd foolishly fallen for against his better judgment. Just like that, he'd become the textbook definition of desperation that he'd been warned about for years. He tried to remind himself that she worked for an allied nation. But such things meant little in the world of espionage. Nathan wanted to trust her more than anything, but how could he when he couldn't even trust himself?

"Forget I said anything," Nathan finally managed.

"That's it. Isn't it? You think I'm using you?" Keira said, the look in her eyes shifting.

"Aren't you?"

Her eyes shot open. "Oh, fuck you, Nathan!" She stood and walked away from the couch. She kept her back to him for a moment before turning around to face him.

"I'm going to assume you're under a lot of stress because in all the months I've known you, you've never once acted like the arse you're being right now. I told you I didn't know anything about Sayyid until recently. Everything before that..." She hesitated, her words faltering. "It was—I mean, that—" She turned away, muttering under her breath, "Bloody hell."

She had a point. Sayyid had said he'd only been in the country for the past month. But that didn't mean she wasn't lying about everything else. And what did she mean by everything else? Sure, she'd flirted with him after he flirted with her, but she was working as a waitress; flirting was part of the job.

Keira turned to face him again, slowly. "You think I put on that display with you so easily because I'm some sort of certified harlot? Is that what you think of me? Go on then—say it."

Nathan wasn't sure what to think. Hearing her confront him forced him to think it through. Did he really see her that way? Even if he did, he'd never say it. There was no reason to offend her. But the look on her face told him he already had. Or was it something else?

"Were you lying the other night?" Keira said.

Nathan's brow creased. "What do you mean?"

"When you held my hand and told me you understood. Were you lying when you said that?" Her voice cracked.

The question hit him like a palm heel to the solar plexus. He wanted to fight back, to tell her she was twisting things. But she wasn't. That night, he *had* understood. Sayyid's revelations had alarmed him to such a degree that he didn't know what to think anymore.

"No," he said finally, the word dragging out. "I wasn't lying. I just..." He stopped, unable to finish the sentence. He had no idea what the hell to say now.

Keira moved directly in front of him, dropping to her knees, grabbing his hands again. "Then what is it, dammit?"

"It's Canada," he shouted. "They're planning something that will cripple the country, and I can't get anyone to listen to me."

"Canada? What? Nathan, you're not making any sense. You need to tell me everything."

He pulled the USB stick out of his pocket and handed it to her. "There's a video. Watch it."

Keira plugged the stick into her laptop and watched the video. She brought her hands up to her mouth when she heard the words "existential threat."

"Dear God. What the hell have we gotten ourselves into?" she said, turning to face him.

Nathan's hands kept shaking. "I don't know. But I know Sayyid. He doesn't exaggerate."

She moved back over to the couch, sitting next to him, much closer this time. "Is that why you've been such a cunt tonight?"

"I'm sorry. I don't know who to trust."

"You said nobody's listening to you. Who else have you told?"

Nathan filled her in on everything. "I had no choice," he said.

"Don't fret it. I would have done the same. Now listen to me. You're not alone. You get me?"

"I don't know what to say."

She frowned. "Nod your head and say yes."

He nodded.

"Well, it's a start at least. Hold here for a minute."

She went into her bedroom. When she returned, she had a satellite phone in her hand. "I need to call this in. And trust me, they're going to bloody listen to me."

Keira entered what looked like an encryption sequence into the phone, then placed the call, putting it on speaker so Nathan could hear.

"Nightgate," a voice on the other end said.

She relayed all the details.

"When and where is the meeting?"

"I haven't asked yet, and I wouldn't say at any rate."

"Understood."

"Can you get the hitters here any sooner?"

"Negative. Hereford's not coming. They've been waved off."

"Waved off? What the bloody hell for? What do you expect us to do out here alone?" Keira demanded.

"Nothing. Your orders are to stand down on all operations. Do not get involved."

"The hell I won't. I gave my word."

"You shouldn't have. Matters have changed. This is for your own good. Stay out of it."

The line went dead.

Keira stared at the satellite phone, pale faced. "I'm not staying out of this," she said, discarding the phone.

Nathan felt something twist in his gut as he watched her. The conviction in her voice, the fire in her eyes. All that doubt, all the unspoken accusations, suddenly felt small and stupid. She wasn't playing him. She never had been. *When did I become so weak and indecisive?* He wondered, not for the first time, if age was catching up with him.

"I can't let you do this."

She turned to face him. "But you can't bloody well stop me, can you?"

"Keira, listen—"

"No. You listen," she interrupted. "Why would the SAS be waved off? And why would Nightgate tell me to stand down from the very assignment he tasked me to?"

She sat down next to him again. "Matters have changed? Nathan, that's code for his hand is being forced. He's trying to protect me from something."

"How can you be so sure?"

"Because I trust him. He's a patriot to his core. King and country and all that jazz."

Keira placed her hand on his forearm. "Nightgate isn't some low-level handler. He's one of the last Cold Warriors. He respects the old ways and isn't easily trifled with. And someone, or something, did just that."

"What do you think it means?"

Keira didn't answer right away. Her gaze drifted toward the dark window, as if she half expected to see the world changing outside it. When she finally spoke, her voice was lower, steadier, but edged with something Nathan hadn't heard from her before: fear.

"It means my government's been compromised," she said quietly. "Corrupted at the highest level. This threat—whatever it is—goes far beyond Canada."

Nathan felt a chill crawl up the back of his neck. For all his years in uniform, for everything he'd seen and done, the idea of corruption that deep inside the British government rattled him in ways no enemy ever had.

"The meeting is taking place at 10 PM tomorrow at Samie's Pizza by the waterfront. But I have to go alone."

"Alone, but not alone," she said.

"We don't want to spook him, Keira. If he disappears on us, we'll never know what we're up against."

"Nathan, Sayyid knows me, remember? He gave me the information to pass on to you. And he's smart. So he knows bloody well that I'll be nearby."

"Who's the hero now?"

Keira leaned into him. "Someone's gotta look after the oldies."

"You never told me who those two punks were following me the other night. You think they're connected to this?"

Keira snorted. "Unlikely." She pointed at the corkboard. "They're with the Circle. One of them fancies me; the other's his mate. They were lurking around my flat like bloody perverts, as usual. When they saw you leave, they assumed you'd had a go at me—made him jealous. So they decided to teach you some manners."

"You knew they were going to be there?"

"Mmm-hmm," she murmured, a playful glint in her eyes.

"Was this some kind of test?"

She laughed. "No, but it was the perfect excuse to have my lads give them a proper smackdown. There are unwritten rules in their world. Causing trouble for anything other than profit is a big no-no. Keeps them from coming at me, but it also stops me from moving against them unless I've got a good reason." She flashed him a quick grin. "Which you, love, so kindly provided."

"Fucking spies," he muttered.

Keira laughed out loud.

"Are your lads going to escort me back to my hotel again?"

She shook her head. "No need. You're staying here with me tonight."

"I am?"

She waved her hands in mock frustration. "Honestly, haven't you been paying attention? You're the only one Sayyid will talk to. There's a pile of terrorists sitting in Belize, and my government's been compromised. You're in danger, Nathan. I'm not letting you out of my sight. And since I'm part of the Circle, I'm under their protection, which makes this the safest place for you to be."

"I guess that makes sense."

They sat on the couch for another hour, trading theories about tomorrow's meeting and the threats it might bring with the occasional barb slipping in between. The tension that had hung between them earlier was gone. Despite the possible danger tomorrow, Nathan let himself relax. He had faith in someone again, and that felt like enough, for now.

Keira rose from the couch, stretching slightly. "I think it's time we got to bed."

Nathan nodded and stretched himself out on the couch.

She stopped mid-step, staring at him. "Oh, piss off, Nathan. Get the hell off my couch."

He looked up at her, genuinely confused. "What?"

She rolled her eyes at him. "Brilliant. We might die tomorrow, and I say 'We should get to bed,' and you play dead on the sofa? Some spy you are."

Nathan found himself caught somewhere between disbelief and mild panic. "Wait. You mean?"

Keira groaned. "Grow a spine already, would you?"

She huffed and disappeared into the bathroom, the sound of running water and a cupboard door snapping shut. When she came back, she was wearing nothing but an old T-shirt that barely covered her thighs. She paused in the doorway, rubbing a towel through her hair before tossing it aside. For a moment, she said nothing, just met his eyes, then tilted her head toward the bedroom before turning and walking away.

"Fuck it," he muttered, pushing himself up from the couch.

He followed her down the hall toward the bedroom, caught sight of her lying in the bed, and let the last of his hesitation fall away.

9

KEIRA STERLING'S FLAT
BELIZE CITY
TUESDAY, OCTOBER 15
11:00 LOCAL TIME

Nathan woke to the slow warmth of sunlight cutting through the slats, thin gold lines tracing across the sheets, Keira's hand gently brushing his shoulder. He squinted, looking up. She was leaning over him, hair falling loose around her face, a faint smile tugging at her lips. "Morning, soldier," she murmured. "Feel better?" He groaned, stretching his arms over his head before wrapping them around her, pulling her against him, and closing his eyes again.

"That's a yes, then," she said.

"What time is it?" he asked, eyes still closed, pulling the sheet over both of their heads.

She chuckled. "11 AM. Slept like a baby, but you snore like a bloody chainsaw."

Nathan threw the sheet back, sitting up instantly and regretting it the moment he opened his eyes.

"Holy shit," he said, wiping the sleep from his eyes.

"Relax," she said. "We've still got plenty of time."

"I've gotta get back to my hotel and grab some things before I meet with Sayyid."

"Best we do that now," she said, crawling out of bed wearing nothing. She rose onto her toes, arms lifted high, back arched as she drew a long breath. Her shoulders rolled back, then she bent slightly forward, rolled her hips before straightening again, and yawned.

For a moment, Nathan could hardly believe he was here. Last night had been a flurry of chaos in his mind, and that was before he'd stepped into her bedroom. When he had, she was lying there, waiting for him. His mind disengaged and stepped out of the way. What happened next was a raw, desperate storm, the kind he hadn't felt in years, maybe ever. Now, in the morning light, he finally took her in: the smooth curve of her back, her slender frame, the way the sunlight traced along her hips and shoulders. It was mouthwatering, but there was more to it than that. He'd been with enough women to know the difference between scratching an itch and whatever that was last night. She hadn't just given him her body; she'd given him something he didn't have words for. It wasn't something that could be performed or chosen. It was either there or it wasn't. There could be no more doubting the genuineness of her actions now. Still, he wondered if she truly understood what had transpired between them. She was young, and God knows when he was her age he couldn't tell his ass from a hole in the wall. Then again, she was a lot more intelligent than he was back then.

"I've got a few rendezvous I have to keep this afternoon," she said, glancing over her shoulder with a teasing half smile. "I'll go to your hotel with you, and then you'll have to come with me."

"How's that going to work?" he asked, getting out of bed and pulling his light-blue jeans on.

She turned around, wrapping her arms around his neck. "You know how I have to constantly put on an act, being an NOC and all?"

"Right," he said, not sure where she was going with this.

"The trick to putting on a good performance," she whispered, rising just enough to reach his ear, "is not having to perform at all."

Nathan frowned at her. "I thought the Brits were supposed to speak English," he said, a hint of playful sarcasm in his tone.

She rolled her eyes and threw up her hands. "Must I spell everything out for you?" She let out an exaggerated sigh before jabbing a finger lightly at his chest. "You're my boyfriend, silly. Why wouldn't I walk to your hotel with you? And why wouldn't you tag along when I meet my shady male contacts? You know, to puff out your chest and mark your territory, obviously. That's a thing around here." She gave him a look equal parts mock-serious and amused. "If anyone's been paying attention, and trust me, the Circle has, they've already seen us carrying on for months at the café. It works perfectly, you dunce."

"I'm not exactly keen on getting mixed up with sex traffickers," Nathan said as he pulled on a simple white T-shirt. "Or even looking like I am."

Keira slipped into a tiny black tank and a short, sandy-coloured wraparound skirt, loose enough to move easily when she walked.

"How very noble of you," she said. "Then I suppose I'll trot off to meet those monsters all by myself, shall I? I'm sure it'll be fine." She paused. "They've got it bad for me. Maybe they'll protect me if something goes sideways."

"Not happening," he said, his expression hardening.

"Then it's settled," she said with a sly smile. "You'll be coming with me."

"Why do we have to waste our time with traffickers today? We need to prepare for Sayyid."

Keira's playful expression faded, something more fragile taking its place. "I'm in too deep with the Circle, Nathan. I can't just vanish on them now. If I stop showing up, if I stop playing the part, they'll know something's off and I won't last long."

Nathan froze for a moment as the weight of her words sank in. He looked at her—past the confidence and the sharp tongue, to the fear she was trying to hide. His chest tightened. For a second, he didn't trust himself to speak. He nodded once, jaw set as he forced down the instinct to pull her close and promise things he knew he couldn't guarantee.

"Fine," he said, his hand rising to her cheek, thumb brushing lightly along her skin. "But when this is all over, we're going to have a chat about your Artemis Circle assignment."

Keira returned his gaze. "Oh, will we now?" she said, the surprise evident in her tone.

Nathan didn't blink. "Yes. We will."

"Alright then," she said, and after a brief pause added, "Dad."

***

They walked hand in hand toward his hotel, looking like any other couple out for a late-morning stroll. Nathan remembered trudging this same street a few nights ago wondering how a man was supposed to feel after hitting the so-called jackpot. He had his answer now. Not spent, not elated, no spring in his step. Just a quiet focus on not tripping over his own damn feet.

"Is that what you've been sleeping on this whole time in Belize?" Keira said, stepping past him as he opened the door to his suite. "That tiny little bed?"

"Afraid so," he said, starting to pack a few things into his backpack: some clothes, a couple of ball caps, and two pairs of sunglasses.

She smirked, leaning against the wall. "Shame you didn't find your balls sooner. Might've treated yourself to a bit more comfort."

Keira kept her eyes on the bed, her expression shifting as if an idea were taking shape. One eyebrow arched. "Had a go with anyone in it yet?"

"No. I was too busy hanging out at your café every night," he said, turning toward his closet.

"So it's my fault then? I suppose I'd better own up and make it right."

Nathan turned just in time to see her easing herself onto his bed, a grin playing at her lips.

"How much time do we have?" he asked.

"Hardly any."

Nathan was done hesitating. He dropped what he was doing and moved toward the bed.

"We'll make a proper spy out of you yet," she managed before his lips caught hers.

They left the hotel ten minutes later, heading toward Keira's first meeting. Nathan revised his earlier assessment. Tripping over his feet was no longer the problem. Getting them to move at all was. Definitely spent, he decided.

Keira briefed Nathan as they walked. The man they were meeting, known as Migs, was a mid-level trafficker with the Circle. He coordinated the local scum who lured girls with promises of work or travel, then handed them off to transporters once they were trapped. Migs was considered reliable, efficient, and ruthless. In the last month alone, he'd delivered twenty-three high-school-aged girls to the Circle. Keira assured Nathan he was near the top of the hit list, assuming the hitters ever got the green light.

Migs was short and broad-shouldered, his bulky frame topped with a thick beard and a shaved head. He had an arrogant smile that never left his face and struck Nathan as the kind of man who had an inflated sense of his own importance.

Nathan listened as Keira and Migs argued over the transport schedule amid the maze of stacked shipping containers in the Port Loyola compound. The metal towers loomed around them, their paint flaking into rust, with narrow alleyways between them puddled with oily rainwater from the previous night's downpour.

Keira fixed Migs with a cool look. "What do you know about boats and coastal traffic? Nothing. That's what. I'm on the water nearly every day. It's too hot right now. Try moving a shipment before next week and it'll get busted and your precious reputation'll sink. You can't hit quotas if you're dead," Keira said, voice flat and sudden. "Or did you forget what happened to Miguel when his shipment got busted?"

Migs sneered, eyes narrowing. "Yuh tink yuh smart, eh? Jus' a likkle cocktease. When di bosses done wid yuh, I put yuh pon one a mi containers," he said, reaching a hand toward Keira's face.

Nathan's blood hammered in his ears as Migs' hand started toward Keira's face. He moved without thinking. His left hand shot up, catching Migs'. His fingers locked around the joint, thumb digging hard against the back of the hand as he twisted outward. The sudden rotation forced Migs' palm to the sky, the bones in his forearm straining against the twist.

Nathan pivoted and dropped his weight, turning the motion into leverage. The torque wrenched Migs off balance, pain flashing through his wrist and up his arm. As Migs stumbled forward, Nathan stepped in close, his right hand clamping down on the man's forearm just above the elbow. He drove the arm down and back in one continuous motion, folding Migs at the waist.

The lock bit deep. Migs' shoulder began to give under the pressure, and his knees buckled. Nathan shifted his stance, bracing with his legs as he pressed down across Migs' trapped arm and shoulder. The man hit the concrete hard, face twisted in pain, his body pinned and immobile beneath Nathan's grip.

"Try and touch her again, and you and I are going to have a very serious disagreement," Nathan said, his voice flat and hard.

Migs howled, then spat a curse, his face twisting in pain.

Keira stepped in, laying a hand on Nathan's shoulder. "Easy, babe. Don't break his arm. Let him up."

Nathan didn't let up. His voice cut through the air, sharp and commanding, that old NCO edge back in full force. "Are we clear?"

Migs grimaced, nodding quickly. "We clear, we clear," he rasped.

Nathan released him but kept his gaze locked, staying inside Migs' personal space, making it clear he was treading on thin ice.

The rest of the meeting went surprisingly well. Migs, now pale and sweating, had found a sudden respect for negotiation. The arrogance was gone from his face, replaced by the wary look of a man who'd just learned the limits of his own importance. He nodded along to everything Keira said, agreeing to delay his next shipment for at least another week. Nathan didn't say a word—he didn't have to.

Once they were clear of the port yard and the noise of the cranes faded behind them, Nathan and Keira started down the cracked pavement toward their next rendezvous. Once they'd put enough distance between themselves and the containers, Keira spoke.

"What the bloody hell was that?"

"Manners," Nathan said.

***

After Keira's business for the day was finished, they made their way to Samie's Pizza on the waterfront where the Sayyid meeting would take place later in the evening. Nathan was a firm believer that time spent on recce was seldom wasted, so they sat down and ordered a pizza. While they waited, he used the time to study the layout, noting the exits, and to map out the line of sight from each cluster of tables in his mind.

Keira's eyes lit up when the pizza arrived, helping herself to a slice and sinking her teeth into it.

"Oh God, this is good," she said. "I love pizza. My favourite."

Nathan chuckled. "I didn't realize."

Keira grinned, wiping a bit of sauce from the corner of her mouth. "You know, it only took two trips to bed before I got you to take me out on a first date. Not bad by today's standards, I'd say." She finished the first slice, then added,

"Oh, and did I mention how long we had to wait to get to this point in the first place? Maybe if you'd moved a little sooner, you'd already know my second favourite food too."

"You're definitely not the stereotypical Bond girl," Nathan said, laughing.

Keira smirked, leaning back in her chair. "I'll make you eat those words the first time you see me in a tight black dress."

He shook his head, smiling, and continued to subtly scan the restaurant. It was larger than he'd expected, bright and crowded with the steady hum of locals and tourists. The place had a weathered charm—whitewashed walls lined with old photographs of fishing boats and sun-faded postcards, mismatched wooden tables worn smooth from years of use, and a long counter where an older man worked the oven with quiet precision. The smell of baked dough and sea salt mingled in the air, carrying the warmth of the kitchen out into the open room.

When they'd finished, Nathan paid the bill while Keira chatted with the owner, effortlessly managing her local cover. It was around 3:00 PM by the time they reached her flat. They spent the next hour going over the plan—not that there was much to it. Sayyid would already be seated at a table when Nathan arrived, keeping the exchange simple and contained. Keira would provide overwatch from a distance, though they both knew there'd be little she could do if things went sideways. Her two surveillants who'd taken care of the Circle thugs trailing Nathan the night before were scheduled to be on a live-aboard dive yacht, leaving just the two of them. So they turned their attention to contingencies instead: Nathan's extraction routes through the surrounding streets and a quiet spot a few blocks away where they could rendezvous afterwards.

"So what do we do now?" Keira said.

"I can think of a few things." Nathan motioned to the hall leading to the bedroom.

"Somebody's come full circle, haven't they?"

A few minutes later, they were tangled together, lost in the heat of it, when a sudden, heavy knock thundered against the front door.

Keira froze beneath him, breath catching. "Wait," she whispered.

They both went still. After a beat, two light, quick knocks followed, then another pause, and again that same powerful knock.

"I don't believe it," she said. "Move. Quick."

Nathan rolled off her as she sprang from the bed, yanking on the same oversized T-shirt that barely covered her thighs. From the nightstand, she drew a sidearm and chambered a round with a soft click. Nathan pulled on his jeans and followed her lead as she moved silently toward the front door.

She took up a position to the side of the doorframe, crouching and motioning for Nathan to move behind her.

"You should know better than to barge in on a girl unannounced," she called out.

"Old habits are hard to break," came the reply—a man's voice, deep, steady, and unmistakably British.

"Maybe you should pick up a hobby," she countered.

"Hobbies are for those who've already moved on."

"Why can't you move on?" she asked, her voice tight now.

"Because the dead demand vengeance."

Keira's face went pale. "Oh my God." She reached for the handle and pulled the door open.

Two men with unmistakable military bearing stepped inside. The first was older, mid-fifties, his black T-shirt stretched tight over a muscular frame, beige board shorts hanging just above scarred knees. The second was younger, maybe mid-thirties, his forearms a canvas of tattoos. Dark hair was pulled into a high knot, a few loose strands falling around a thick, unkempt beard. A white polo and navy shorts did little to soften the edge about him.

"Warrant Officer Class 2 Gareth Loughton, his Majesty's SAS—retired," the first man said.

"Sergeant Randy Ashford, Royal Marines," the second man said. "Also retired."

Keira straightened abruptly, tugging at the hem of her T-shirt before it could ride any higher. "Keira Sterling," she said quickly, nodding toward Nathan. "And this is Warrant Officer Nathan Cutler."

Loughton's eyes flicked to Keira, barely covered by her T-shirt, then to Nathan, standing there in half done up jeans. He exchanged a look with the younger man beside him and said, "Should've become a bloody spy instead."

Keira's cheeks flushed crimson. Nathan could've sworn it was the first time he'd ever seen her blush.

"Uh, right," Keira said, looking down at her uncovered lower half. "I'll go put on something a little less distracting." She quickly retreated to the bedroom.

Nathan buttoned his jeans, pulled a black T-shirt from his backpack, and slipped it on. "Sorry about that," he said, extending a hand to the two men.

"No need," Ashford said, taking Nathan's hand and offering a wink.

Keira returned a minute later. She'd swapped the T-shirt for a white bikini top and her short, sand-coloured skirt.

"Less distracting, huh?" Randy quipped, grinning.

Keira hesitated for a minute. Nathan didn't think he'd

ever seen her do that before either, though she seemed to recover her nerve quickly enough.

"What? It's the Caribbean. You can't expect me to wear a bloody snowsuit," she shot back.

Loughton cleared his throat. "We have much to discuss."

***

"So you're both MI6, then?" Keira asked as she paced back and forth.

Up to this point, she'd been calm, collected, in control. But now Nathan could see she was just as terrified as he was; she'd merely done a better job of pushing it to the side. He found himself admiring her even more. It was one thing to be a fearless robot. They were rare, but they existed; he'd met enough to know. But to be afraid and conquer it? That was something else entirely.

"No. I'm a hill farmer from North Yorkshire, up near the Pennines," Loughton said.

Keira glanced at Ashford. "And you?"

He grimaced and looked down for a moment. "Knocked up a Canadian gal. Decided to leave the Marines and make a go of it with her in Ottawa. Currently unemployed."

Keira's expression sagged. She sat down on the sofa next to Nathan, shoulders slumping.

"Who sent you then?" she asked.

"Nightgate," Loughton said. "Something foul's happening in London. He reached out not long after your sat call. The Ministry of Defence is paralyzed, and the SAS has been sidelined. I owe him a few favours. He called one in. He assigned me to support you here in Belize, but he never made it to our face-to-face. I waited half an hour before I noticed two men watching me. I left, and they followed."

"You lost them, I take it?" Keira asked.

Loughton's expression barely shifted. "I dealt with them," he said. "No IDs. They were each carrying a Glock."

"What about Nightgate?" Keira asked, an edge of alarm creeping into her voice.

Loughton shook his head. "Unknown," he said. "He's either on the run, been taken, or something worse." His expression darkened as he spoke. "That's all I know. Don't know why I'm here or what I'm supposed to be helping you with. I contacted Ashford and asked him to meet me here. Had to make our own way down."

"What about the Foreign Office?" Keira asked.

"Like I said, that's all I—"

A series of frantic knocks erupted across the front door. "Get me your sidearm, now," Loughton whispered as he motioned for Ashford and Nathan to move to the opposite wall.

Keira sprinted to the bedroom and returned, passing the gun to Loughton, and huddled beside Nathan.

Loughton approached the front door like a predator, making sure not to place himself directly in front of the door. He reached for the handle with his left hand.

"Could someone please hurry up and help me?" a young man's voice called from the other side of the door, British, polite, and strained. "My bag's quite heavy. I can't drag it all the way up here."

Loughton frowned. "Who the hell are you?"

"Oh, right... um, just a sec." A brief shuffle followed, then the voice again, uncertain but oddly cheerful. "I'm the bringer of vengeance... for dead people, I think. Something like that, anyway."

"Bloody hell," Loughton said as he yanked the door open. His left hand shot out, grabbing a fistful of hair, and he hauled the young man unceremoniously inside before slamming the door shut. The newcomer hit the floor with a thud, tall and lanky, thick-framed glasses askew, a bow tie hanging loose against a white shirt and grey slacks.

The young man scrabbled up on his elbows, eyes wide and wet. "Oi—my bag! You can't just drag me in and leave my bag down there," he said. "Bloody brutes."

Loughton gestured to Ashford. "Check his bag over and then bring it up."

Ashford nodded, moving toward the door.

"Don't touch anything in there," the young man insisted.

Nathan looked over at Keira. "Do all your ops go so smoothly?"

She shot him a glare. "Don't even get me started," she said, offering a hand to the newcomer. "Let's get you off the floor, then. Have a seat on the sofa."

The young man stumbled over to the sofa and took a seat, his face red and clearly flustered.

"What's your name?" Keira asked softly, sitting next to him.

"Oliver Haversham," he said, straightening his glasses.

"Ollie, then," Keira said, moving his bow tie back into place. She made introductions for the group, then Ashford disappeared down the stairs and returned a minute later, hauling an oversized duffel slung over one shoulder. As he stepped through the doorway, he set it down with a heavy thud.

"Tinkerbell wasn't exaggerating," he said, rubbing his shoulder. "Bloody thing weighs a ton. How did you manage an SDR with this thing strapped to your back, mate?"

"An SDR?" Ollie asked incredulously. "Are you mad? I took a taxi from the airport."

Keira buried her face in her palms. "My safe house is now a frat house. Brilliant."

"Well, I'm sorry. I wasn't exactly given much in the way of resources," Ollie shot back.

"Alright, everyone. Let's take a deep breath," Nathan said, sitting in the chair across from the young man. "Ollie, can you tell us why you're here?"

"I'm here because of you, mate," Ollie said, jabbing a finger in Nathan's direction. "Nightgate got in touch right after your communique from the consulate. He's been on the run ever since. That message you sent sparked a firestorm in half of London. One day everything's business as usual, the next it all goes to hell."

Nathan shook his head. "That makes no sense. I can't imagine Global Affairs moving that fast, let alone passing it to London so quickly."

"They didn't," Ollie said. "No sign they've even looked at it yet. If they have, they're keeping quiet. Someone on our side intercepted and decrypted your message. Only GCHQ has the capability to do that and they swear they know nothing about it. Now there's a warrant out for Nightgate's arrest." He paused, then pointed at Loughton. "Yours too.

"There's more," Ollie went on. "There's always been a bit of a turf war between the Ministry of Defence and the Foreign Office, but now it's turned into a full-blown internal civil war. Intelligence operations worldwide are at a standstill as bureaucrats clash over control. There are even whispers the government itself might collapse."

"The bit about the government isn't much of a shocker. It's collapsed twice before in the past year," Ashford said.

"Right. But that was always political, wasn't it?" Keira said. "And it was telegraphed through the media. It wasn't a surprise to anyone. There's been nothing public about anything that would topple the government right now."

She got up, started pacing again, and then moved to her corkboard and began rearranging it. Nathan stood behind her and watched her work as she mumbled to herself. It looked like she was building a new link analysis with the pieces of information they'd just learned about London along with what they knew about Sayyid and his revelations.

"What are you thinking?" he asked.

Keira turned to face the group. "Someone with the ability to hack high-level communications is desperate to keep what's inside Sayyid's head buried. If GCHQ is telling the truth, someone outside the government, but close enough to it, is pulling some heavy strings. It all ties back to what Sayyid said in his video, doesn't it?"

She looked at Nathan. "Shall we show it to the lads?"

He nodded.

***

When the video ended, Loughton leaned forward, forearms resting on his knees. "We've got to assume the meeting with Sayyid's blown," he said, his voice low and measured. "Whoever cracked that transmission from the Canadian consulate could've broken the cipher just as easily. They'll know where and when it's happening. This Sayyid fellow's in danger, and so are you, Nathan."

Keira looked at Nathan, concern in her expression. "That settles it, then. We have to call it off. You're not going."

"I have to go," Nathan said. "If I don't, he's dead. Sayyid's never let me down before. I won't let him down now. And we need the information he has."

"My team tracked him down before. With the four of you, I can do it again, and we can warn him off," Keira said, almost pleading.

"In the next few hours?" Nathan asked.

"Probably not," she admitted, sinking into the sofa.

Nathan shifted his gaze from Keira back to the group. "I can't ask any of you to—"

"Don't need to ask, mate," Loughton interrupted. "I've never backed down from a fight before. Not gonna bloody start now."

Ashford crossed his arms across his chest. "Any cunts threatening the UK or Canada need a bullet in their face. Count me in."

"Speaking of bullets," Ollie chimed in, "I've brought some toys. Go on, open the bag."

Ashford unzipped the duffel and the room filled with the smell of gun oil. Inside were countless neat stacks of U.S. hundred-dollar bills wrapped in brown paper bands, two carbines with short barrels and sound suppressor-ready rails—the L119A1 variant of the MRR uppers the British military favoured, two full-size Glock 17s, a pair of compact Glock 19s, several spare magazines, and dozens of ammunition boxes.

"That'll do nicely," Loughton said.

"Courtesy of the SIS," Ollie said. "There's enough cash in there to fairly compensate the three of you for your service to the Crown"—he motioned to the two former British soldiers and Nathan—"plus extra to facilitate operations. There are also my gadgets," Ollie said with a proud little grin. "Prototype short-range comms system—team-based, fully encrypted. Brand new, straight out of the lab, so there's no way anyone's hacked it yet." He hesitated, then added with a nervous laugh, "Well… I *hope* not anyway."

"How does it work?" Nathan asked.

"Quite simple, really," Ollie said, flipping open a black case. Nested neatly inside were several smaller boxes, each snugly fitted with tiny devices. He picked one up delicately between his fingers. "You pop this little beauty inside your ear—not like an earbud, *inside* inside. You'll hear everything your teammates say within about 500 metres and they'll hear you. No buttons, no push-to-talk, nothing. Completely silent to anyone else. Short of taking a serious knock to the head or digging it out with a finger, it'll stay put. Only catch is it's an open mic, so try not to natter unless it's important."

"Interesting," Ashford said, slipping one of the tiny devices into his ear. "Can barely feel..."

He stopped short, blinking as his expression twisted in surprise. A second later, he wobbled, lost his balance, and pitched forward, landing face-first on the duffel bag.

Ollie winced. "Ah, yes—forgot to mention. Causes a bit of vertigo at first until your inner ear recalibrates. Best you all plug yours in now; get it over with."

"One more gadget," Ollie said, opening one of the smaller boxes. "This little microchip will let me track your locations over a long range. Mostly an insurance policy, but one can never be too careful." He looked up, grinning faintly. "Fair warning. Hurts like a bitch to install."

"Install?" Nathan asked, frowning.

Ollie pulled out a slender tool that looked suspiciously like a pair of tweezers. "You've got to slide it under a toenail," he said matter-of-factly.

Loughton slapped a magazine into a Glock 19 and passed it to Nathan.

"I reckon you remember how to use one of these."

Nathan pulled the serrated slide hard to the rear and let it slam forward, the slide stripping a round from the magazine and feeding it into the chamber. He eased his thumb up the slide and gave it a quick press check, moving the slide back just enough to verify the round was where it ought to be.

"I sure do."

Keira tipped her head, eyes glittering with equal parts exasperation and affection. "Damn you, Nathan. Why must you always insist on playing the bloody hero?"

Nathan met her eyes and felt something shift inside him like the weight of memory settling into place. He felt the quiet certainty that used to come before a mission during his days in uniform, the calm voice in his head that told him what he was meant to do. It wasn't so much courage as it was the absence of doubt.

He drew a slow breath and said, "There's no such thing as heroes in war. Only those who stand and those who don't."

The words came out steady, but inside he felt a throbbing ache that came with the knowledge that he might not live to see her again. He wished he'd acted sooner and had had more time with her. But as he watched Keira's face tighten, his certainty hardened, cold and final. He'd already chosen what kind of man he would be.

"Let's work through a new plan," he said.

10

SAMIE'S PIZZA
BELIZE CITY
TUESDAY, OCTOBER 15
22:00 LOCAL TIME

Nathan moved along the narrow stretch of sidewalk on Marine Parade Boulevard, the humid October night thick with sea salt and diesel from the passing traffic, and the heavy scent of fried food and beer. The streetlamps cast a yellow haze over the wet pavement, still slick from an earlier rain. To his left, the parking lot outside the Midpoint Bar & Grill was crowded with rental cars, their windshields glinting under the lights like dull glass eyes. The bar itself pulsed faintly with music, the low throb of bass leaking through its open doors. Just beyond it sat Samie's Pizza, its own small gravel lot full. A covered patio ran along the front, every table occupied. Canvas umbrellas stood open above them, strung with small white lights that gave the area a steady, even glow.

"One taxi approaching from the south," Ashford reported from his perch atop the Central Bank of Belize, four stories up and directly across the street. "Three men stepping out."

"I'm telling you, Mum, he's *so* the one," Keira's voice came next, bright and sure of itself. "Well, of course I'm sure. Come meet him if you don't believe me."

"Confirmed. Op is a go." Ollie was parked in a Land Rover on Hudson, roughly 250 metres away from Samie's.

"In position," Loughton said, stationed by the rear door of the restaurant used by staff only.

Nathan, wearing a black ball cap, tugged the brim lower to shadow his face. A pair of sunglasses hung from the collar of his black T-shirt. The combination of the cap and the placement of the glasses was a signal only Sayyid and his men would recognize: *We're compromised. Follow me.* The revised plan was simple. Nathan would lead Sayyid out through the back entrance, where Loughton stood by, then Ollie would extract them. Keira and Ashford would link up and make their way on foot back to her flat.

He crossed into Samie's small parking lot, scanning automatically before his eyes settled on Keira for half a second. She sat alone on the patio, a half-eaten pizza in front of her, phone pressed to her ear as she continued talking to herself. The wide-brimmed hat, oversized linen shirt, and thick pink frames of her glasses gave her an easy tourist look.

"Gotta go, Mum," she said, putting her phone away.

Nathan passed one of Sayyid's men who stood by the entrance, offering a slight nod. The man stiffened slightly when he saw him, returning the nod and readying himself. Nathan walked into the pizza shop with Sayyid's guard, the now familiar smell of fresh dough filling the air, and scanned for Sayyid.

"I've got eyes on a quad of old Hilux-style chassis approaching from the north," Ashford reported. "One of 'em's painted in an odd blue-red pattern."

"That's a Circle convoy," Keira said. "Probably just passing through. They never operate in this part of town."

Nathan spotted Sayyid in the far-right corner, head down over the menu. The guard opposite him sat with his back to Nathan. *Just great.* Between the two of them, the position provided a clear line of sight across the restaurant and coverage of every exit, but it was also the furthest point from the rear door.

"Convoy's splitting up," Ashford said. "Two moving left toward the rear of Samie's; the other two will pass in front."

"Ollie. ETA?" Loughton asked.

"100 metres out, but stuck in a wee bit of traffic," Ollie said.

Nathan directed the guard to cover the front entrance, then stepped through the line of customers, angling toward Sayyid, doing his best to look casual, wishing his old friend would pull his head up from the menu.

"We've got trouble," Loughton said. "The two trucks approaching the rear just split lanes—one's pulled into oncoming traffic. They're side by side now, blocking both lanes, and stopped. Eight men getting out. Armed."

"Shit," Ashford said. "The two trucks to the front just pulled over. Four men stepping out."

"What the hell," Keira said.

"Change of plan," Loughton said. "Get Sayyid out the front now. I'll hold these eight as long as I can."

Nathan broke into a run toward Sayyid, who finally looked up from the menu. At first, he smiled—then his expression shifted to alarm as he tapped his guard's arm.

"We've gotta move now. No time to explain," Nathan said. Sayyid and his guard rose to their feet and followed Nathan, who was pushing his way past the lineup of patrons.

"Engaging," Loughton said.

Nathan heard muffled pops to the rear of the restaurant as he waved the two men forward.

"Keira, get back to your table," Ashford barked. "Stay out of my scope. Nathan, don't leave the restaurant yet, and try to get the civvies away from the bloody door."

"I've got a better idea. Randy, hold your fire," Nathan said. He raised his voice over the noise in the restaurant. "Bomb! There's a bomb. Everyone out, now!"

Startled cries broke out as chairs scraped and plates shattered, the room erupting into chaos while people surged for the front exit. Nathan forced his way through the panic toward the rear door, planting himself there to block anyone from trying to escape that way.

He drew his Glock 19 from the waistband at the small of his back and waved it toward the crowd. "Move! Hurry up!"

"Bloody brilliant, mate," Ashford said. "The crowd's busting out the door. Ran one of the cunts over. Let me know when the restaurant is clear, and I'll take them out."

Sayyid and his two guards closed in beside Nathan, drawing their sidearms. "What is happening, my friend?" Sayyid asked, his voice tight with alarm.

"No time. Take cover behind the counter," Nathan said.

"Two down," Loughton reported. "Advancing."

"I'm bloody stuck. Traffic's not moving," Ollie said.

"It's probably another blockade. We never get traffic like this around here," Keira yelled over the chaos as patrons ran from the front entrance, colliding with others trying to escape the patio.

"Fuck's sake. I'm pinned down in a crossfire," Loughton said. "Bunch more coming up on my six. Can't stop them. Expect company, Nathan."

Nathan motioned one of the guards. "We need to set up a defence. We're about to be hit through the rear door."

He wasn't an expert in close-quarters battle like a Tier-1 operator, but he knew enough from his days in the infantry and his three tours in Afghanistan. The key was to create a fatal funnel. Never stand in the open path of a doorway; instead, make the enemy cone through one narrow space where only a single man can fight at a time.

There was a narrow hallway that ran from the north side of the dining area to the rear door, and it gave Nathan an idea.

"Help me with this table," he said to one of the guards then pointed to the other guard. "Stay with Sayyid behind the counter." Nathan and the guard shoved the nearest prep table down the hall until its legs bit into the threshold of the rear doorway. Nathan stripped off his leather belt, looping it once around the handle and twice around a table leg. He pulled until the strap tightened, then cinched the buckle and tested the latch with a hard tug. The door held. They repeated the process with the guard's belt, locking down the interior door that opened into the hall.

A burst of heavy gunfire erupted behind the building, the sharp rattle of automatic fire cutting through the night and shaking dust from the ceiling tiles.

"One more down, but I'm taking heavy fire," Loughton said. "They're throwing a hell of a lot back my way. I make it ten men closing on the rear entrance. Not Circle guys by the looks of them." A pause. "Make that nine. I just bagged another one."

If the men coming up behind Loughton weren't Circle, then who were they? Nathan hoped they weren't professionals. He took a breath and scanned the room. The belts would hold for a minute, maybe two if the hinges didn't give first. He considered pushing through the front door with Sayyid and the two guards to make a run for it, but there was still too much chaos out there. If they exited the front door now, there was a good chance that civilians would get caught in the crossfire between his group and the Circle men.

"Another group of men approaching the south side windows," Ashford said. "I've got a clear line of sight. Engaging now. Keira, keep an eye on the four in the front."

Nathan and the guard hopped over the large U-shaped counter that extended outwards from the kitchen to the back of the restaurant.

"Positions," Nathan said, low and calm. "Sayyid, cover the hallway with me. You guys," he said to the guards, "watch the windows to our rear."

***

The hell with this, Ollie thought, gripping the wheel so tightly his knuckles went white. *I've got to do something.*

He jerked the Land Rover across the centre line and into oncoming traffic, flooring it. The tires screamed, the engine roared, and the few cars that did appear swerved and honked as if he'd lost his mind. *Not entirely wrong.*

A minute later, he saw it. A large white panel van had wedged itself sideways across both lanes, blocking the entire road. "Brilliant," he said, slamming the steering wheel. The shoulder was too small for the Land Rover to fit through, and there was no way he could push through the column of vehicles on the right. He glanced down at the digital map glowing on the dashboard. The only option was to double back the way he'd come and take an alternate route. *Five minutes at a minimum. Might as well be five bloody years.*

His pulse hammered in his throat. *I hope there's nobody left in that van.* He didn't have much in the way of tactical training. Ollie was never meant to be in the field like this, but the team had needed a driver, and he'd be damned if he was going to sit in Keira's flat and do nothing. He shot at paper targets a couple of times a year because MI6 said he had to. *I hope people are easier to hit than bloody paper.*

He had a Glock 17 and the initiative. *Surely that's got to count for something right?*

Ollie slipped out of the Land Rover, drew his weapon, and started inching his way forward. *As long as I don't shoot myself in the face by accident, I might have a chance.* The driver was still inside, facing away, leaning forward as if trying to get a view of the chaos near the restaurant. Ollie closed to within 2 metres, arms shaking violently. He pointed the Glock at the back of the man's head, pulled the trigger—and missed.

The driver whipped around, eyes wide, hand diving for a weapon. Ollie squeezed his eyes shut, and pulled the trigger again and again and again, until the slide locked back with a sharp click. *I'm not dead yet.* He opened his eyes, breathing hard. The man was slumped forward against the steering wheel. Ollie caught the smell of cordite and saw blood and brain matter oozing down what was left of the man's head.

Ollie stumbled back and doubled over, his stomach convulsing in violent spasms. He vomited until bile burned his throat and flooded his nose, eyes streaming, vision blurring as the world swam in front of him.

He wiped his mouth and eyes with his sleeves, swapped in a fresh magazine with clumsy hands, and forced himself to move. Thankfully, the back of the van was empty. He circled to the front, opened the door, and tried to haul the driver out. The man was much bigger than he was, and Ollie nearly gave himself a hernia dragging him onto the road.

He dropped into the seat, slammed the van into reverse, and manhandled it into a rough three-point turn, then he heard Nathan's voice. "They've broken through." A pause. "Two down." Then a sharp yell. "Shit. Sayyid's hit." Followed by a dull, muffled thud.

"Nathan!" Keira screamed.

"Oh no," Ollie said, stomach turning again. He jammed the van into drive, slammed the accelerator, and hurtled toward the restaurant.

***

Ashford tracked the last gunman approaching the south side window through his scope as the man scrambled for the shattered window. He squeezed the trigger of his L119A1; a single, clean shot cracked through the humid air, and the attacker collapsed. Shifting his aim toward the front entrance, Ashford caught sight of Keira pulling her pistol and firing into the chaos outside. One of the gunmen spun and fell; without hesitating, she broke cover and sprinted into the restaurant.

He still didn't have a clean shot at the remaining three men. *Bloody hell.*

Ashford grabbed his patrol pack, thumbed it open and clipped a locking carabiner to the braided rope inside. He cinched the rope around the rooftop railing, ran a safety wrap, fed the rope through the carabiner, and fed the spare tail through his belay loop—small checks he'd done a hundred times. He swung the patrol pack up and shrugged into the straps, settling the weight high across his shoulders, then slung his carbine across his chest, tugged on leather gloves, clipped the carabiner to his harness, and tested the knot with a hard pull. Then he leaned back over the edge. The rope took his weight without complaint as he rappelled down the side of the building.

He heard four sharp cracks from inside the restaurant.

After his feet touched ground, he unfastened the rope then sprinted toward the front wall. At the last step, he planted hard, drove upward, and vaulted over, catching the edge with his gloved hands. His body swung once against the brick, then he kicked off and dropped cleanly to the ground on the other side.

"Keira, report," Ashford said.

"Sayyid and his guards are dead. Nathan's been hit," Keira said, voice cracking. "They're still coming."

Two more sharp cracks rang out from inside the building.

Ashford bolted across the street, vaulting over the hood of a car that screeched to a stop just in time. He hit the pavement running, carbine up at the high ready, and charged straight for the restaurant's front entrance. He trained his weapon on the nearest gunman. The young woman standing between them saw the weapon and leaped to the side. He fired twice into the gunman's back, killing him. Ashford pushed his way past another five people as the next gunman spun around just in time to take a round to the face.

Through his earpiece, he heard a thud followed by struggling and someone gasping for breath. Then Keira's voice broke through, strained and furious. "Get your bloody hands off me!"

"Outta my way!" Ashford barked, shoving through the panicked crowd. He burst through the doorway, rifle up, and fired two quick rounds down the hallway into the man by the rear door. Without breaking stride, he pivoted right and sent two more shots into the last man still on his feet.

He swept the room, stepping over several bodies and broken glass. The air was thick with smoke and the stench of cordite. Nathan and Keira were nowhere in sight.

"Keira! Nathan!" Ashford shouted.

Nothing.

The only sound he heard was the raging gunfire from the rear of the building. *Loughton.* He unloaded his mag, feeding a fresh one in its place, then moved down the hallway to the rear door.

Ashford canted right and saw two vans speeding away. He swung left and caught sight of Loughton, four men closing on him. Loughton's carbine lay useless beside him as he emptied his Glock 17 at his attackers.

Weapon raised, Ashford advanced. He sighted the first man sprinting toward Loughton and squeezed off a controlled pair; the rounds punched clean through the man's chest, dropping him mid-stride. The second attacker pivoted toward the muzzle flash, and Ashford caught him with another two rounds, folding him over the bonnet of a nearby car.

Loughton took advantage of the distraction. He fired his Glock four more times. One assailant spun and went down hard; the other staggered back clutching his throat before collapsing beside the curb. The street fell quiet.

Ashford ran to his older comrade. "You alright, mate?"

Loughton lowered the pistol, his chest heaving. His face was a mask of grime and sweat, eyes raw with disbelief. "They made off with Nathan and Keira," he said, voice rough as gravel. "And Sayyid's dead. No, I'm not bloody alright."

Ashford had never seen him like this. The old warrior had walked through fire in four wars. Now he was standing in the middle of the street, looking utterly hollow.

"I'm in the white van out front," Ollie said. "Big ugly thing. Can't miss it! Come on, before the coppers show up and start asking awkward questions."

11

EXCALIBUR INDUSTRIES
CANARY WHARF, LONDON
WEDNESDAY, OCTOBER 16
07:00 LOCAL TIME

Al-Najm stood by the glass, arms folded across his chest, the black keffiyeh casting his reflection into something almost spectral against the pale dawn over London. The city sprawled beneath him, its citizens completely oblivious to the fate that awaited. But for the first time in years, he felt rage rather than satisfaction. Khalid's arrogance had swollen beyond restraint, blinding him to caution and leaving his name whispered in a place it never should have been heard. Now the quiet stroke against Canada he'd planned had erupted into a spectacle of gunfire and bodies before the plot had been hatched, placing the entire operation in jeopardy.

Behind him, Volk sat at his ridiculous desk, feigning calm but radiating the restless impatience that had always betrayed him. Fairfax, the one Al-Najm had entrusted to keep him grounded, had floundered.

"What I fail to understand," Al-Najm said, his voice low and edged with menace, "is what possessed you to bring the Under-Secretary into play long before my instructions required it."

Volk's tone was tight with justification. "The SAS—"

"Had already been delayed by a week," Al-Najm interrupted, turning to face Volk. "More than enough time to silence al-Mazari and allow Khalid to complete his task."

He turned back to the glass. There had been a time when he would have viewed it differently. As a boy, he'd believed the world could be remade through intellect. His teachers had called him gifted, his ambition noble. He had dreamed of shaping minds with ideas. But the world had taken something from him, and grief had taught him what scholarship never could: that strength determined whose ideas survived. Reason was the purview of how to apply strength. Violence could be a valuable tool if wielded by someone who knew how to use it effectively. His brother had never understood that truth, mistaking brutality for purpose. That ignorance had cost him his life and doomed Al-Najm to watch an empire rebuild itself from the ashes.

"We cannot afford to repeat the mistakes of the past, Mr. Volk." Al-Najm let the silence linger, then turned to face him. "Tell me, Mr. Volk. How much power do Al Qaeda or ISIS wield today?"

Volk glanced at Fairfax, then back to Al-Najm, apparently searching for an answer. "Well... they still stage the occasional attack," he said, the words tumbling out awkwardly. "A few cells—"

"Academics, pundits, and strategists are quick to equate the Global War on Terror to another Vietnam," Al-Najm interrupted again, "but they miss the point. Al Qaeda and ISIS have been all but destroyed."

He fell silent for a moment, the only sound the low mechanical hum of the tower's systems threading through steel and glass. When he spoke again, his voice was softer, almost reflective. "Neither organization has the power, capability, or influence they once enjoyed. Why?"

Volk didn't answer. Like everyone else, he lacked the wisdom and foresight to understand.

"They lacked patience," Al-Najm said. His gaze shifted to Fairfax, then back to Volk. "And if you do not learn from their failure—if you cannot master your own impulse to act before instructed—then your foolish desk, and all the power you think you wield, will vanish just as completely as theirs did."

Volk's jaw tightened, the flicker of defiance in his eyes dimming to something closer to unease. He said nothing, but the message had landed; Al-Najm could see it in the way the man's posture straightened, his bravado retreating behind calculation. Satisfied that the lesson had taken root, Al-Najm turned to the next matter at hand.

"Have you reviewed my instructions, Ms. Fairfax?"

Fairfax stood with her tablet in hand. "I have. All major outlets are running the Belize City story as a gang-on-gang shooting. The Canadian and the British agents will be reported as killed in the exchange. But it's unlikely to hold."

"It doesn't have to," Al-Najm said. "It need only delay their response. A day or less is enough."

"A response from who?"

"The Canadians," Al-Najm said.

12

CANSOFCOM HEADQUARTERS
OTTAWA
WEDNESDAY, OCTOBER 16
08:00 LOCAL TIME

Lieutenant Colonel Marc Tremblay sat at his desk, listening as his newest intelligence officer, James Carter, a tall, athletic man in his early twenties, delivered the morning briefing. His office, buried deep within Canadian Special Operations Forces Command, reflected the man himself: practical, disciplined, and quietly warm. Geopolitical maps lined the walls, and a stack of reports waited on his desk for review. A large monitor displayed live intelligence feeds from both domestic and international sources. Behind him, framed photos of his old unit, JTF2, served as reminders of his years leading Alpha Team before he took a commission and later rebadged as an intelligence officer. On his desk, a small display case held a single maple leaf pin, a simple emblem of service.

"Open source reporting indicates gang-on-gang violence in Belize City continues to escalate. A large-scale gun battle at a waterfront tourist venue erupted last night. One Canadian was reported killed in the incident. That concludes this morning's brief, pending your questions, sir," Carter said.

Tremblay, now in his late forties, ran a hand through what was left of his grey hair and set his thin-framed, circular glasses back in place before letting out a slow breath.

"Are you reading me the news, James, or providing me insight?" he asked.

James was one of the intelligence branch's more gifted recent graduates. The instructors at the Canadian Forces School of Military Intelligence had sung his praises, naming him the top candidate in his intelligence officer course. Yet he lacked the confidence that only experience could bring, something Tremblay was determined to correct. The staffing crisis had hit the intelligence branch as hard as every other element of the CAF, leaving it stretched thin and in need of capable officers.

"Intelligence is about giving the commander a decision-making advantage," Tremblay said. "If I walk into the commander's office with that bit about Belize, what exactly is he supposed to do with it?"

"Honestly, sir, I don't know the first thing about Belize. I have no idea what to make of it beyond what the media are reporting."

"Most of us know as much about Belize as you do. But when I stand in front of the general, that's not an excuse I can use." Tremblay leaned back slightly, his voice firm. "Excuses are like assholes, Lieutenant. I want solutions."

He paused, glancing toward the map of Central America on the wall. "I remember reading something about Belize recently, but I can't put my finger on it. You have one hour to dig up everything we've got. Intelligence reports, open source material, whatever you can find. Get one of the collators to help you if you're struggling."

"On it, sir," Carter replied before heading out.

Tremblay watched him leave. The kid seemed to have an endless supply of enthusiasm buried somewhere under that uniform. Tremblay suddenly felt old and wondered what fate had in store for Carter. Canada might be at peace for now, but the special operations units under CANSOFCOM never were. They were always fighting wars the public never heard about or stopping them before they started.

He wasn't sure if he had the energy to take someone new under his wing.

Tremblay turned his chair toward the wall and stared at a photo of him and Matt Lion, both of them smiling. His jaw tightened as the memories came rushing back.

"Tabarnak," he muttered.

He opened a desk drawer and pulled out one of several stacks of toonies, tossing a coin into the large swear jar on his desk. It was nearly full again—he had emptied it only two weeks earlier, donating the proceeds to a veterans' suicide prevention charity.

The picture haunted him, yet he kept it on the wall all the same. It had become a ritual. Each morning, he forced himself to look at it. To remember. Matt's grin in that photo mocked him, a reminder of everything he couldn't protect. He should have known better, but he couldn't see it until it was too late. He'd raised Matt from a promising recruit into a leader of warriors only to watch him disappear into the fog of shadow wars. Others might have called it reflection or self-growth, but Tremblay knew better. It was penance. Every glance at that frame was a confession, a daily act of self-inflicted punishment for a sin he didn't know how to atone for.

***

An hour later, Carter burst into Tremblay's office with another young officer in tow, Lieutenant Isabelle Reid, nearly startling him. He'd been completely absorbed in a stack of urgent classified reports coming out of Russia.

"I'm sorry, James. It'll have to wait," Tremblay said, eyes returning to the reports on his desk.

The door to his office clicked shut, drawing his attention up again. His expression shifted to mild irritation until he saw who had closed it. Standing there was his sergeant major, Master Warrant Officer Richard Harlan. In his late forties, he was roughly Tremblay's age, but Harlan still had a full head of thick grey hair—something Tremblay both envied and quietly resented.

"This can't wait, sir."

Tremblay sighed and motioned for the group to take the seats around the coffee table he used for small team meetings. He joined them a moment later. "Alright, James," he said. "What's going on in Belize?"

"So I talked to the Latin America and Caribbean analyst over at CJOC J2," Carter began. "He told me that while gang violence in Belize has been rising slightly, and he really emphasized *slightly*, it's virtually unheard of for it to spill into the tourist areas of Belize City. Certainly not a major gun battle like the one being reported in the media.

"The analyst put me in touch with their OSINT team. They sat down with me and ran a comprehensive search of everything they could find related to Belize. They dug much deeper than I did, crawling social media and uncovering several eyewitness videos."

Carter picked up his datapad and tapped the screen. "One of them shows a guy with a rifle strapped to his chest rappelling down the side of a four-story bank building. He sprints across the street, nearly gets run over by a car, and carries on like it's nothing. Then he drops three armed men surrounded by civilians in front of a pizza shop."

He turned the screen toward Tremblay and hit play.

"This guy's white," Carter said. "He's wearing a tac vest, multicam patrol pack, and the weapon he's carrying is a—"

"L119A1," Tremblay interjected. "The British adaptation of our C8 SFW."

"That's right, sir," Carter said. "And those weapons don't show up on the black market. We think he's some kind of British operator. Look at how he moves—controlled, deliberate—and how easily he takes these guys down. Then look at this." He paused the video mid-frame. "He goes out of his way to avoid shooting civilians. That's not gang behaviour.

"Now look at this next video," Carter said. "It comes from the same person who filmed the first one. Watch how he moves into the building."

Tremblay slipped his glasses back on, leaning forward as the footage played. "Standard CQB," he said. "Alright, so he's an operator. What's the so *what* here, James?"

Carter adjusted the volume and replayed the final few seconds of the clip. The man's voice shouted, raw and urgent. "Keira! Nathan!"

"And who the hell are they?" Tremblay asked.

Isabelle Reid spoke next. In her early twenties like Carter, she was far less excitable—tall, composed, with long dark hair pulled back into a tight bun.

"Sir," she began, "I was the CANSOFCOM J2 duty officer a couple of days ago. I received a phone call from someone identifying himself as retired Warrant Officer Nathan Cutler. He said he'd come across a potential threat to national security. I stopped him before he could say more and advised him to report it in person at the Canadian consulate. I told him they could pass the information to us through secure channels." She paused, her tone measured. "He assured me he'd do it first thing the next morning."

"And did we receive anything from Global Affairs?" Tremblay asked, though he already knew the answer.

"No, sir," Reid said. "I followed up this morning and got nowhere, so I brought it to the sergeant major."

"Sir," Harlan said, his tone edged with frustration, "I've been on the phone all morning getting the runaround from Global Affairs headquarters. Someone there hinted that the PMO might've tied their hands." He leaned forward. "So, I called a friend of mine at the consulate in Belize. He checked the logs and confirmed that Warrant Cutler did show up that morning. He couldn't tell me what was discussed, but the records show they transmitted a classified message to Global Affairs addressed to us."

"Bien colis de tabarnak," Tremblay said, then caught himself and winced, halfway out of his chair to feed the jar.

"I've got this one, sir," Harlan said, tossing a ten-dollar bill into the nearly full swear jar on the desk.

"What do we know about Cutler?" Tremblay asked.

"Former infantryman turned HUMINTer," Carter said. "A damn good one, too. Did two tours in Iraq and was credited with recruiting one of the most valuable sources during the Mosul campaign."

"I'm assuming Cutler was the Canadian you said was killed in the attack?" Tremblay asked.

"That's what the media are saying," Carter said. "They didn't name him—just referred to him as a Canadian—but they showed his face. The OSINT guy pointed out that none of the other victims were shown, which he thought was odd.

"But look at this," Carter continued. "Another witness video taken from the back of the restaurant. You can see two people being dragged into a van. A middle-aged white male, looks dead or unconscious, and a young white female."

Carter zoomed in on the footage. "We can't really see the man's face, but the build and clothing match Cutler's description. The young woman, though, her face is clear. Here. Take a look." He angled the screen toward Tremblay.

"We ran her face and the name *Keira* through our database and got several hits," Carter said. "She's suspected of being involved in the Artemis Circle's Belize operation. Her full name is Keira Sterling. According to her file, she's a marine biology grad student at the University of Essex. She's a Brit.

"Now, let's go back to the British shooter inside the restaurant—the one yelling *Nathan* and *Keira*," Carter said. "Before that, he does a detailed sweep of the place, checking each body quickly. Based on what we're seeing, I'm assessing that Nathan and Keira aren't among the dead. They're the two who got taken in the van."

He paused, zooming in on the footage. "And the guys who grabbed them don't look like local gangsters. More like Middle Eastern and professional."

"Sir," the sergeant major said, his voice firm. "We've got enough int here to suggest a possible national security threat to Canada that Cutler stumbled onto. He tried to warn us and ended up either killed or kidnapped for his trouble. I think this is actionable."

The evidence was compelling. There was no smoking gun, but in the intelligence world there rarely was. If there were, there'd be no need for intelligence in the first place. Even President Obama had ordered the assault on Osama bin Laden's compound in Pakistan based on intelligence just as circumstantial as what his team had just laid before him.

Tremblay swore in both English and French several times under his breath. "Isabelle, get this to J3 and have them briefed. Sergeant Major, get me the National Security and Intelligence Advisor on the line now. James, take all of this to Sergeant McLeod and have him start working it. Then reach out to Talia Maris on the Hill and begin coordinating with her."

He paused, his expression hardening. "And Isabelle, once that's done, tell J3 to spin up JTF2."

Tremblay pushed back his chair and stood. He walked to his desk, pulled open a drawer, and took out an entire stack of toonies. After a long look at the overflowing swear jar, he sighed.

"Someone get me another goddamn jar," he barked.

He had a feeling Belize was going to cost him a lot of money.

13

DWYER HILL TRAINING CENTRE
OTTAWA
WEDNESDAY, OCTOBER 16
18:00 LOCAL TIME

Rocky sat in silence, eyes fixed on the frozen image of Sayyid al-Mazari's face projected on the screen at the front of the mission planning room. His words echoed in Rocky's mind: A blow that will cripple Canada. The rest of Alpha Team sat equally still, seated around the long modular planning table, its surface crowded with annotated maps and overlays of the Chiquibul rainforest. Along the side wall, a bank of monitors displayed satellite imagery, drone reconnaissance, and comms status feeds, casting a faint wash of light across the operators' faces. Toward the rear of the room, several officers and intelligence staff stood observing the briefing, notebooks in hand.

"Khalid al-Rashid," Champs said aloud. "I'd love a chance to rid the world of his carbon dioxide."

Rocky nodded. A hit on al-Rashid would rank alongside JSOC's takedown of Abu Ayyub al-Masri and the strike on Zarqawi in 2006. Al-Rashid had the blood of Canadian and allied soldiers on his hands; he'd been responsible for the ambush that had hit Rocky's platoon in Afghanistan back when he was a corporal with First Battalion, Royal Canadian Regiment. He thought of the two friends he'd lost that day, their bodies torn apart by the roadside bomb.

"When do we launch?" Rocky asked.

Belanger held up a hand. "That's not the mission priority," he said, leaning over the table. He gestured to Talia, who sat at her workstation, a compact setup of triple monitors, along the right wall. Behind her, analysts worked quietly at three desks arranged against the wall, each with their own secure terminal.

The image on the screen shifted. "You're looking at retired Warrant Officer Nathan Cutler and Keira Sterling, likely an MI6 NOC. They're being held by al-Rashid and his men in a small compound deep inside the Chiquibul. Your primary objective," Belanger said, "is to bring them home. Your secondary objective is to take out al-Rashid."

Rocky's calculus shifted. A kill-or-capture was one thing; a hostage rescue was another. A rescue put a clock on the plan. Speed and certainty mattered more than retribution. A delay to set up a strike could cost the hostages, and a blunt assault could get them killed. The jungle complicated things further. It could be as much an adversary as al-Rashid's men. He ran options in his head: a small extraction element to get the prisoners out first, then a deliberate strike on al-Rashid or a simultaneous snatch-and-neutralize with over-watch. Any option that increased Cutler's or Sterling's risk was off the table. But if they could extract the hostages and still put al-Rashid down, Rocky would take it in a heartbeat.

"Joint op with SAS?" he asked.

"It's a solo run," Tremblay said, stepping forward. "What I'm about to tell you doesn't leave this room. It doesn't get spoken out loud or transmitted through any means of communication whatsoever."

He drew a steady breath, eyes on the screen, then on each face around the table. "I've spent the afternoon on secure calls with my contacts in London and Hereford. Something isn't right. SAS and MI6 ops are stalled or cancelled. I think it's tied to the video and the prisoners."

Tremblay's voice hardened. "Al-Mazari was killed in what we're assessing as an assassination. Cutler and Sterling may be the only people left who can clarify the threat to Canada. This is a no-fail mission."

Hangman sat up in his chair, rotating a pen around his fingers, his typically cavalier expression fading.

"How are we supposed to find them?" Spooky asked. "The Chiquibul is a big-ass jungle."

"You won't have to," Belanger said with a grin. "That's already handled." He nodded toward Talia again, who switched the display to reveal three more faces.

"I'll be damned," Rocky said. "Gareth Loughton. Who are the other two?"

"Randy Ashford, former Royal Marines, and Oliver Haversham, MI6," Tremblay said. "We got a secure sat phone call from Haversham not long ago from a safe house in Belize City. The three of them were backing Cutler and

Sterling off the books. They were the ones on the other side of the gunfight in Belize City." He paused, then added, "Haversham's got a way to track them. He's already sent us coordinates for where they're being held and expects Loughton and Ashford to be on site within a few hours. They'll be doing a full recce workup in advance of your arrival."

"That'll make things faster," Rocky said. "What's their disposition?"

"They're driving toward the signal in a Land Rover," Tremblay said. "They plan to ditch it and hide it within 5 kilometres of the signal then hump the rest of the way in. They're both carrying L119A1s and Glocks, wearing shorts and T-shirts, and not much in the way of food or water."

Rocky shared a glance with Champs. "I want two extra sets of equipment drawn for them with plenty of extra water and rats. That jungle will dehydrate them fast; they'll probably be half dead by the time we get there."

Champs scribbled in his notebook. "I'll figure it out."

"They've got a sat phone, but we don't expect them to get a signal under the jungle canopy," Belanger said. "You'll link up with them after insertion. They've agreed to provide any support you need for the assault."

Talia pulled up satellite imagery of the Chiquibul and keyed a red circle over the compound. Rocky stood, crossed to the table map, found the spot, and began studying the surroundings. Eyes on the target ahead of time would save Alpha Team from gathering pattern-of-life data once they arrived. He'd worked joint ops with Loughton before. The old warrior was top-shelf; he'd have the ins and outs mapped long before insertion. The real problem was getting there undetected.

"We'll leave you to it," Belanger said. "Bob will coordinate whatever logistical support you need, and he'll set up a

TOC with Talia in Belize. I want everyone wheels up before midnight."

Belanger, Tremblay, and the rest of the staff left the room, clearing space for Alpha, Talia, and Green to plan the particulars of the mission.

Once they left, Green spoke up. "I've sent warning orders to CSOR, 427 SOAS, and 1 CAD. The Air Force is assembling a Special Operations Air Task Force and has a Globemaster being loaded with three CH-147 Griffons in case you need them. Recommend we prioritize the air picture to provide 1 CAD as much lead time as possible."

"Agreed," Rocky said. "Let's get to work."

Talia tapped a console, generating digital overlays on top of the compound area on the main screen. "As you can see, we can't penetrate the canopy over the target area," she said, eyes on the display. She flicked a waypoint and highlighted a narrow corridor of lighter cover. "There might be tiny openings here allowing enough starlight through to make NVGs viable, but I can't guarantee it."

She tilted the image to show a profile view. "The canopy tops out around 20 to 25 metres in places. Don't expect clear, open areas under the trees. It's going to be thick with bush and natural obstacles."

Talia lit up several lines across the screen. "The Las Cuevas Access Road runs north to south, roughly five klicks west of the target. From there, a series of small trails branch east into the Chiquibul. We assess that small vehicles can travel from the access road to the compound. We can task a CE-145 Vigilance for route ISR, which can provide early warnings of vehicles or dismounted movement along those trails."

She sighed before continuing, "But the canopy is going to be a problem. You'll need to raise an antenna above the trees to keep a comms link open or it's useless."

"Should be doable," said Bambam, the team's jungle warfare specialist.

"How many bad guys?" Spooky asked.

Talia frowned. "All we have to go on is al-Mazari's video indicating that he saw fifty armed men, but that doesn't mean there aren't more that he didn't see," she said. "I am not confident in this assessment."

Their best chance of getting a clearer picture of the size of al-Rashid's force rested with the two British operators on the ground. But unless the Brits had a portable antenna that they could extend through the jungle canopy, they would have no way of reporting their findings to Alpha Team in advance. Rocky figured Loughton and Ashford probably didn't have an antenna on them. He wouldn't get a clear picture of enemy strength until they were on location.

"What condition are the prisoners in?" Whiskey asked.

"We think Cutler sustained a gunshot wound and is unconscious. So far as we know, Sterling didn't take any hits before the apprehension. But our information is a day old," Talia replied.

"Can we expect anything from the host nation?" Rocky asked.

Green leaned forward in his chair, forearms resting on the edge of the table. "The Belizean government authorized the use of their airspace and airfields. They're willing to assist, but they don't have an air force to speak of. The handful of Hueys they have are old and unreliable. They've got a small SOF unit that could be used as a quick reaction force, but I'd prefer we use CSOR as our first option in our own helos and put the Belizeans on third line."

Whiskey ran a hand through his thick, black, wavy hair.

"I don't think three CH-146 Griffons are going to cut it," he said. "If we're planning on using helos to exfil, we need at least two birds, one for each det and another for the QRF. So figure you can get a full CSOR section on the third. Where do we put Cutler and Sterling? If they're in bad shape, they'll be horizontal, which will take even more room."

"Can we get more CH-146 Griffons to Belize?" Rocky asked.

"Yes, but it will take a lot more time," Green said.

Rocky threw his pen across the table in frustration. "Al-Rashid isn't known for keeping his hostages alive for long. We have to assume they're in bad shape and that we're running up against a clock. That means a ground exfil is a no go. At least for Cutler and Sterling."

"We're going to need at least one Huey from the Belizeans," Champs said.

"Looks that way," Rocky agreed.

Hangman leaned back in his chair. "So who's drawing short straws and hitching a ride on the Huey?"

"Forget about that for now," Rocky said. "We've got bigger problems. The helos can't land at the compound, which leaves us three options. Challilo Lake to the north, the Macal River to the east, or the trail network to the west."

He rubbed a hand over his jaw, eyes flicking between the map overlays on the table and his notepad. "If we go in by the lake or the river, we're carrying Cutler and Sterling out on stretchers for three clicks through rough ground. If we go west, it's five clicks, but the terrain's friendlier."

Miles leaned forward, his voice flat. "If this turns into a fighting withdrawal, it's going to be an absolute shit show."

An idea began to take shape in Rocky's mind. The road and trail network would be the hinge, especially if Cutler and Sterling were in bad shape. "How many CSOR guys can we get?" he asked.

"They've got an entire high readiness platoon getting ready at Pet now; just waiting for the order," Green said.

"Think you can pull about eight vehicles out of your ass?" Rocky asked.

Green's jaw shifted once, muscles tightening as his eyes stayed fixed on the map. He exhaled slowly through his nose, then rubbed the bridge of it with two fingers. When he finally looked up again, his gaze swept to the screen. "I'll find a way," he said.

"Okay, ladies and gentlemen," Rocky said. "Here's what we're going to do."

He laid out the plan to the group, making slight adjustments as valid points were made. Once the details were settled, one of the collators went to fetch Belanger and Tremblay, who both reviewed the plan.

Tremblay whistled. "That's a lot of moving parts."

"True," Belanger said. "But given the circumstances, I think it's the best play."

Tremblay looked up at the screen, staring at it for a long while, then shifted his gaze toward Rocky, then back to Belanger. "I'm not seeing anything else."

Belanger nodded, then looked at Rocky. "Approved. Now go and get after it."

The team exchanged fist pumps with each other and the two officers.

"Let's go get jocked up," Rocky said.

Green approached Rocky as everyone filed out of the room. "A word."

Goddamn this guy. The last thing Rocky needed right now was another lecture from Green. He steeled himself, vowing not to lose his temper this time.

"Warrant."

The ops warrant sighed and hesitated for a moment, his expression softening from the stone face that was his natural state. "Look, I'm sorry about how things went down the other day. I should have approached you man-to-man. I wasn't thinking."

Rocky, still focused on self-control, said nothing.

"I can't begin to imagine what you're going through," Green said quietly. "I know you two were close. Matt's loss hit everyone hard. Between you and me, I think the whole situation's bullshit. There's stuff they're not telling us. And despite what I said the other day, I think he's still out there somewhere."

Rocky opened his mouth, but the words didn't form. Green was mission-focused, above all things. He'd pulled off some incredible feats downrange, but he'd always lacked that human quality necessary for leadership.

Green rubbed a hand over his jaw and looked away for a moment, his tone softening. "But I meant what I said about moving on," he said. "The lives of your men and those prisoners depend on you keeping a clear head downrange. You don't have to forget about him, and you sure as hell don't need to be him." He stepped forward, placing both hands on Rocky's shoulders. "Truth is, you're one of the finest tactical leaders in this unit. There's only one person who doesn't know it yet, and that's you."

Rocky lowered his gaze, staring at a scuff mark on the floor by his feet. "I don't know what to say."

Green's voice rose slightly, giving Rocky a slight shake.

"You don't need to say anything. Now put all this out of your head. You get down there and bring those people home."

14

CC-177 GLOBEMASTER III
SOMEWHERE OVER BELIZE
THURSDAY, OCTOBER 17
23:15 LOCAL TIME

The deep thrum of the CC-177 Globemaster III filled the cabin as Alpha Team closed in on the drop point. The Canadian Armed Forces had an almost comical habit of renaming every piece of imported kit, turning the C-17 into the CC-177. It didn't do much to soothe Canadian sensitivities about sovereignty, at least not in Rocky's view, but it did a hell of a job confusing everyone. It was a trivial thought, irrelevant to the mission, but his mind tried to cling to it anyway and failed. He'd accepted that Alpha was his team to lead, for now at least, but he still couldn't bring himself to use the Alpha One callsign. It didn't feel right. Neither did running a live op without Lion. The bitter irony wasn't lost on him. He'd nearly wrecked his relationship with Lion out of anger for being passed over as team leader, yet now that he was the one in charge, he found no satisfaction in it. It took the fun out of operating. He used to tell his wife he'd never survive in any job, which always puzzled her. "It's not a job when you love what you're doing," he'd explain. But lately, he wasn't so sure he loved it anymore. Maybe that was the problem.

After years of working for Lion, he'd come to prefer being the grease between the wheels. The fixer. The guy who smoothed out the rough edges while Lion handled the big picture. Now Champs was the fixer—his fixer—which, to be fair, was a blessing since he'd caused no end of problems for Champs to fix over the past nine months.

Rocky's thoughts were interrupted when the jumpmaster called out to the team. "One hour until jump time." He nodded and motioned to Alpha. They knew the drill. They clipped their masks on and hooked up their oxygen bottles.

Soon, they would jump out of a perfectly good aircraft from an altitude of just over 30,000 feet. The high altitude low opening, or HALO, technique was by far one of the most dangerous and daring insertion techniques available to special operators. It wasn't simply the danger of turning into bug splat on the sudden stop at the end of a jump gone wrong that made it dangerous. There was also the risk of hypoxia and decompression sickness to contend with. The air thinned fast at altitude, starving the body of oxygen. Hypoxia set in before an operator even realized it, clouding thought, slowing reaction, then knocking them out cold. Decompression sickness, or the bends, was the other threat. Nitrogen bubbles formed in the blood, joints locked, and vision faded. The warnings in training had scared the hell out of Rocky, and for good reason.

So every jump began the same way: pre-breathe pure oxygen, flush the nitrogen, trust the gear, and stay sharp. A careless mistake up here could cripple a team before they even hit the ground because where JTF2 went, often nobody else followed. If the insertion went wrong tonight, they would be on their own for several hours.

427 SOAS was providing three CH-146 Griffons for extraction, but those birds first had to be offloaded from the Globemaster in Belize City, reassembled, and fuelled, which took time. A quick reaction force from CSOR, a section-sized element, depended on the same aircraft; without them, there would be nothing quick about their response.

Green was leading the ground extraction. He'd sourced eight Toyota Hiluxs from local contacts, giving the team another option. The trucks would carry another section's worth of CSOR operators, but they too needed time to get into position, and there was no guarantee they wouldn't run into environmental obstacles or hostile elements deep in the jungle.

Red tactical lights lit the cargo hold where the operators sat, leaving enough light for preparations while ensuring the operators jumped with their night vision intact.

The plan called for Alpha Team to free fall for most of their descent. They would stabilize themselves mid-air, keeping close together as they plummeted at nearly 200 kilometres per hour. They would deploy their parachutes at low altitudes, around 2000 feet, to minimize the time spent in the air and reduce the chances of being spotted. It would take approximately two minutes from the time they jumped until their boots touched the ground. There were no clearings in the jungle canopy near the compound, so the drop zone would be the Macal River, just south of where it joined Challilo Lake. From the river, they would have to push 3 kilometres southwest to reach the compound. The terrain between would be rough going, with steep limestone ridges, tangled vines, and a canopy so dense it turned daylight into a green haze. The ground would be slick and uneven, the air thick with moisture and insects, every step a slow battle through mud, roots, and undergrowth.

The compound itself remained an intelligence gap. There was no record of it on any Belizean map, and the Vigilance that would provide ISR support couldn't penetrate the canopy. The best its sensors could do was monitor movement along routes, trails, and rivers, which was useful, but not nearly enough. Their intelligence on the compound would be limited to what the two British operators provided Alpha Team on their arrival.

Plenty of opportunity for things to go wrong. Being spotted or compromised in the middle of a Belizean rainforest would be problematic at best.

"The canopy is thick with large trees up to 25 metres high," Talia had warned during the mission planning session. "If you get caught in one, it could mean your life." She looked directly at Hangman, earning a round of laughter from the team. Rocky hadn't bothered saying anything. He knew it didn't matter how often Hangman was told not to get tangled in trees. It would happen anyway. He literally couldn't help himself.

"Don't worry, babe. I got it this time, honest," Hangman said.

Talia tried to glare at him, but instead she smiled, shaking her head. Rocky wondered if perhaps all her rejections of Hangman's advances were merely an act to deflect attention.

He was tempted to ask Hangman about it but decided not to. The two tended to clash as it was. Rocky could be overly serious while Hangman was cavalier and lighthearted. In the past, their conflicts were usually more comical than serious. Their loyalty to Lion kept things in check. A simple glance from him was often enough to defuse the tension. Besides, if Talia and Hangman had something going on and it didn't affect the team adversely, he saw no reason to care.

The jumpmaster's voice brought Rocky back to the present. "We'll be over the DZ in 10 minutes." The team gave a thumbs-up before beginning their final equipment checks. The red lights overhead flickered to green, signalling the countdown to jump. Rocky took one last look at his men, then walked out the back of the C-17.

He felt weightless for a moment. The air rushed past him as the world below stretched in a dark, endless expanse. He spotted the silhouettes of his men keeping tight formation. The dense Chiquibul Forest loomed below. Its thick canopy was barely visible in the dim moonlight.

The team plummeted toward the earth, dropping through the humid night air. Rocky's altimeter numbers were ticking down fast: 2000 feet.

A moment later, he pulled the ripcord, deploying his parachute.

The sudden jerk yanked him upright as the chute deployed. The tension in the straps immediately steadied him as the wind caught the parachute. He floated above the vast jungle momentarily as he scanned the river below. Rocky adjusted his descent, steering the chute carefully toward the water.

He noted the trees, some of which were nearly 100 feet tall. They were the biggest threat during this phase of the operation. One wrong move, and they'd be tangled in the massive branches, exposed and vulnerable.

Rocky broke through the mist and hit the river with a clean splash, the parachute spreading across the surface as he dropped beneath it. He released the harness, surfaced, and grabbed the nylon before the current could carry it away. Kicking hard, he inflated his flotation collar and towed the chute toward the bank, keeping low in the water until he reached the shallows. Once his boots found silt, he pulled the gear bag behind him, hauling both himself and the chute to the treeline. There, under the dripping canopy, he buried the chute beneath mud and palm fronds before stopping to catch his breath.

"Alpha Two down," he whispered through the comms as he scanned the area. The rest of the team would be landing shortly.

The team reported their landings one by one until only Alpha Six remained: Hangman.

"Fucking Hangman!" Rocky cursed as he looked around, trying to spot his missing teammate.

A rustling above caught his attention. True to form, Hangman was tangled in a massive tree about 65 feet up. *He just had to pull this stunt on our first mission without Lion.* Rocky's face reddened and his pulse quickened. Knowing it would happen and not blowing his top when it did were two entirely different things.

"You've got to be shitting me," Rocky said, shaking his head. The rest of the team stifled their laughter.

"Don't worry, Alpha Two. I came prepared this time." Hangman's voice came through Rocky's earpiece, followed by the sound of gear shifting. To everyone's surprise, Hangman had rigged a makeshift bungee rappelling kit.

With some effort, he hooked it to a sturdy branch and, to the team's amazement, began to rappel down from the canopy.

As Hangman finally touched the ground, Champs grabbed him, pulling him prone. "Where the fuck did you pull that from?" he whispered.

"Outta my ass," Hangman whispered in response. "Besides, you're all wet and I'm nice and dry."

Rocky glanced around before looking at his watch. He prayed nobody had spotted or heard their less-than-smooth insertion.

The team stayed in a prone position, each one positioned to provide 360-degree coverage. They listened, their eyes scanning the tree line and ears attuned to any sound that might suggest nearby patrols. The Chiquibul Forest was alive with the noises of nocturnal animals, the rustling of leaves, and the occasional call of distant birds. The air was so humid and thick that it felt like Rocky was breathing fluid. Fluid that was alive. He tried not to imagine how many species of tiny insects he inhaled with each breath. *I fucking hate jungles.*

"Jupiter, Alpha Two. Optimus. Charlie Mike."

"Alpha Two, Jupiter. Roger. Good hunting," Talia said from the TOC.

Previous intelligence on al-Rashid indicated that his men were highly trained and disciplined. Though Rocky assumed the enemy didn't have much in the way of jungle experience, he wasn't willing to discount the possibility of reconnaissance patrols.

He flashed a clenched fist, then two fingers forward, signalling the team to move out cautiously. One man took the lead, a second stayed a few steps behind to cover him, and the rest formed a single line with 3 to 5 metres spacing between them. The last man kept watch over their six, making sure nothing followed. In places where the canopy opened slightly, two men drifted outward to watch each flank. When the jungle closed in tight again, they drew back into line. No one spoke. Hand signals passed orders down the file. There were no machetes or bush hacking. The lead man used his knife to lift vines and let them drop quietly back into place. Every 50 metres, Rocky called a short SLLS halt to stop, look, listen, and smell, counting a slow fifteen before continuing.

It was slow going, every step a risk of giving away their position, but if any recce patrols were out there, Alpha Team would be ready.

15

KHALID AL-RASHID COMPOUND
CHIQUIBUL FOREST, BELIZE
FRIDAY, OCTOBER 18
03:31 LOCAL TIME

Rocky's boots sank into damp leaf litter as darkness pressed tight around him. The jungle breathed and shifted in shadow, every rustle, drip, and whisper sharpened against the heavy air. Fireflies pulsed faintly between the trunks, their light mirrored by the occasional glint of a spider's eyeshine. Frogs called in irregular bursts, deep-throated and close, while the higher trill of katydids and crickets filled the canopy. A night bird gave a short, hollow cry somewhere in the distance, and then, up ahead, a branch snapped.

Rocky froze mid-step, hand up, the patrol locking still behind him. The jungle's chorus carried on, indifferent.

No one moved. The patrol stopped like a breath held, boots locked in place.

Each man's eyes swept his respective arcs, ensuring 360-degree coverage, but light was sparse, and NVGs provided a grainy, low-contrast picture. Rocky slipped his carbine to the high ready, safety lever switched to semi-automatic. A slow count ran in his mind—fifteen, ten—while the team remained as still as a statue.

He heard a rustle, then the faint drag of fabric through wet leaves. Those weren't the sounds of nocturnal animals, and in this part of the jungle, anyone making them likely came from the compound. Rocky traced a shallow arc with two fingers, then slashed his hand down: *split and peel.* Hangman and Spooky dissolved into the foliage, moving flat and quiet. Whiskey and Bambam eased left to cover the flank.

Hangman's eyes flicked up from his low posture as the undergrowth ahead shifted. Two figures stumbled over a root, armed with AK-47s. Hangman had already drawn his combat knife, a flush, tactical fixed blade. The men paused, whispering in Arabic. Hangman glided forward. His left hand sealed over the nearest man's mouth and nose, his momentum carrying them both off balance. The blade punched down between neck and collarbone, a single, deep drive that sank into the lung. The sound was a quiet, wet give. He eased the body down, following it to the ground, hand still clamped until the man's last breath stuttered out.

To his right, Spooky moved in tandem. The second figure barely turned before Spooky's arm locked across his face, muffling the startled inhale. His knife found the same gap, same angle, same outcome—a muted exhale, a soft collapse into vines and earth.

The team held their position for a few minutes. Satisfied there was nobody else nearby, Rocky pointed forward, and Alpha Team continued its silent approach toward the compound. Save for a chance encounter with a snake, which nearly caused Spooky to cry out like a baby, the approach to the compound's perimeter passed without further incident.

The team moved in silence, senses tuned sharp, each step measured and deliberate through the damp undergrowth. It was a gruelling and tedious process. The humidity was unrelenting. Rocky had stopped wiping the sweat from his brow an hour ago. His fatigues clung to him like a second skin. Not for the first time, Rocky decided human beings had no business in jungles. Whether desert or jungle ranked as the worst place on earth was still up for debate—though tonight, the jungle was winning.

Then, somewhere ahead, close but hidden, a voice whispered from the dark.

"Halt."

Rocky froze, making a fist. The rest of the team followed suit.

From the same patch of darkness ahead came another whisper.

"Oscar Hotel."

Rocky smiled. "November Foxtrot," he whispered back.

"Advance one to be recognized," the voice ahead said.

Rocky raised his weapon above his head and moved forward slowly until the whisper came again.

"Halt."

He froze where he stood. The voice came again, low and measured through the dark.

"How many in your party?"

"Twelve, myself included."

"Call the next man forward," the whisper ordered.

Rocky gave a silent hand signal, and Spooky stepped out a moment later. He confirmed him as part of the team, and the process repeated. Each man was called forward, identified, and cleared until all of Alpha stood accounted for and no movement showed behind them.

A figure rose from the darkness behind them.

"About bloody time, mate," Loughton said.

"How the hell do you do that?" Rocky asked.

The crusty old Brit grinned.

"Magic."

Another shape rose from the dark, barely 2 metres off Rocky's flank.

"Randy Ashford," the man said.

Rocky embraced Loughton, then looked the older man and his comrade over. "You boys look like shit."

"Not as young as I used to be, and it's been a rough few days in this bloody sauna."

Champs and Bambam shrugged off their rucks, each carrying another lashed on top. They handed the spares to the British pair.

"Brought you water, rats, and kit," Rocky said, then signalled Hangman and Spooky forward to cover the group.

The two men wasted no time. They stripped down to their waists, wiped away the grime and sweat with the towels packed inside, then pulled on fresh fatigues. From the same rucks they drew out CamelBaks, slung them over their shoulders, and drank deeply.

Miles and Davis unhooked the spare tac vests from their gear and passed them over. The Brits slipped into the vests, unfastening the helmets clipped to them and pulling them on.

"Damn," Ashford said, adjusting the chin strap. "You blokes hauled an extra set of body armour all this way? Bloody studs."

Next, Loughton and Ashford dug into the rucks for fresh socks and boots, swapping out the soaked ones without a second thought.

"How'd you lot get our sizes?" Loughton asked, tugging at a boot lace.

"Some dude named Ollie," Champs said.

Ashford shook his head in disbelief. "How'd he get our... Ah, never mind, not important."

Master Corporal Liam McKay, Alpha's second medic and machine gunner, stepped forward, handing Ashford his C9 light machine gun and ammo drums.

"This bitch only comes in one size," McKay said.

Ashford took the C9, unloaded it, racked it, and ran a quick safety check before reloading. He smiled at the weapon, brushed a thumb along the rail, and kissed it lightly. "You and I are gonna get on just fine," he murmured.

After the two Brits finished their rations, they briefed Rocky and the team. Keira was alive and unharmed for now, but Nathan had taken a round just below the right collarbone, slightly left of the shoulder. It went clean through, but he'd lost a lot of blood. Loughton had talked Keira through how to stop the bleeding over the earpieces Ollie had supplied, which were still functional. Keira followed every instruction, tearing up the oversized shirt and skirt she'd been wearing to improvise bandages. Nathan seemed stable for the moment. So far, al-Rashid and his men hadn't touched them, aside from bringing bread and water.

"At least we know they aren't planning on killing them right away," Rocky said.

"My thoughts exactly," Loughton said. "Though I'm surprised they haven't tried questioning them yet."

Loughton and Ashford each led a pair of Alpha operators around the compound's perimeter, closing to within 10 metres to get eyes on. They guided the men into position, pointing out every fold of terrain, every blind spot and approach route they'd mapped over the past few days. Together, they selected a small clearing where a climber could rig and push an antenna through the canopy to establish a signal.

"Have at 'er," Champs said to Hangman.

"What? Why me?" Hangman protested. "I know how to get down from trees, not climb them."

"That's half of the battle right there," Champs said. "I'm sure you'll figure it out. Now get to it. I want comms established before first light."

Rocky and Loughton scanned the compound together. Two large wooden structures stood among the roots of enormous trees that punched straight out of the ground. Most of the undergrowth had been hacked away leaving a rough but open floor of mud and trampled vines. Two campfires burned near the centre, each watched by a pair of guards. The easy posture of the sentries told Rocky they weren't expecting company this deep in the jungle.

The compound's layout came into focus as Rocky and Loughton studied it from Alpha's position south of the perimeter. Two structures dominated the clearing, forming a rough L-shape. The long side of the L was a single-story building stretching across most of the compound, which they figured served as a barracks. The shorter leg was a two-story structure running lengthwise toward them, with a small shed-like annex jutting from the near side. Together, the buildings boxed the open patch of ground. The northwest corner of the compound led to a network of trails and small dirt roads that extended toward the main road 5 kilometres away.

Random two-man patrols moved around inside and outside the compound perimeter at irregular intervals. Everyone would have to stay sharp and ready to shift position fast; an encounter this close wouldn't go unnoticed.

"Nathan and Keira are being held on the ground floor of the two-story building," Loughton said.

"How do you know?" Rocky asked.

"She can hear footsteps overhead. Only one place she can be to hear that."

"Got it," Rocky said. "What about al-Rashid?"

"Don't know for sure, but my gut tells me he's on the second floor of the two-story," Loughton said.

"That fits the profile we have on him," Spooky said. "Arrogant. Sees himself as a divine messenger. He wouldn't mix with the rank and file and wouldn't want to lower himself to the same level as his prisoners."

"Jupiter, Alpha Six. Comm check, over," Rocky heard Hangman repeat three times through his headset.

A moment later, Talia's voice filled the headset. "Alpha Six, Jupiter. Roger. You're broken and distorted but readable."

Rocky looked up just in time to see Hangman flash a thumbs-up right before he lost his grip. He dropped fast, the harness stretching tight and yanking him to a stop about 3 metres above the ground. The bungee cord snapped him back upward, then down again, bouncing him in like a yo-yo between air and earth.

After a few wild swings, Hangman managed to snag a nearby tree trunk. He steadied himself, unhooked from the harness, and began the careful climb down. When his boots finally hit the ground, he gave the team an awkward grin, the colour drained from his face.

"All part of the plan," Hangman said, stumbling a step.

"What in the bloody hell is that man doing?" Loughton asked, disbelief cutting through his whisper.

"Don't get me started," Rocky said, glaring at Hangman.

Ashford strolled over to Hangman, grinning ear to ear. "That was cool as fuck, mate."

Talia's voice cracked through the comms, tense and clipped. "Alpha Six, Jupiter. I say again, report."

"Jupiter, Alpha Two. Prime," Rocky said. "Situation normal. We are Charlie Mike, on schedule."

Rocky thought he heard her mutter "*Fucking asshole*" under her breath before she stopped transmitting. He smothered a grin.

Champs seized both Hangman and Ashford by their gear and hauled them back toward the group. "Don't fucking encourage him," he whispered to Ashford.

Talia spent the next few minutes bringing them up to date on the ISR feed from the Vigilance. No vehicles or foot movement had been observed on the main road or along the network of trails leading to the compound. Two individuals were seen moving near the shoreline of the lake. Likely one of al-Rashid's patrols, Rocky figured.

Boxcar, Green's motor convoy, had been delayed leaving Belmopan but was now making good time. In Belize City, the CH-146 Griffons and a pair of Hueys were spooled up and ready, along with the CSOR contingent and a Belizean Special Forces platoon standing by.

So far so good. Rocky briefed the two Brits on the plan, receiving nods in return.

"Sounds good to me, mate," Loughton said.

"Where do you want me?" Ashford asked.

Rocky glanced at Champs, who grabbed a twig nearby, marking a spot on the makeshift map they'd created out of mud, leaves, and branches. "I want you in this elevated position on the east side," Champs said, pointing.

"You'll have line of sight over the courtyard and the approaches into the compound. Your job is simple: If we get into trouble, fuck 'em up. But do not open fire until we have positive control of the prisoners unless you're explicitly ordered to."

"Count on it," Ashford said.

"Miles, you'll set up position with him," Champs said. "Davis, I want you here on the west side, north of the route network. You'll be covering our exfil."

The snipers nodded.

"Gareth, how do you feel about joining the stack?" Rocky asked.

"Tip top, shit hot," Loughton replied.

"Sun's coming up soon. You two go to ground and catch up on sleep," Rocky said, pointing at the two Brits. "Daytime routine for the rest of you. Pair up. Sleep in shifts. Maintain comms with Jupiter and report any changes. We launch after dark once the camp goes into their evening routine."

Loughton nodded then spoke. "Keira, we're grabbing some winks. If anything changes, make some noise. I'm a light sleeper. It'll wake me up."

He paused for a moment, listening to the device in his ear. "You're doing great, lass. You just hang in there. We're gonna bring the rain."

"Hell of a young woman, that one is," Loughton said to the team, before finding a spot to close his eyes.

"Champs, go put your head down. I'll take first watch," Rocky said.

08:30 LOCAL TIME

Khalid al-Rashid sat at a small table in the two-story building that had housed him for the past few weeks. He had already been in Belize far longer than he had planned, and his frustration was growing. He had other pressing concerns that required his attention in Palestine. But Al-Najm al-Saghir had sent him here, and whatever Al-Najm wanted took precedence. His mission was simple—to negotiate terms with the La Sangre Sagrada drug cartel—yet the rationale behind it escaped him.

They were the most feared drug cartel in Central America, known for their vicious brutality. Its members consisted of ex-special forces personnel from neighbouring countries. They were as efficient as they were cruel. They trafficked drugs and weapons across borders with impunity, and they had recently entered the market of human trafficking. The scope of their international operations was so vast that the volume of business they conducted dwarfed the GDP of many Central American countries.

Khalid didn't trust them, which was why he had brought seventy of his most trusted warriors with him. As far as he was concerned, the members of the cartel were godless infidels that served no higher purpose than their own pocketbooks. Khalid understood the value of wealth. He had spent years cultivating his own, but not for luxury or entertainment. No. He had little interest in such trivial things. He saw himself as a humble pilgrim. One who did the work of God's hand. He had been entrusted with this most important of tasks, and he would see it through. He served a calling. A calling so profound that he had dedicated his entire life to it. He saw the Western way of life as a threat to everything he believed in. Everything he held dear. *Why couldn't they understand the folly of their ways?* He didn't hate the West or its people. He saw them as hapless victims who needed to be saved from themselves. From their selfishness. From their trivial pursuits. *Freedom is the poison that has corrupted them. But not for much longer. Soon they shall be liberated from freedom. Soon they shall see.*

He wasn't above killing the innocent to see his work done. *Everyone has to sacrifice. This was their sacrifice.* Khalid had done his share of killing over the years. He took no pleasure in it, but he didn't hesitate either until recently. His thinking on the matter had shifted. *Why teach them the error of their ways if they were all going to die anyway?* Perhaps he was growing weak in his old age. He'd been at this for decades. Were it not for his faith and absolute certainty in the cause, he would have lost his way years ago.

There was a knock at the door.

"Enter," Khalid said.

"The cartel is approaching," Omar Haddad, one of his most trusted devotees, reported.

"Good," Khalid answered. "I grow tired of wasting time in this godforsaken jungle. But you seem troubled. Speak your mind, my son."

Omar shifted uneasily, his eyes flicking to the window. "They come with many soldiers, well armed. We cannot win if blood is spilled." His voice carried a nervous edge, his fingers twitching at his side.

Khalid looked at Omar with calm, unwavering eyes, a faint smile playing at the corners of his lips. "Fear not," he said, his tone almost serene. "We are here to treat with them, not fight. But if it comes to that, God will welcome us."

"As you say," Omar said, though his tone suggested he harboured doubts.

Khalid's voice was firm but measured. "Have your men take a defensive posture." His gaze drifted toward the compound's entrance. "Show them we are not weak. But offer no aggression." He approached the window, peering at the tree line where the cartel's convoy would soon appear. "Show them in as soon as they arrive," he said. "We have something they desperately want. They aren't here to fight. They seek merely to intimidate to gain more favourable terms." His confidence radiated. His posture was that of a man convinced of his superiority and divine purpose. He knew the cartel wanted what he had to offer.

"And what about the prisoners?" Omar asked.

Khalid stroked his long, grey beard. The truth was he had no idea what to do with them. He'd never planned on holding prisoners in the first place. He wished they had been killed in the gun battle, but some of his newer men were out to impress. They thought he would welcome having hostages. He couldn't blame them for their logic. In the past, he had produced several videos, some of them live, of him beheading people to send a message to his enemies. But that was a different time, and as Al-Najm had made clear, they were fighting a different kind of war now. What enemy would he be sending a message to if he killed the ex-soldier? Canadians would barely notice, let alone care. Two terror cells had each taken a Canadian citizen hostage a few years ago and killed them when the government refused to negotiate. That didn't surprise Khalid—Western governments rarely negotiated with him either—but the Canadians hadn't bothered launching a rescue attempt. Whatever media attention the ex-soldier's death garnered would be pointed at Canada's politicians in a futile attempt to shame them. It wouldn't benefit him or Al-Najm.

The young British woman, on the other hand, would command considerable attention. A few years ago, he would have leaped at the chance to behead her on a live social media feed. But the British government was about to tear itself apart, and so her death wouldn't serve his purpose either. At least not right now. And even if it did, he suspected that Al-Najm would have his head if he were to pull such a stunt now. Publicity for the cause was something Al-Najm had insisted needed to be avoided.

"They will kill themselves," Al-Najm had preached passionately a few years ago. "We need only let them and provide a few helpful nudges along the way."

Khalid had initially thought the man was out of his mind, but then he reconsidered. Al-Najm's logic was difficult to rebut. Khalid's own tactics had brought them no closer to achieving the Muslim Brotherhood's goals than they were a few decades ago, and not for lack of trying. The Brotherhood was most effective when it managed the narrative, painting itself as the victim and Western governments as the enemy. Khalid no longer served the Brotherhood; he'd cut ties with them after meeting Al-Najm.

He turned to face Omar. "I do not know yet. I will pray on it later and come to a decision. Ensure the cartel does not learn of their presence. They would insist on selling them, which would bring unwanted attention."

"And if they do learn of their presence?" Omar asked.

Khalid locked eyes with Omar. "You will ensure that the cartel does not take my prisoners."

***

"What the fuck." Spooky moved to Rocky and nudged him a little harder than he intended. "Boss, wake up. Something's going down."

Miles whispered into the comms. "This is Alpha Five. I've got four times SUVs disgorging heavily armed men. Full body armour. Compound guys look like they're panicking."

Rocky snapped himself awake, rubbing his eyes as he groaned beside Spooky. "Show me," he ordered, reaching for his binoculars.

"Looks like a confrontation is brewing down there, boss," Champs said as his brow furrowed in confusion. "What the fuck are these guys up to?"

After a moment, Rocky spoke quietly into the comms. "All stations. Take no action. Observe only. If they start shooting at each other, let them. Let this play out. I want to see what's going on."

***

Diego Morales entered the room. "Odio a estos locos (*I hate these nutcases*)," he muttered as he pulled up a chair.

Khalid didn't move. The white thobe he wore over his tall frame remained still. He was content to let a few moments pass before addressing the portly, greasy infidel behind him.

"Senior al-Rashid, I don't have all fucking day, and you're no deity. Tell me why you called this meeting, or I'll shave your beard and make you eat it for wasting my time."

Khalid sighed. The infidels never had patience. They were bred from greed, concerned only with immediate gratification. But that would serve his purposes today. He turned and smiled at the Sagrada cartel member, running him through the offer.

Diego's voice was edged with skepticism. "You want us to supply the Canadian market with cheap fentanyl and opioids? Why would we do this? We don't even bother with Canada. They are cheap enough, and our competitors already work there."

"Wealth." Khalid shrugged his shoulders. "This is your goal, yes?"

Diego gripped the chair arms so tight that his knuckles started turning white. "There is no wealth to be gained by handing out free drugs."

Khalid finally took a seat, locking eyes with Diego as he smiled at the simple-minded man. "Do this for us, and Al-Najm al-Saghir will grant you access to Eastern Europe. Do not, and we will meet with your competitors next. You choose. Wealth for you or your competitors?"

Diego appeared to be taken aback. His organization had long tried to penetrate the Eastern European market but had failed at every turn. The criminal networks there were just as vicious as Sagrada, and their backyard gave them a competitive edge. Khalid knew that if Diego could secure access to Eastern Europe, his masters at the pinnacle of Sagrada would reward him. That was the only pressure point he had over the drug lord.

"This offer intrigues me. But there are challenges. I haven't bothered with Canada before. I have no contacts there. Plus, my competitors will resist me. It could start a war with the others," Diego said.

"We can assist you with all of this," Khalid insisted. "Al-Najm will commit to bringing your competitors to heel."

Khalid could imagine the gears turning in this simple man's mind, weighing the risk against the monetary reward.

Infidels like Diego seldom surprised him. Greed dictated all their actions.

After a long moment, Diego extended a hand to Khalid. "Tell Al-Najm he has a deal."

"Tell him yourself," Khalid replied, scribbling contact information on a small card. "You will reach out to Sienna Fairfax and confirm your acceptance. She will liaise with you. We will have no further dealings. I have more pressing matters to attend to."

"As you wish," Diego said as he rose to leave with a large smile.

"Would you be so kind as to leave one of your vehicles behind? I want to leave this place tomorrow," Khalid asked after him.

Diego turned to face him one more time. "For Eastern Europe, you can have all the vehicles you wish."

Khalid sighed. It was too easy. *Why waste me on such a simple task?*

***

Rocky watched as the small-statured, fat man entered the main building. The forces he'd brought with him appeared to be in a standoff with the fighters at the compound, though it didn't appear that the newcomers were too concerned.

The fat one emerged half an hour later with a big smile and an extra spring in his step. "Looks like Khalid and the new guy just became friends," Hangman whispered through the comms. "I bet Logan's leftover ravioli that he's drug cartel."

"Agreed," Spooky said. "The only people in the region with that kind of gear are the La Sangre Sagrada drug cartel. Those guys don't fuck around. Rank one assholes."

Lion had often speculated that it was only a matter of time before terrorists and transnational criminal organizations got into bed together. "Imagine the logistical benefits a drug cartel could offer a terror group," Lion had said. Organized terrorists faced enormous difficulty moving in and out of Western countries after 9/11—but drug cartels didn't. Still, Lion's theories had gained little traction within intelligence circles. Even the Americans seemed unconvinced. The prevailing view was that criminal organizations cared only about profit and would never risk partnering with terrorists for fear of provoking a full-scale crackdown. That logic had always puzzled Rocky. Why weren't they dropping the hammer on the cartels in the first place?

He thought about it some more. If al-Rashid was planning to use drug traffickers to enter Canada, that would indeed be a grave threat to Canada. Maybe that's what Sayyid was trying to warn Cutler about? It was time to get some answers.

"Mission update," Rocky said over the comms. "Priority objective remains Cutler and Sterling. Secondary objective now capture, not kill. I want to find out what these guys are talking about."

16

ALPHA TEAM OBSERVATION POST
CHIQUIBUL FOREST, BELIZE
SATURDAY, OCTOBER 19
01:52 LOCAL TIME

Rocky didn't like what he saw through his handheld thermal monocular. The cartel convoy had pulled out of the compound soon after the meeting between their leader and al-Rashid, but one SUV stayed behind, parked near the northwest corner of the perimeter by the dirt road network. Outside the two-story building's entrance, six cartel gunmen who'd stayed behind were engaged in another confrontation with al-Rashid's men, and things were getting tense. Neither Rocky's team nor their two British allies spoke Arabic or Spanish, but Keira knew enough Spanish to understand what was happening. Loughton kept Rocky updated on everything Keira said, which painted the unfolding picture.

"So that's it, then. They know we're here. Must be why there are six of you lads with rifles now," Keira said to the guards.

Rocky was beginning to understand why Loughton held Keira in such high regard. The young woman had kept her composure under pressure and found creative ways to pass intelligence using her conversations with the gunmen as cover to keep the team informed.

This was the fifth confrontation between the two groups and by far the most intense. There was only one reason Rocky could think of for the repeated clashes: Keira Sterling.

Al-Rashid's men were clearly intent on keeping the cartel away from their prisoners, which was both a blessing and a curse. On one hand, the increased presence of al-Rashid's men protected Keira from horrific trauma, but it also meant Nathan and Keira now had six armed guards in the room with them at all times, with another six just outside the building.

A stealth assault would be more difficult now. Once his team slipped past the perimeter they'd have to take out the two groups arguing outside before they could even think about breaching the door. Sure, a gunfight might draw the six guards inside the room out into the open, which could simplify extracting Nathan and Keira, but it would also put the entire compound on full alert, forcing a firefight with a force at least five times Alpha's size. The CSOR element riding with Green's convoy would help, but they were still holding position 3 kilometres out. Bringing them forward by truck would make too much noise, and moving on foot would take too long. The second CSOR element, waiting aboard the CH-146

Griffons at Belize International, could launch at any time, but even then it would be a thirty-minute flight, plus the time needed to move from their insertion point to the compound on foot.

The door to the two-story building opened, and a tall figure with a long beard emerged.

"Positive ID on al-Rashid," Miles said from his sniper perch.

"Ack," Rocky said. "All stations, stand fast."

Rocky watched as al-Rashid appeared to be shouting at the cartel group, stabbing a finger their way. A minute later, the gunmen backed off and returned to their SUV.

"How long do you want to wait?" Champs whispered.

"Let's give things enough time to settle down," Rocky said. "I want these guys asleep before we make our move."

"Nothing new from Keira," Loughton said.

Rocky nodded and waited, deciding once more that patience was a virtue for now.

The humidity was wearing him down. He hadn't stopped sweating since Alpha first set down, and their water supply was running low. His fatigues were drenched—first from the river, then from the endless sweat. Every man on the team was hungry, exhausted, filthy, and just as soaked as he was. Conditions like these tested the patience of even the most disciplined soldier, but that was the job.

Another hour crawled by. Then his snipers on overwatch came over the net with a report.

"Four cartel members shooting the shit—two posted at the front of the SUV, two at the rear. Looks like the other two are passed out inside the vehicle," Davis reported.

"I've got eyes on fifteen al-Rashid men. Mostly engaged in idle conversation. Two pairs of sentries at each of the fire pits, another pair patrolling the perimeter, four pairs stationed by the entrance of the target building, and a solo wandering around," Miles reported.

Rocky glanced at Loughton, who said, "No change."

"Looks like the rest of the camp's gone to ground, boss," Spooky said.

"Based on what we've observed the past few days, this is likely as good as it's gonna get, mate," Loughton said.

"Agreed," Rocky said.

"Jupiter, Alpha Two. Launch Hammer."

"Alpha Two, Jupiter. Acknowledged. Launching Hammer."

The jungle was alive with noise—the constant hum of cicadas and crickets, the clucking of tree frogs, and the deeper croaks of toads nearby. A howler monkey's distant call rolled through the canopy, followed by the faint rush of wings as a nightbird moved overhead. Water dripped steadily from leaves, pattering against mud, while somewhere close something small pushed through the brush and went silent again. Rocky focused on drowning out the sounds as he steadied his breathing.

He decided to split his assault force into two elements: a three-man det led by Champs, and an eight-man team under his own command.

Rocky waited another twenty minutes before giving the order. "Champs, you have the cartel and the rear entry. I'll take the guys out front and the main entry," he said. "Miles, Davis, you have the fire pits, the patrol, and the wanderer. Move."

Champs' three-man detachment moved first, angling slightly west from Alpha's hide site roughly 80 metres south of the perimeter, tight to the underbrush to mask their approach toward the SUV. Rocky followed with his det, NVGs pushed down over his eyes; he picked up the faint strobes of Champs' team ahead and matched their pace. His movements were deliberate and measured, every step chosen to avoid dry leaves and snapping twigs. The eight men stayed close, weapons at high ready, each covering assigned arcs. Once they passed the western edge of the target building, Rocky peeled right toward the annex shed, keeping a shallow offset so trees and foliage continued to provide concealment. He turned, pointed at Savard, then swept his hand to the window; Savard nodded, dropped to a kneeling position, and trained his weapon on the glass. Rocky gave the signal and the det crossed the 5 metres of open ground, entered the shed, and cleared it methodically: no contacts. He turned and motioned toward Savard, who moved slowly toward the shed, weapon remaining trained on the window. They reformed tight on the shed's south corner, stacked and ready to pivot left and engage the eight gunmen posted at the main entrance, holding position.

Miles' voice cut through the headset. "Assault group two in position."

"Assault group one in position," Davis said.

Then Miles again. "Go on my mark. Three—two—now."

Rocky's det peeled off the shed's corner, moving left as one body. He spotted eight figures through his NVGs. Spooky and Hangman fired two suppressed rounds each into the near pair—short, compact muzzle pops with a thin, high crack from the rounds. The two men crumpled to the ground, but one continued moving. Hangman fired another round into the man's head. Loughton and Whiskey trained their weapons on the next sector, shoulders and barrels aligning on two separate targets—four more sharp pops; each pair of shots landed, and the two hostiles collapsed. Each fired a third round into their targets, who didn't move again. At the same time, Rocky and Savard took a step away from the wall, crouching and firing rounds into a third pair of men, while Monty and Wood, standing directly behind them, fired into the final pair of men.

It never ceased to amaze Rocky how seamlessly they moved together. Reading each other's body language was faster than speaking. Besides, once the CQB began, words not only got in the way, but they could be heard by an adversary. To Rocky, it was beautiful in its own brutal way. When that kind of precision met initiative combined with violence of action, anyone on the receiving end rarely stood a chance.

He gave a sharp hand signal, and his detachment started dragging the bodies into the shed before Spooky captured images of the bodies.

***

Champs led his det forward through the underbrush, NVGs casting the scene in grainy dim green. The SUV came into view ahead, the four cartel gunmen standing outside it smoking. The faint smell of cigarettes hung in the humid air. Champs raised a fist, halting the team, then pointed to McKay and gestured toward a north-facing window of the target building. McKay nodded, moved off a few paces, and took a knee, MRR covering the window.

Turning to Bambam, Champs gave a quick hand signal, and the two advanced while McKay held his position. They moved low through the last stretch of brush, closing to within 5 metres of the SUV. The four cartel gunmen outside were relaxed, talking quietly, AK-47s slung, smoke drifting from their cigarettes.

Champs gave a short nod and moved toward the front of the SUV while Bambam slipped to the rear. Through his NVGs, the two cartel fighters appeared in crisp, green silhouette—their faces ghostlike in the image intensifier's glow, cigarettes burning as bright white pinpoints against the dark. One leaned on the hood; the other exhaled smoke into the air. Champs fired twice in quick succession at close range, one suppressed round into each skull. Both went down instantly. He heard two more muffled pops as Bambam did the same at the rear of the vehicle—two more instantaneous kills. Champs then stepped to the passenger side, angled his muzzle through the open window, and fired one suppressed headshot into each of the two men inside the vehicle.

He swept the area through his NVGs for movement, then moved back to the front of the SUV and hauled the two bodies into the nearest underbrush, concealing them from view. Bambam mirrored him at the rear, dragging two more into cover. They left the corpses inside the vehicle where they lay, then slipped off toward the western side of the target building, stacking against the rear door. McKay fell in beside them, rifle up and pressed to the wall, covering the north-facing window as they closed.

***

Rocky heard four low, concussive thuds from the C14 Timberwolf MRSWS sniper rifles, each muffled report marked by a thin, high-pitched crack as the .338 rounds broke the sound barrier.

"Fire pit sentries down," Miles said over the comms.

A beat later, another muted thud and crack followed. "Wanderer down," Davis reported. "No eyes on the two-man patrol."

Hangman crouched by the main entrance and glanced up the doorframe. The hinges showed it opened outward. He tested the knob; it turned freely. He gave Spooky a short nod—the door was unlocked. Rocky glanced over his shoulder at the stack behind him, each man hugging the wall to the right of the door, weapons up, eyes forward. Spooky squeezed Hangman's shoulder once. Hangman turned the handle and eased the door open, stepping aside to clear the line.

Spooky and Rocky moved together through the gap like a practised pair. Spooky entered first, driving past the threshold and angling left toward the near corner of the large hallway, and fired twice at an armed man standing by a door along the way then shifted his line of sight to sweep the centre as he moved. Once at the near corner, he held that sector and worked his way along the wall to the far left corner. Rocky followed almost simultaneously, taking the opposite jamb and sweeping right along the far wall. Spotting a figure through his NGVs, he fired a three-round burst into the man then shifted his attention back toward the far corner. Both men kept their weapons trained on their immediate sectors, folding the space into managed pieces.

Loughton and Whiskey came next, taking the left and right centre lanes. Savard and Monty followed immediately, moving down the hall toward a perpendicular corridor. Savard peered toward the right without exposing himself, then confirmed the way was clear. Monty closed with him, and they held the intersection.

Farther down the hall, a door opened. Bambam moved through and angled left toward Savard; Champs moved right and angled down the opposite side with McKay slotting in behind him. Champs' det consolidated at the stairwell while Savard advanced to secure the rear door they had come through.

Wood and Hangman entered last. Wood dropped in with Rocky's element, now positioned to the left of the door, while Hangman took up rear security at the main entrance to make sure nothing moved in behind them.

Based on the building's size and the angle of the hall, Rocky concluded Nathan and Keira were in the room beyond the door, guarded by six fighters. He caught Loughton's eye; the other man seemed to have reached the same conclusion and gave him a quick nod and thumbs-up.

Spooky checked the door. It opened inward and was locked. He signalled Hangman forward, switching places with him.

Hangman slung his rifle, drew the breaching shotgun, and waited for Rocky's squeeze. One blast shattered the lock. Hangman kicked the door hard, forcing it open, then pivoted clear as Rocky surged through, sweeping right and firing two controlled shots into the man crouched in the near corner. Loughton came in tight behind, hooking left and cutting down the fighter in the opposite corner. Two more gunmen lifted their rifles, but Whiskey and Wood entered next and dropped them with short bursts. Rocky heard two sharp pops as Loughton fired at a gunman who was swinging his weapon toward Nathan and Keira, both huddled on the floor against the far wall. Rocky took a final shot at the fighter who was kneeling next to the two prisoners.

Whiskey dropped to one knee beside Nathan, shrugging off his medical satchel. Keira, tears streaking her face, clung to Nathan's side. Loughton stepped in, eased his arms around her, and pulled her clear so Whiskey could work.

"They started beating him," she choked out, anger and disbelief twisting through every word.

"I know, lass," Loughton said. "Try to calm down. We're going to get you two out of here."

Rocky turned to him. "You knew?"

"They started on him as we crossed the perimeter," Loughton said.

"Why didn't you say anything?"

"Because your team was already moving as fast as humanly possible," Loughton said evenly. "If I'd told you, it would've only slowed you down."

Rocky nodded. "Good call." He keyed his mic. "All stations, Alpha Two. Citadel."

"Alpha Two, Boxcar," Green said over the comms. "We're moving to you now."

Rocky looked at Nathan lying on the wooden floor against the wall, his black T-shirt torn and clinging to his skin, darkened where blood had soaked through the makeshift bandage across his upper chest. The strips of Keira's clothing were knotted tight, crusted and uneven. His face was pale and slick with sweat, his lips cracked, his eyes glassy. A deep bruise shadowed one eye, with several more running along his forearms and shins. Clearly, he'd tried to shield himself from the beating. Rocky hoped most of the strikes had hit his limbs and not anything vital.

He glanced over at Keira. She was down to a white bikini top and short yoga shorts, her skin streaked with blood, sweat, and dirt, her expression a raw mix of panic and fury, hands shaking as Loughton tried to calm her.

"Are you hurt?" Rocky asked, kneeling beside them.

She shook her head.

"I'm going to do a quick check," he said, running his hands over her body to feel for wounds or bleeding. "Looks like you're good."

Rocky shrugged out of his tac vest and body armour, pulled a dark green T-shirt from a rear pouch, and slipped it over her head. "I know it's gross, but it'll help break up your outline."

He fastened the vest and armour around her, tightening the straps as best he could to fit her frame. It wasn't perfect, but it would have to do. Next, he removed his helmet, adjusted the padding inside, and settled it on her head. Ideally, the team would have brought extra body armour for the hostages to protect them in case something went wrong during extraction. But carrying that weight for Loughton and Ashford on the approach had been one thing, dragging it into the assault would have cost speed and invited failure. Giving his body armour to Keira left him exposed, but he wasn't the mission. Nathan and Keira were.

Rocky looked back at Whiskey and Nathan. Whiskey tore away the makeshift bandage, the knotted strips of fabric coming loose in his hands, then cleaned the wound as best he could. He packed it tight with combat gauze, sealed it with a proper pressure dressing, and cinched it down until the bleeding stopped. He listened for breath sounds and felt along the ribs.

"It went straight through," Whiskey said. "No lung hit."

He pinched Nathan's fingernails, watching how long it took the colour to return, then glanced up. "He's dry," Whiskey said. "He's got severe blood loss." Whiskey pulled an IV line from his med kit, inserted the needle, and secured it with tape. A small saline pouch followed, half filled, followed by a shot of tranexamic acid and a measured dose of ketamine. Nathan's eyelids fluttered, his breathing evened slightly.

"We're going to lose him if I don't start pumping him with plasma now," Whiskey said. He pulled an AB plasma bag from his kit, spiked it, snapped the line into the IV, and opened the clamp to start the transfusion.

***

Champs angled his MRR upward as he reached the stairwell and signalled for Savard to join his det. Monty stepped forward from the intersection and took over security at the rear entrance. Champs started moving up the stairs slowly as McKay, Bambam, and Savard followed, weapons up.

Before reaching the landing, Champs leaned out just enough to check upward. A fighter was looking down the stairwell. Champs fired once, the round taking the man clean in the forehead, then moved up to secure the landing as the rest of the team closed in behind him.

The team moved toward the second floor. The staircase terminated at a closed door positioned flush with the wall, leaving no lateral space for a stack or prep. It was a straight, confined approach. Champs glanced back at his det, ensuring they were ready. McKay squeezed his shoulder. He pushed the door open and slipped into the room with his carbine sweeping right. He spotted a hostile near the window and fired. The man dropped, his body slumping against the glass. Champs moved further into the room to make room for the next man, scanning for threats.

McKay entered right behind him, flowing to the left. He spotted a second hostile standing by a table and fired twice, dropping the man before he could react. The body hit the floor hard.

Bambam was next, his carbine sweeping the far corners of the room. Two more hostiles came into view near the back wall. He fired twice at the first man just as Savard came in, hitting the second.

As the last man dropped, al-Rashid stood, trying to reach for an AK to his left, but Champs, McKay, and Bambam were on him with a tackle that the most talented stunt coordinator couldn't have choreographed better.

Champs sprang forward, leaping into al-Rashid, driving his shoulder into the man's midsection, wrapping his arms around al-Rashid's arms and torso. In the same instant, McKay leaped forward, wrapping his arms around the man's legs. The two assaulters hit al-Rashid simultaneously, driving him to the floor. Bambam stood over him with his weapon pointed at al-Rashid's head. "Don't fucking move."

As the others dealt with al-Rashid, Savard secured the rear of the room. Seeing no threats, he nodded and whispered, "Clear." He then took up a position guarding the entrance to the room.

Rocky's voice came over the comms. "All stations, Alpha Two. Citadel."

Champs rolled al-Rashid over into a prone position, then planted his right knee firmly into the man's back, securing him in place. McKay grabbed al-Rashid's arms, positioned them behind his back, and tied his wrists together with zip ties.

"All stations, Alpha Three. Jackpot. Starting sensitive site exploitation."

While Bambam stood guard over al-Rashid, Champs and McKay gathered two laptops, four cell phones, four manila envelopes, and a few stacks of documents before taking pictures of all the dead fighters.

"Alpha Two, Alpha Three. We've gathered everything we can. On our way to your pos now."

***

Rocky watched as Champs and his det moved al-Rashid into the room where they had found Nathan and Keira. He heard two short bursts of suppressed fire echo from the corridor.

"Two hostiles down," Wood's voice came through over comms. "I think that might be the missing patrol."

"All stations, Alpha Two. Prepare for exfil via Boxcar."

McKay rushed to Whiskey's side to help with Nathan.

"Alpha Two, Boxcar. Ten mikes to your pos."

"Ack," Rocky replied, then turned to Whiskey. "How much longer until we can move him?"

"At least twelve mikes."

"You've got eight. Find a way to make it happen."

Rocky was about to address al-Rashid, hoping to get something useful out of him before they moved, but Keira beat him to it. She had already gotten to her feet, eyes burning as she stared him down.

"Tables have turned, haven't they?" she said coldly. "You're my prisoner now." Champs and Bambam shoved al-Rashid into a chair, forcing his shoulders down until he stopped struggling.

Al-Rashid said nothing. He kept his head still, eyes fixed on the floor, refusing to even glance in Keira's direction.

Keira picked up a chair from the floor, moved it directly in front of al-Rashid, and took a seat.

"Cat got your tongue, then?" she asked.

He didn't answer, still refusing to look at her.

She gave a small, amused exhale and leaned forward, elbows resting on her knees. "Really, Khalid? Fraternizing with drug cartels? How far the mighty have fallen."

Rocky watched the exchange in silence, eyes flicking between them. Al-Rashid's composure held until Keira mentioned the cartels, then something shifted. It was barely perceptible—a tightening around his jaw, the faintest twitch at the corner of his mouth—before he caught himself. It looked like Keira saw it too. Her eyes sharpened, a flicker of satisfaction crossing her face.

"What's it like," Keira said softly, almost conversationally, "to spend decades grinding away at your grand little objective only to fail so completely you end up a common thug?" She smiled faintly, tilting her head just enough to make the words sting. "All that ideology, all that fire, and now you're just another petty criminal with a price tag."

"I cannot be bought," he said with a heavy Arabic accent, voice low and fierce. "My motives remain pure." He jerked his head up, finally meeting Keira's stare, eyes burning. "Someone like you"—the words were spat out between clenched teeth—"would never understand."

Keira giggled. "You're right."

He glared at her, confusion in his eyes.

"I've never spent decades on a cause only to end up a footnote in someone else's trafficking log."

Al-Rashid fell silent again, chin tucked as if weighing whatever scrap of dignity he had left. Rocky watched him. The motion was small but telling; a young Western woman calling him out this bluntly must be knotting the man's stomach. Rocky wasn't sure what her game was. He'd heard from source handlers and interrogators that rapport usually beat confrontation or force. He couldn't tell exactly what Keira was trying to coax out of the man. Humiliation? A confession perhaps or a crack in his pride? Or maybe she was just pissed off. In any case, he was content to let her work her angle until Whiskey finished preparing Nathan to move.

"Tell me the truth," Keira said. "Was any of it ever about God, or has it always been about you, just like it has for all the others..." She let the sentence trail off, then added, "What will God think of you now? What will your followers think when we broadcast to the world that you're nothing but a selfish criminal?"

"You arrogant little bitch. I should have killed you when I had the chance." He struggled against the restraints, eyes wild. "You know nothing, but you will see soon enough.

When Canada succumbs to drugs and burns, you will finally see the weakness of your society and why it needs to be saved."

Keira smirked, then leaned forward, giving al-Rashid a pinch on his cheek. "Thank you, Khalid. You've been most helpful." She patted him on the head.

Rocky thought the man was going to explode. Thankfully, Champs, who had been standing behind al-Rashid, gagged the man before he could start screaming.

"All stations, Jupiter. Be advised: multiple dismounted contacts moving into the route network from the brush to the north. They're en route to the compound and will be there in minutes. Thermal showing twenty heat signatures, maybe more."

Before Rocky could react, he heard automatic gunfire erupt to the west of the building, rounds punching into timber, sharp, staccato cracks that echoed down the corridor.

"Time's up," he said to Whiskey.

Whiskey and McKay spread a tarp across the floor. Together, they rolled Nathan onto his side, slid the tarp beneath him, then eased him back onto it, securing his position for transport.

"Contact west," Wood said. "Six moving toward the rear entrance. I can't hold them."

That didn't make sense. They would've seen that many fighters moving out of the compound, and Ashford hadn't reported any such movement either. These had to be reinforcements from somewhere else. A cold weight settled in Rocky's gut. Extracting toward the lake or the river through that thick jungle with two men burdened by Nathan's weight was a nonstarter. The sound of the gunfire alone was sure to wake every fighter still asleep in the barracks. A fighting withdrawal over three klicks of dense terrain would be suicide; they'd be overtaken long before they reached the exfil point. But heading west toward Green's convoy was just as impossible. They'd be too exposed.

"For fuck's sake," Rocky said. They were facing at least seventy armed men, minus the ones they'd killed, and the element of surprise was gone. The enemy now held the initiative. Outnumbered and exposed, everything had just gone sideways. *What the hell do I do now?*

17

KHALID AL-RASHID'S COMPOUND
CHIQUIBUL FOREST, BELIZE
SATURDAY, OCTOBER 19
03:09 LOCAL TIME

Rocky forced himself to think past the self-doubt rising within, trying to picture what Lion would do in his place. Gunfire continued rattling against the walls. Through Rocky's headset, Ashford's voice broke in. "Lights just came on in the barracks." Then Champs, standing next to him. "What's the play, boss?" He didn't answer. The question hung there, swallowed by the steady roar of automatic fire. His thoughts ran in circles. *God dammit. If Lion were here, he'd know exactly what call to make.* Lion made split-second decisions with little to no information all the time, and they always turned out to be the right call. He had a natural intuition for this sort of thing. Something not easily taught.

Rocky needed to find a way to even the odds. If he could get both CSOR sections into the fight, they'd have a chance. Green was almost there, but one section wouldn't be enough. He needed the one on the CH-146 Griffon, which was due any minute now, but their best bet was to land by the main road, and then run, in the middle of the night, through trails across 5 kilometres. They were tough enough to do it, but it would take too long. Alpha Team could sustain heavy firepower on an enemy for eight minutes at best before they ran out of ammo. He needed reinforcements fast. Dragging Nathan out on a stretcher without CSOR would be suicide.

Think, Rocky, think. How does Lion always come up with the answer on the spot? That's when it hit him. Lion rarely had to come up with an impossible answer on the spot, because he'd already come up with one. Rocky thought back to those mentally taxing "work the problem" evolutions, then remembered something that had sounded so outrageous at the time, but now, it might just give them a fighting chance.

"Hangman," Rocky shouted, "how big was that clearing you put the antennae through, and how high was the canopy?"

"Barely a metre wide," Hangman said. "Maybe 17 metres high."

Rappelling through a jungle canopy was one of the most dangerous insertions imaginable and damn near impossible at night. The helicopter had to hover above the treetops, high enough to avoid the rotor wash tearing the canopy apart or sucking branches into the main or tail rotor, which could cause a deadly crash, to say nothing of the fact that lowering a fast rope through a tiny gap in the trees while maintaining a hover in total darkness was pure madness. But that's exactly what they were going to do.

"Get your ass back up that tree," Rocky ordered. "And make sure you have a glow stick. I've got an idea."

He keyed his mic. "Ashford, Miles, Davis. Cover Hangman. He's exiting the main doorway and running back to our observation post. Light up anything that moves."

Rocky thought of something else Lion was fond of saying. "Expect and prepare for the worst. If you do that, the only surprises you'll get are pleasant ones."

He turned to his second in command. "They're going to breach the rear entrance, then come down the corridor and into the hallway and slaughter us in this room. I want traps on the rear entrance, another in the corridor, then another where the corridor and hallway intersect. And pull Wood back here."

Champs motioned to Bambam and Savard, then led them to the rear doorway where Wood was struggling to hold back a growing wave of gunmen—at least ten now—trying to force their way inside. Wood tossed a grenade at them and pulled back as Champs planted a Claymore near the threshold, out of sight of the attackers. His det repeated the process for the next two traps. Once they were set, Wood and Savard dragged the bodies of the first two men that the team had neutralized to the intersection and concealed the final mine beneath them.

"Monty, can you blow a hole in this wall and create an alternate exit without collapsing the building or getting us killed?" Rocky asked.

"Think so."

"Good enough for government work. Set it up."

Monty pulled a roll of flexible linear charge from his pack. He pressed the charge flat against the wooden planks, tracing a perfect three-foot square. He secured it with strips of high-strength tape, jammed a detonator into the corner, and ran the line back toward the team.

"Listen up, everyone," Rocky said, keying his mic. "We need to buy ourselves as much time as possible until we can get both QRF elements into the fight. Conserve ammo as best you can."

He looked at Hangman, who nodded in return.

"Go."

Rocky heard the C9 light machine gun erupt in the distance, its report a harsh, metallic chatter that split the humid air. From 80 metres out, the bursts arrived with a rolling sharpness. Each crack distinct at first, then collapsing into a stuttering roar.

"Five baddies down by the barracks main entrance. Get ready for incoming."

Champs took position at the hallway intersection, weapon trained on the rear doorway. Bambam crouched behind him, thumb poised over the first Claymore clacker.

Champs fired two rounds at the first man that came through the doorway, killing him. "Get ready," he said.

A second later, two more gunmen moved through the doorway in standard CQB fashion. "Now."

The Claymore erupted with a flat, concussive crack that rolled into a savage metallic roar, a sound like tearing steel and thunder compressed into a single heartbeat.

Spooky, still holding security by the main entrance to the building, fired multiple bursts from his MRR at anyone that made it past Ashford's machine gun.

"They're probably going to start coming out the back door of the barracks where I don't have line of sight," Ashford said.

"RPG!" Spooky shouted as he hurled himself inward across the floor.

The RPG detonated with a deep, gut-punching blast that shattered the wooden facade, ripping through the structure in a thunderous crack of splintering timber and rolling flame.

"Spooky!" McKay shouted, sprinting from the room where Alpha Team was holed up, grabbing Spooky by the vest and hauling him back across the hall into cover.

"RPG gunner down," Miles said.

Rocky crouched beside Spooky while McKay checked him over; several large splinters jutted from Spooky's face.

"Thank God for ballistic eyewear," Spooky muttered, spitting a gritty mix of blood and sawdust onto the floor.

"He got his bell rung pretty good," McKay said. "But he should be ok."

Another pair of low concussive thuds rang out from one of the C14 Timberwolfs.

"Two hostiles down from the twenty-man group moving up the trail, but I'm taking heavy fire. My position's blown," Davis reported.

"Get out of there," Rocky ordered, just as the Claymore in the corridor detonated.

"Four more down," Champs called, bursting into the room with Bambam at his heels. "One trap left. After that, we're getting overrun."

Rocky considered the options. The hallway leading into the room they were in provided a choke point and tactical advantage, though a grenade thrown into the room by one of al-Rashid's men would be catastrophic. But the options were limited. Leaving the building too early would expose them to heavy gunfire.

"Prepare to defend this room," he ordered.

***

Captain Steve Thorne, commander of CSOR's First Squadron, listened through his headset aboard the CH-146 Griffon as it skimmed above the dense canopy of the Chiquibul rainforest. *That's a hell of an idea.* A dangerous, maybe even stupid idea, but it could work. And judging by the ass-kicking Alpha Team was taking below, it was probably their only chance. He ran it by Sergeant Moore, who nodded in agreement. He keyed his mic and relayed the information to the pilot.

"That's fucking crazy," the pilot, Captain Desjardins, responded.

"Will you do it?" Thorne asked.

"Hell yeah I'll do it. What kind of stupid question is that?"

The CH-146 Griffon banked hard and accelerated away from the Macal River, racing toward the compound.

"We're looking for a red glow stick in the trees below," Thronc said to the section of CSOR operators onboard. "Keep your eyes open."

"I see it," one of the men said. "Two o'clock. Waving back and forth."

The CH-146 Griffon rotated. "I got it," Desjardins said.

Moore cracked a blue glow stick and secured it to the end of a 120-foot rope.

The wash of the rotors flattened the canopy below into a rippling dark sea. Moist air and the scent of crushed vegetation surged through the open doors.

"Line coming out!" Moore shouted.

The crew chief kicked the coil of rope toward the door. The 120-foot fast rope spilled out in a heavy brown spiral, the blue glow stick marking its end like a bead of light against the darkness. It streamed down through the rotor wash, swaying violently as it broke into the humid night.

Thorne leaned out the door, one hand on the frame, the other gripping the intercom cord. The glow from the cockpit instruments painted his sleeve green. "Bring her right five, Desjardins. The stick's off our nose, maybe twenty degrees."

"Copy, right five."

The CH-146 Griffon eased sideways, nose dipping slightly as the pilot compensated for torque. Below, the canopy shifted beneath the downwash, leaves and debris twisting in spirals. A faint red pulse flickered through the trees—the signal light the JTF2 assaulter was waving back and forth like a madman.

"There! Hold it there," Thorne barked. "Lower us ten!"

The helicopter sank slowly. The rope's glowing tip wavered, missing the opening by a few feet. Thorne craned out, judging angles through the shuddering vibration. "Forward twenty! Steady... Steady... Good. Right there!"

The red and blue glow sticks drew close in the blackness until they almost touched, then the blue stick swung away.

They made several more failed attempts. "I don't think this is going to work," Desjardins said. "The wash is pushing the rope back and forth like a pendulum."

"Keep trying," Hangman's voice crackled over the radio.

Thorne watched as the blue glow stick swung back and forth. Then he saw a figure leap from the tree. *What the fuck?*

"I got it!" Hangman called over the radio. "Start giving it some slack."

"You're gonna get yourself killed," Thorne said over the radio.

"Trust me," Hangman said.

Thorne nodded at Moore and the crew chief. "Start lowering him—slowly. Keep us steady," Thorne said to the pilot. "We've got a nutcase hanging from the line now."

Thorne watched the spectacle as the red and blue glow sticks slowly descended until he couldn't see them anymore.

"I'm on the ground," Hangman said. "Anchor in progress."

The CH-146 Griffon held position, the pilot fighting the air's uneven pressure. Sweat ran down Thorne's temple beneath his helmet. He stared at the altimeter—barely 10 metres of clearance to the canopy—and prayed Desjardins' skids didn't kiss the branches.

"Line's secure. You're clear to send the first man," Hangman said.

Thorne clipped in and swung his boots over the skid. He gripped the rope, testing the friction.

"Wait for my word to send the next man down," he said. "If I fall to my death, abort."

"Well you better not fall then," Moore said. "If I abort and tell the men they can't shoot at the bad guys, they'll throw me overboard after you."

Thorne took one last breath and slid off the skid.

The roar of the CH-146 Griffon's rotors turned into a deep, physical pressure that pounded against his ribs as he hung suspended in the rotor wash. The rope trembled in his gloved hands, a living thing, alive with vibration. 10 metres of clearance wasn't much. One gust, one wrong movement from the pilot, and the rotor tips would chew the trees to splinters.

He eased his grip, feeding rope through the descender. The motion was jerky, too fast at first, then too slow. The harness dug into his hips and he felt the pull in his stomach.

"Jesus Christ," he muttered.

The canopy rushed up beneath him, a chaotic mesh of leaves and branches flashing under the blue glow from his wrist light. He tried to steer himself away, but the next second a branch cracked across his shoulder. Then another tore against his leg, knocking his boot sideways.

He kept moving, feeding rope. A sharp branch slid under his arm and snagged the webbing on his plate carrier. He twisted, swore, and yanked free, feeling bark scrape his cheek under the visor.

The air below grew darker. The smell of soil and rot rose, thick and damp. He risked a glance up. The CH-146 Griffon's silhouette was just a shadow in the blackness above, blades a furious blur. Something brushed his helmet, then his boots hit a limb. It bowed under his weight but held. He crouched on it, catching his breath, then stepped off into open air.

He dropped the last few metres, knees buckling as his boots hit the forest floor, harder than he would have liked. The shock went straight up his spine. He unclipped and staggered backward, chest heaving, heart hammering like a jackhammer.

The rope hung above him, still swaying. Leaves and bits of bark rained down through the hole he'd made in the canopy.

He felt a hand slap his back. "See, that wasn't so bad," Hangman said, standing next to him.

Thorne turned and looked at him in disbelief. He shook his head, then keyed his mic.

"Rope's clear. Send the next man."

Static crackled. Then Moore's voice came back, half laughing, half relieved. "Roger that, sir. Try not to die down there before we join you."

Thorne leaned against the base of the tree, staring up at the dark hole above, realizing how small that opening really was and how lucky he was to have made it through alive.

He heard a burst of automatic fire ripping through the night. Short, savage bursts that echoed up through the trees. Thorne dropped instinctively to a knee, rifle raised toward the sound. The jungle absorbed the noise, turning it into a deep metallic hammering that rolled through the trunks and leaves.

"RPG!" someone shouted over the comms.

A streak of orange light tore through the darkness, its motor whining for half a heartbeat before it slammed into the compound. The blast wave hit Thorne a second later, a hot slap of pressure at this distance.

He pressed his body flat to the ground as the echo rolled away, replaced by the rising crackle of small-arms fire, steady and disciplined, overlapping. Alpha Team was still in the fight, but they were taking hell.

He exhaled through gritted teeth, the smell of cordite and burned foliage mixing with the wet, earthy air. "Jesus… they're right on top of them." He clutched his C8 SFW tighter.

Another burst of gunfire answered from deeper in the compound, louder now, closer. Each shot like a hammer striking iron.

The next man hit the ground, boots sinking into the loam. Thorne rose, grabbed the man's shoulder, and pointed forward through the shadows. "Cover that arc," he ordered. The operator moved low, rifle shouldered, disappearing into the undergrowth to establish a perimeter.

One by one, the rest of the CSOR operators made it down, unclipping and spreading out into the darkness, forming a tight perimeter around the small clearing.

"Alright, Hangman," Thorne said. "Let's get in the fight."

***

Champs motioned for Bambam to take position in the top right corner of the room, covering the hallway, with a direct line on the intersection with the corridor. The rest of the team huddled up in the top left corner of the room. Keira picked up an AK-47 from the floor and snatched some extra magazines from one of the dead bodies. Nathan and al-Rashid were pushed up against the upper wall with Alpha members standing in front of them, shielding them with their bodies.

The chainsaw rhythm of the C9 continued rattling in the distance. "They're flanking from both sides of the barracks and closing on the target building," Ashford said over the comms. "They're going to breach both front and rear doors. I'm keeping their heads down as best I can, but there are too many of them, and I'm going to be Winchester soon."

"Davis, report," Rocky said.

"I've pulled back about 30 metres. I'm still engaging the twenty-man group. They've just breached the perimeter. I've taken four out, but they're still advancing." Rocky heard more low concussive thuds mixed with the C9. "These guys are disciplined as fuck. We won't be able to extract without going through them," Davis said.

"Fire in the hole!" Bambam shouted. A split second later, the Claymore detonated at the corridor junction with a gut-punching blast that rocked the walls and sent a hot pressure wave ripping through the hallway. Dust and smoke rolled out in a pulse, and Rocky felt the floor shudder beneath his boots.

"There's nothing else between us and the bad guys entering through the rear door," Bambam said.

Bambam yanked a grenade from his rig, pulled the pin, and lobbed it down the hallway toward the corridor. It detonated with a deafening crack. A split second later came the screams, raw and short—proof that a few of the bastards had been caught in the blast.

Rocky motioned to Monty. "Blow the wall."

Monty slapped the firing switch. The planks tore outward in a howling shower of splinters and dust as a concussive crack split the air; a large, ragged hole yawned where wood had been, smoke and the sharp smell of singed timber pouring through the gap.

"I've got incoming," Bambam shouted.

"Go," Rocky ordered.

Wood and Savard flowed through the jagged aperture first, slipping out of the building and onto the compound, immediately dropping into low firing stances. Their MRRs barked suppressed rounds in tight, disciplined bursts into the gunmen that were in the process of breaching the doorway, catching them completely off guard. Loughton and Monty followed, carbines joining the rhythm, followed by Keira firing her AK-47 into the advancing men. Whiskey and McKay came next, lugging Nathan on the tarp, his face pale and fluttering at the edges of consciousness.

"Let's go," Champs said. He yanked al-Rashid through with Spooky's help and shoved him toward cover.

Rocky and Bambam held the door to the hallway, meeting every attempt to push through with controlled fire. Hostiles tried to force their way down the hall; each time they surged, Rocky and Bambam answered with precise bursts that snapped bodies back into the smoke and splinters. They bought the rest of the team the seconds they needed to get clear.

Two more gunmen charged toward them from the corridor with a third close behind. Rock and Bambam dispatched the first two seconds before cutting down the third man. As the man fell, he lobbed a cylindrical object toward them.

"Out!" Rocky barked, grabbing Bambam by the vest. They sprinted for the breach, diving through the hole just as the grenade went off. The blast hit like a hammer—heat, dust, and shards of wood chasing them through the air. Rocky slammed into the ground outside, the impact driving the breath from his lungs. Pain flared hot across the backs of his thighs and lower back. He rolled, gasping, and did a quick check. Three shallow shrapnel wounds, one in each leg and another low on his back above the left hip bone. It hurt like a bitch, but everything still worked. He could move, and more importantly, he could still fight.

He looked at Bambam, sprawled face-down in the dirt, not moving.

"Shit. Bambam!" Rocky crawled to him, the pain in his own legs forgotten. He reached him and froze. The back of Bambam's plate carrier was shredded, torn open by shrapnel. Blood poured from the wounds, soaking through his uniform and pooling beneath him. His eyes were half open, glassy, his mouth slack.

Rocky caught a flicker of movement inside the smoke-choked room, the faint silhouette of a rifle rising. Instinct took over. He snapped his carbine up, sighted through the chaos, and squeezed the trigger in rapid succession at the men trying to advance through the building.

The rest of the team opened up at once, their weapons thundering in a furious, overlapping rhythm that drowned out everything else. The air turned to smoke and noise. Brass casings sprinkled everywhere. The sharp, mechanical chatter of MRRs and the C9 merged into a single, deafening roar as the team poured fire into the advancing fighters. The gunfire was relentless, a solid wall of lead and noise that kept the enemy pinned. Every few seconds another magazine hit the ground, replaced by a fresh one. The air stank of burnt powder. Over it all, Rocky could still hear himself shouting orders, hoarse, barely audible, trying to be heard through the storm.

"McKay, get Bambam out of here!"

McKay dropped beside Bambam, grabbed him under the arms, and hauled him backward, boots sliding through the dirt. Blood smeared the ground in his wake as he dragged the limp body toward the shed where Whiskey crouched over Nathan and Keira stood guard beside al-Rashid, weapon trained on the treeline.

"Peel back to the shed," Rocky ordered.

The team moved instantly, executing a textbook Aussie peel under fire. The man on the far flank fired a short, suppressive burst, then turned and sprinted backward past the line. As soon as he cleared, the next man took his place, firing before pulling back. The rhythm was fast and violent—fire, move, fire, move—each man laying down a wall of lead before peeling back in turn.

Shell casings bounced off the packed dirt as they fell into a tight rhythm, leapfrogging through smoke and debris toward the shed.

Rocky was the last to move. He fired a final burst down into the building, then turned and sprinted for the shed as rounds tore through the air around him.

A searing sting ripped across his left ear. Before he could process it, another round grazed his right side, punching through his shirt and carving a line of fire along his ribs. He stumbled but kept running, adrenaline drowning out the pain.

"I'm Winchester," Ashford reported over the comms. "Dropping the gun. I'm going to try and flank them with my carbine and draw their attention."

The team was already at the structure, diving behind its splintered walls. Rocky threw himself in after them, landing hard against the dirt floor. The sound of gunfire hammered against the outside, smacking into wood and tin. He pressed a hand to his side, came away with blood, then checked his ear—half of it was gone, but it was still attached enough to hurt like hell. He drew a steadying breath, grabbed a fresh mag, and slammed it home.

"Contact treeline," Champs yelled.

The words cut through the chaos like a knife. Gunfire erupted from the west. New muzzle flashes lit up from the foliage beyond the shed. Splinters burst from the wall beside Rocky's head as rounds tore through the wood.

For a split second, he processed it all. The enemy in the courtyard hammering from the east, and now another element closing from the west. They were boxed in, caught between two advancing forces with nowhere to go. Rocky's stomach dropped. He glanced at his men. They were tired, bloodied, and running low on ammo. That's when he realized they weren't making it out of this alive.

18

KHALID AL-RASHID'S COMPOUND
CHIQUIBUL FOREST, BELIZE
SATURDAY, OCTOBER 19
03:21 LOCAL TIME

Empty clicks filled the shed, the last echoes of their rifles dying under the roar of incoming fire. Rocky dropped his MRR, drew his SIG Sauer P320, and continued shooting. The pistol bucked in his hands as he squeezed off round after round at the silhouettes charging from the courtyard, brass flashing in the dim light. Around him, the rest of the team had made the same transition. Sidearms barked in defiance, each shot a refusal to quit. *I'm not going down until I've fired every last bullet.* Rocky clenched his teeth as he reloaded with shaking hands. Outside, the snipers were still firing, dulled, desperate thuds from somewhere beyond, but it wasn't enough.

The SIG P320's slide locked back with a sharp metallic clack, the recoil dying in his hands. The weapon felt suddenly lighter, dead weight instead of purpose. Smoke curled from the barrel, the acrid scent of burnt powder mixing with sweat and blood. The chamber gaped open, empty, the slide frozen to the rear. A silent confirmation that he'd just fired his last round.

As Rocky prepared for the end, his thoughts drifted to Lion and the way things might have gone had he still been in command. Alpha had been trapped before, staring down death more than once, but Lion always found a way to turn the impossible not only into survival but into success. Nobody had been torn up under his watch the way Bambam had. One final memory surfaced through the haze, Lion's voice cutting through the chaos in his mind. "If you can still breathe, you can still fight. There's a reason we're here and the countless others who failed selection aren't. We don't quit. Ever."

Rocky drew his combat knife. "Prepare for hand-to-hand," he ordered. The men fell back a few feet, blades coming free as they bought themselves a few more seconds of life. He had no idea how to turn things around, but he'd be damned if he gave up before he was dead.

"Advance to contact!" a commanding voice bellowed from behind. Rocky snapped his head around, and for a heartbeat, he thought he was hallucinating. What he saw charging out of the treeline made his breath catch.

"Alpha One, Hammer One. Hold your position and take cover. This one's on us," Thorne said over the comms.

They came out of the brush from behind like a ghost patrol. Hangman, Thorne, and the eight-man CSOR section, faces slick with sweat and cam paint, weapons up. Two

C9s opened up from the flanks; their linked belts began feeding a relentless stream of fire into the courtyard, brass cascading around their boots. The rest of the section advanced with C8 SFWs, each fitted with an underslung M203 grenade launcher, their bursts punctuated by the deep *thunk-thunk* of 40mm rounds leaving the tubes.

The first grenades landed with deep, throat-punching blasts that folded the courtyard in on itself. Shockwaves overlapped, thudding through the earth beneath Rocky's hands. Each detonation sent bodies tumbling, fragments and limbs twisting through the haze. The explosions mingled with the hammering C9s and the sharper rhythm of C8 fire until it became one continuous, punishing storm. Through the smoke and flying dirt, Rocky watched as the formation of fighters in the courtyard broke apart. Men flung to the ground, silhouettes collapsing one after another until the enemy gun line disintegrated.

The CSOR element pivoted as one, shifting their fire toward the western flank. But most of the fighters there had already broken, panic rippling through their ranks as they turned and bolted straight into the overlapping fields of fire from Davis and Miles. The snipers opened up, their rifles cracking in rapid succession, dropping men mid-stride. The CSOR section pressed forward through the chaos, closing the distance and finishing the job.

Then Rocky heard a fresh eruption of gunfire from the northwest, louder and heavier than before. The sound rolled through the trees in violent waves, a storm of automatic fire and sharp, cracking bursts overlapping in chaotic rhythm. He turned toward it, catching faint muzzle flashes through the haze beyond the compound. Another fight was raging up the trails. By the volume of fire alone, he guessed at least two dozen fighters were pushing hard against an unseen force somewhere along the approach.

"All stations, Boxcar. Moving into position. We've got dozens of contacts approaching on us from behind the barracks."

"Boxcar, Hammer One. Advancing for a pincer. Standby."

Thorne's CSOR section reached the shed at a run, sliding into cover beside Alpha Team. Without a word, they began handing out spare magazines. The Alpha assaulters grabbed their MRRs, slammed the mags home, and racked the charging handles with sharp, mechanical snaps. Fresh rounds chambered, eyes up, they were back in the fight.

Whiskey and McKay were already on Bambam, hands slick with blood as they stripped his gear off, their voices low and urgent. Rocky struggled to stand, forcing himself upright despite the pain in his legs, back, and side. He reached for his carbine and tried to steady himself.

Loughton caught him by the shoulder, pressing him back down. "You're sitting this one out, mate."

Rocky started to protest, but before he could speak, Champs stepped in, voice cutting clean through the chaos. "Spooky, Rocky, Keira—stay here. Watch al-Rashid and the wounded." He checked his carbine, eyes scanning the treeline. "We've got this."

"Let's move out," Thorne ordered.

"Damn it, Bambam," Whiskey muttered under his breath as he peeled back the shredded fabric of Bambam's shirt. Two jagged pieces of shrapnel were lodged deep in his back, and blood poured from the wounds in dark rivulets. He reached for the QuikClot in Bambam's med kit. His fingers were stained with blood as he packed the gauze deep into the wounds. The hemostatic agent started working immediately, but the bleeding wasn't slowing fast enough.

"Come on," Whiskey growled, ripping open a pressure bandage. He wrapped it tightly around Bambam's torso, taking care to wrap it around the wounds, not over top of them. He pressed hard against the gauze to stem the flow of blood. The bandage was slick with red, but Whiskey pulled it tighter with McKay's help, securing it firmly.

"Stay with us, man," he said as they worked.

Once the bleeding had slowed, Whiskey leaned back with sweat dripping down his forehead. "He's lost a lot of blood."

"Let's get him started on plasma," McKay said.

Whiskey shook his head in defeat. "Can't. I used it all on Nathan."

"I've got the same blood type," Rocky said. "We're doing this now. Set up the transfusion."

McKay nodded as his hands moved. He grabbed an IV kit from his pack, then inserted the needle into Rocky's arm, watching the blood collection bag slowly fill.

"Bambam's pulse is fading," Whiskey said.

McKay connected the IV line to Bambam. The blood started to flow slowly into his veins.

"We need to get antibiotics in him," Whiskey muttered. He fished out a vial of moxifloxacin, grabbing a syringe.

Whiskey found another vein and injected the antibiotic directly into Bambam's bloodstream, attempting to stave off infection from the shrapnel wounds.

"You're not dying on my watch, Bambam," Rocky said. "You hear me? Stay with us."

Bambam didn't respond. His face was pale, and his breathing was beginning to falter.

Whiskey pulled a bag-valve mask from his med kit and positioned it over Bambam's face, ensuring a tight seal. His hand gripped the bag, rhythmically squeezing, forcing oxygen into Bambam's lungs.

"Come on, buddy. Stay with us," McKay said under his breath.

The gunfire tapered off a few minutes later, echo fading into the jungle until only the hum of insects remained. A moment later, Rocky heard the clucking of tree frogs once again. The jungle had already moved on, as if the battle had never happened.

The last fighters hadn't stood a chance. Caught between two converging CSOR elements and a rearmed Alpha Team, they were torn apart in the crossfire. The compound was a ruin of smoke and bodies, the dirt slick with blood and littered with spent brass.

Spooky, who'd been watching al-Rashid, raised his pistol until the SIG's muzzle hovered against the man's mouth. "All this," he said, voice low and tight, "just to traffic drugs into Canada? Tell me why I shouldn't put a bullet in your mouth right now."

Keira's hand landed on Spooky's forearm. "We need him alive," she said, eyes on al-Rashid. "He's got a lot more to tell us. I've got some off-the-books types that'll make sure of it."

Rocky looked up at Spooky, feeling slightly light-headed. "She's right, man. Let her team have at him."

Spooky lowered his weapon slowly.

"None of this was supposed to happen," al-Rashid said, a hollow, empty look on his face.

A Toyota Hilux skidded to a stop beside the shed, its engine growling through the fading smoke. Green and the driver jumped out, boots hitting the dirt in unison. They pulled two stretchers from the bed and ran over.

"Let's get the wounded loaded up," Green said, voice steady but urgent.

They moved quickly and with care, rolling Nathan onto a stretcher and lifting him onto the truck's bed. His face was ghostly pale, eyes flickering open for a moment before sliding shut again. Keira climbed up beside him, one hand gripping the side rail, the other clasping his. She kept her eyes on him as the team worked, her expression caught somewhere between focus and relief. "You're going to be fine," she said.

Whiskey and McKay carefully rolled Bambam onto the second stretcher, lying him face-down to keep from aggravating his wounds. Rocky, still feeding blood into Bambam, tried to stand, but his legs couldn't find the strength. They gave out halfway.

"Easy, buddy. We've got you," Green said, stepping in with the driver. They hooked their arms under his shoulders and hauled him upright. Rocky tried to protest, but the words wouldn't come. The two men guided him to the truck, lifting him onto the bed beside Bambam, where Whiskey and McKay were already working over the body in a desperate, rhythmic silence.

A short while later, Green's convoy rumbled out of the jungle and onto the main road where three CH-146 Griffons idled with their rotors turning. The aircraft lights cut through the dust and darkness as Alpha Team brought the wounded aboard followed by al-Rashid and their British allies.

Back at the compound, Thorne's CSOR operators held position, weapons trained on the sixteen surviving fighters who had thrown down their arms. They kept them secured and under guard, maintaining a tight perimeter until the Belizean Special Forces arrived to take custody and secure the site.

Moments later, the three CH-146 Griffons lifted off, banking northeast toward Philip S. W. Goldson International Airport where a waiting C-17 sat on the tarmac with its ramp lowered. The mission to rescue the hostages was over, but the fight to save Bambam's life had only just begun.

19

AL-NAJM AL-SAGHIR'S HEADQUARTERS
MOROCCO, UNKNOWN LOCATION
THURSDAY, OCTOBER 24
19:00 LOCAL TIME

The loss of Khalid was an unfortunate development. Despite his shortcomings, Al-Najm valued the terrorist leader for his willingness to get his hands dirty. Now, he would have to play a more direct role unless he could find another suitable proxy. But first there was the matter of his cabal, all of whom were proving to be as impatient as Volk, if not more, the Chinese general being the notable exception.

"Your master stroke against Canada has failed," Reznikov, the Russian GRU commander, said. "If you can't even destabilize Canada, how can you expect to topple the Americans?"

The Iranian and North Korean generals nodded in agreement.

Al-Najm, still facing his map of the globe tacked against the war wall, turned slowly to meet the Russian's gaze. He was beginning to lose patience with the group's collective lack of patience. The irony wasn't lost on him, and he allowed it to show in his tone.

"Is that your assessment, General Reznikov?" Al-Najm said, locking eyes with him, unflinching. He'd chosen to wear red contact lenses this evening, giving him an almost supernatural look, covered by his dark keffiyeh. "That the plan failed?"

Reznikov hesitated, looking around the stone chamber for support and finding none. The rest of the generals decided to let the exchange play out before playing their hands.

"Is it not obvious?" Reznikov asked, his tone quieter.

"By all means, General, enlighten us," Al-Najm said, waving his arm toward the rest of the gathering. He crossed his arms, waiting for a response. He knew that the GRU had a robust presence in Canada, the northern country's security measures being what they were made it easy for Russian intelligence to gain entry, mainly as a means of getting into the United States. Still, their intelligence collection capabilities in Canada were nearly unmatched. Did Reznikov truly not understand? Or was he posturing for power within the cabal? Al-Najm suspected it was the former.

"Canadian military forces slaughtered your men, captured al-Rashid, and rescued the hostages. How is this not a failure?" Reznikov said at last.

"Perhaps," Al-Najm said, walking toward Reznikov, "if pride were a factor used to determine whether an objective were achieved, I might agree with you. But it is not."

Reznikov lowered his eyes to the large steel table he and his co-conspirators were seated around. His jaw flexed as his brow creased. Al-Najm let the silence sit. Power in conversation was the art of saying much while speaking little.

"Point taken," Reznikov said, letting out a breath, leaning back in his chair.

Al-Najm walked past Reznikov, circling the stone cavern as he spoke. "We have achieved much, my friends."

He paused as he reached the head of the table, turning to face the men seated around it. "The La Sangre Sagrada cartel has already started flooding Canada with cheap opioids. It won't be long before their precious health-care system collapses in on itself."

"How is this possible?" General Zhou asked. "With al-Rashid already in custody…" He let the words fade, the implication clear.

"Al-Rashid was merely the messenger," Volk said. "He held negotiations before his capture. The cartel reached out to my associate immediately. Terms were finalized on the spot. My enterprise will manage it."

"So we've caused their health-care system some trouble," Khorasani said. "How does this contribute to our goals? Why not attack them?"

Al-Najm shook his head. No wonder nobody had managed to challenge Western supremacy. They all clung to outdated notions of victory. He leaned forward, placing both palms on the steel table.

"Attacking Canada directly with kinetic force would have accomplished little, but their time is coming," Al-Najm said, addressing the group, but his gaze lingered on Reznikov. The confidence in his tone left no room for argument.

As Al-Najm walked them through the next phase, he caught a shift in the room. The generals' questions turned constructive. For the first time, they seemed genuinely enthusiastic about the plan. They were starting to believe in it. Sensing the moment, Al-Najm revealed the core of his strategy: Every move was crafted so that Canada and its allies would serve his agenda regardless of the outcome.

"They won the battle in the jungle, but in so doing, they have brought us one step closer to winning the war," Al-Najm concluded, his voice low and cold.

He turned back toward the global map on the wall, eyes zeroing in on Canada. *Now that I've stripped what little unity they had left, I will rob them of their reputation. After that, I will crush them.*

20

JACKSON MEMORIAL HOSPITAL
MIAMI, FLORIDA
FRIDAY, OCTOBER 25
11:30 LOCAL TIME

The voices reached him from far away, muffled and meaningless at first. He floated in warmth and darkness, wrapped in the heavy comfort of oblivion. Then came a tug. A hand on his shoulder, gentle but insistent, and a voice that pierced the fog. "Sebastien... Sebastien, wake up for me." Rocky didn't want to. But the voices wouldn't stop. Light pressed against his eyelids, too bright, and the sterile scent of antiseptic filled his nose. Someone squeezed his hand. "Sebastien, can you hear me?" He groaned, the sound rough and unwilling. His throat burned. Every part of him wanted to retreat, to drift back down into the dark where sleep still waited, but the damn voices wouldn't stop.

He opened his eyes and saw two beautiful women wearing light-blue scrubs leaning over him. *Nurses?* For a moment, he was certain he'd died. Nurses were only gorgeous in movies and TV shows. He'd seen enough in person to know better.

"Welcome back, Sebastien," one of them said, smiling.

"Go away," Rocky said, closing his eyes again.

"Quit being such a baby."

Rocky's eyes shot open, looking to the left and saw Bob Green sitting in a chair with a tablet on his lap, reading glasses sitting low on his nose.

"It's about goddamn time," Green said. "We don't pay you to sleep."

Rocky started to sit up, but pain tore through his torso and legs, sharp enough to steal his breath. The nurses' hands were on him instantly, firm but gentle, guiding him back down. Between the ache in his body and their steady pressure, the effort was useless. Rocky sank into the mattress, wincing in pain.

"Please don't try to move," the nurse said. "The doctor will be in to see you shortly."

Why does everything hurt so damn bad, and where the hell am I? He looked around in confusion. The room was large enough to fit four patients, but he was the only one. It almost had the look of a fancy hotel room. He'd never seen anything like it before, not even in Germany.

"What the hell..."

"Adrenaline's a funny thing," Green said, standing and approaching Rocky's bedside. "Drowns out the pain pretty good. But once it's gone?" He shook his head. "The whole world goes to shit pretty fast."

"Where am I?"

Green chuckled. "The Americans do hospitals a bit differently than we do in Canada."

The walls were a soft, neutral beige broken by polished wood accents and a wide window that framed the skyline in bright light. Stainless steel equipment stood discreetly in the corners, half hidden behind curtains.

"Ryder Trauma Centre at Jackson Memorial in Miami," Green said.

"How long was I out for? Wait... Bambam! How's Bambam?"

Green's expression faltered, concern etched across his face. "I won't lie to you," he said. "It's not good."

"Is he going to make it?"

"We don't know yet," Green said quietly. "His back got torn apart by the same grenade that shredded you. He lost a hell of a lot of blood, even with you damn near killing yourself to give him yours."

"Killing myself?"

"The pain you feel in your side is courtesy of a 7.62 round from an AK-47," Green said, pulling his glasses off and setting his tablet on a table next to Rocky's bed. "It didn't hit anything serious, but you were losing blood, too."

Green shook his head. "The medics didn't realize it right away, between the way you were acting and the shape Bambam was in." He gave a short, humourless chuckle. "Once Whiskey assessed you, he was gonna stop the transfusion. He said you threatened to kill his cat if he did."

Rocky frowned. "I don't remember."

"Doesn't surprise me," Green said. "You were delirious. Anyway, the docs say Bambam suffered a spinal injury from the grenade frags. They've put him into a medically induced coma."

Green paused, taking a deep breath. "Even if he does make it. He may never walk again. It's just too soon to tell."

"I need to see him," Rocky said.

"No can do. He's being flown out to James A. Haley Veterans Hospital in Tampa. Apparently, they have a unit that specializes in this stuff. The rest of the team is airborne with him. It's just you and me here."

"When can I get out of here?"

"A couple of days," another man answered.

Rocky shifted his gaze toward the door of his room and saw a short, bald man with dark blue scrubs entering.

"I'm Dr. Chavez," he said as he approached, extending his hand first to Rocky, then to Green. "I've heard a lot about you guys. It's an honour to meet some of you in person." The doctor smiled. "Ex Marine here. Turned in my rifle for a scalpel."

"A pleasure, doc," Green said. Rocky nodded respectfully.

They spent a few minutes exchanging pleasantries and some lighthearted war stories.

"So what's the prognosis, doc?" Green asked.

Chavez swiped a few times across his tablet before he spoke.

"I removed the shrapnel from your thighs, left glute, and lower back. They were deep soft tissue wounds, but nothing vital was hit. I also closed the wound in your side. The round passed through muscle but missed all major vessels and organs. You'll be on your feet in a few days, and back to full strength in a few weeks, though those muscles are going to hurt like hell until they heal."

Green pulled out a notepad from his fatigues and started writing in it. "Okay, doc, I want to make sure I understood you correctly. For the record, you're saying that Sergeant

Ray here got his ass blasted apart. Is that correct?"

Chavez, clearly catching on, smiled and nodded enthusiastically. "Yes, that's exactly right."

"Could I get you to sign my little notepad right here?" Green said, passing it to him. "You know, for the citation and all."

The doctor laughed. "Sure thing." He scribbled his signature.

"I'm thinking AssBlast should be your new nickname moving forward. It even says so right here," Green said, waving his notepad in Rocky's face.

The three men laughed as Rocky occasionally winced in pain. They spent another few minutes shooting the shit before the doctor spoke up again.

"I almost forgot," he said, looking at Rocky. "My colleague was able to repair your ear. You probably won't feel much there again, but it should look normal." He paused, then added, "Ish."

"Sergeant Moore found the top half of it on the ground by the shed," Green said. "You owe him a couple of beers."

"Are you the one who operated on Bambam?" Rocky asked, his tone shifting back to something hard and serious.

Chavez shook his head. "No, I was too busy patching you up." His tone was light before his expression darkened. "A full trauma team handled him." He hesitated, forcing a faint, reassuring smile. "He's in good hands. Some of the best in the country."

They spoke about Bambam and the implications for the next few minutes before the doctor took his leave to finish his daily rounds.

"There are a few things we need to talk about, Rocky," Green said once the room had cleared. His voice was low, steady. He pulled a chair closer to the bed and sat down, elbows on his knees. "The team's not doing so good, man. Between Matt and Bambam, they're taking it hard." He paused, rubbing a hand over his face. "Things spiralled while you were under. Champs did his best to keep everyone together, but they're in pain."

Green looked up, meeting Rocky's eyes. "The brass has decided to pull Alpha out of the rotation. The team's being stood down for now. You're all under lockdown. Ordered to stay in Tampa until things settle down. They're arranging for a specialist to assess everyone in the meantime. I've been told she's quite the miracle worker."

Rocky's eyes narrowed. "We don't need a goddamn shrink. We need some fucking answers, and we need Bambam on his feet again."

"I get it, man. I do. But it's out of my hands," Green said, pulling out a mobile phone. "Use this to call Charlotte. After that, you're all stuck in radio silence."

"What the hell are we supposed to do?" Rocky said, wincing in pain.

"Be with Bambam. Take in Tampa. Try to enjoy the time off and use it as an opportunity to put the team back together. We need you back out there."

"But—" Rocky started, his voice rough. Green cut him off before he could say more.

"Call Charlotte," Green said, already standing. "I've got a few things to take care of, but I'll be back around dinner." He nodded toward the bedside table. "Feel free to use the tablet."

Without waiting for a reply, he turned and walked out, the door clicking shut behind him.

Rocky took a deep breath before dialling. *Time to face the music.*

The phone rang long enough that he thought it might go to voicemail.

"Yes, hello?"

"Hey, babe. It's me."

There was a sharp intake of breath on the other end. "Oh my God, Sebastien! Hold on. I need to grab someone to cover my class."

He waited, listening to the faint sounds of movement and muffled voices. A moment later, she was back, her voice trembling. "I've been so worried. Mike Belanger stopped by the house the other day. He said you'd been hurt."

"Yeah, well... You should see the other guy."

"Sebastien, this is serious." Her voice broke as she started to cry.

"Hey, hey..." he said softly, his voice losing its edge. "I know it is. But I'm okay, I promise."

"Don't you dare lie to me," she said through her sobs. "Guy's wife came by, too. She said Alain might not make it. What happened?"

Rocky closed his eyes, struggling to fight back the tears. "Babe, you know I can't talk about that."

"Oh no, you don't. Not this time." Her voice shook. "This is too much, Sebastien."

Here comes the music. He knew the drill. Unfortunately, he'd been through this with her a few times already. Rocky listened quietly as she vented, cursed, and occasionally screamed. All he wanted to do was fly home and hold her. He hated that she was in so much pain because of him. It wasn't fair to her. They both knew it, but there wasn't anything he could do about it, short of pulling the pin and releasing, but he still had a few more years to go before he could walk away with a pension.

"Are you sure you're okay?" she asked, her voice softening as she began to calm down.

"I'm in some pain," he said. "Probably will be for another week or so, but the doctor said I'll make a full recovery."

"When can I see you?" she asked, sniffling.

Rocky finally broke down. The iron dome he'd built around himself over the years shattered under the weight. Lion, Bambam, the burden of command. Listening to his wife's voice crack on the other end was too much. His chest tightened, breath catching as everything he'd been holding back came crashing through at once. Between uneven breaths, he told her about the lockdown, that Alpha had been stood down, and he wouldn't be able to call for a while. He wasn't sure when he'd be home.

"I understand," she said softly. "I'm sorry I got so upset. I just love you so much… I was so scared."

Tears slid down his cheeks. Moments like this made him oddly grateful that Charlotte had such terrible taste in men. If she hadn't, he never would've stood a chance with her in the first place, let alone been able to hold on to her through all this hell.

***

Rocky was bored out of his mind, flipping through the tablet in a half-hearted attempt to distract himself from the pain. He opened the CTV News app and tuned in to a live broadcast. Sarah Bouchard, Canada's famous war correspondent and political analyst for *The Globe and Mail*, was being interviewed by CTV's anchor Miranda Reeves.

Bouchard, young and undeniably attractive, was a favourite among the troops. She was reporting on the surging death toll from an unprecedented wave of opioid overdoses sweeping across the country. After years of failed attempts to manage the crisis, it had erupted into a full-scale catastrophe. It wasn't just addicts and users. Emergency rooms were collapsing under the strain. Patients with heart attacks, infections, and even children with high fevers were being left untreated as hospitals buckled under the flood. People were literally dying in waiting rooms. In Ottawa, parliament had descended into chaos during Question Period, MPs shouting over one another as the government scrambled for answers.

That's when Rocky realized a terrible truth—despite their hard-won battle, the enemy had still won. He watched in disbelief as the broadcast cut to live footage from hospital waiting areas in turmoil. Families pleaded with staff, voices breaking as loved ones slipped away without care.

"My sources tell me the government is preparing to invoke the Emergencies Act," Bouchard said. She glanced down at her notes, then back to the camera. "Despite this government's refusal to increase military spending, the Canadian Armed Forces, already stretched to the breaking point, will be called on again. The reserves are being mobilized to help maintain order at medical facilities."

Rocky leaned forward slightly, regretting it immediately as the pain reminded him to keep from moving.

"Their medics will be deployed to relieve overwhelmed hospitals," Bouchard continued, brushing a loose strand of hair behind her ear. "Retired medical personnel are being recalled to service, a move already sparking fierce debate over whether the government can legally compel civilian retirees to return to work."

Reeves cut in, her silver hair catching the studio lights as she leaned toward the camera. "Just to clarify, we're talking about former health-care workers, not retired military personnel?"

Bouchard shifted slightly, her tone turning more deliberate. "It's both," she said. "The government can legally recall former military personnel under certain conditions. But forcing provincial health-care workers—people who've never worn a uniform—back onto the job? That's a whole different ball game."

Her expression darkened slightly, the composure in her voice thinning. "As your viewers know, Miranda, many health-care workers walked off the job after the COVID crisis due to burnout, while others were dismissed for refusing vaccination. Some military personnel were also dismissed over the vaccination policy. Now, those divisions are resurfacing, reopening an old wound in an already fractured political landscape."

Rocky paused the feed. After everything Alpha Team had endured over the past week—the jungle, the firefight, Bambam bleeding out, the burn of damaged muscle continuing its sharp sting of pain—he felt hollow. His country was descending into chaos. He felt old and obsolete.

A thought was beginning to take shape when a soft knock sounded at the door.

"Come in," he called.

The door opened and Nathan stepped in with Keira beside him. Nathan looked better. The bruising on his face had abated slightly. His right arm was in a sling and fresh bandages were visible beneath his shirt, but he was steady on his feet. Keira looked untouched by comparison, though the fatigue in her eyes told a different story. Loughton, Ashford, and Ollie came in right behind them, the three moving together as if they hadn't been apart since the fight.

"Damn, you look like utter dog shit, mate," Loughton said, grinning.

Rocky laughed, grimacing.

"Don't make me laugh, you bastard," Rocky said. "What are you guys still doing here?"

"We ain't leaving here until you do, brother," Loughton said.

A nurse stepped in quietly and injected something into the IV line at the top of his hand.

"What are you shooting me up with?" Rocky asked, watching the clear fluid push through the tube.

"Something for the pain," she said with a faint smile, "and something to help you sleep."

Rocky wasn't sure how he felt about pain meds after what he'd just seen on the news, but a split second later, the pain vanished, as did the thought.

The group talked for a few minutes, sharing their perspectives on the past few days. Ollie confessed to barfing his guts out after shooting a man with his eyes closed, earning a few laughs.

"What's next for you guys?" Rocky asked.

"A slight bit of unfinished business in Belize City that needs a wee bit of taking care of," Keira said.

"What about our mutual friend?" Rocky asked.

"Gonna squeeze that rotten piece of shit for everything he has," Loughton said, a slight menace to his tone. "I'm a wanted man now. Might as well go all the way."

Nathan spoke next. "Listen, Sergeant... Rocky," he began, his voice unsteady, "I just wanted to thank you and your team for everything you did." He paused, swallowing hard before continuing. "You've renewed my faith in Canada. Anytime, anywhere, no matter what you need... You call me, and I'll be there."

"Both of us," Keira added, placing her hand in Nathan's.

"No need to thank us. You know how it is," Rocky said. "Never leave a fallen comrade behind."

Ashford left a card on the small table by Rocky's bed. "I'm living in Ottawa now. Call on me if you're ever up to it."

Rocky's mind slowed as the meds took hold, softening the edges of thought until everything drifted. His words slurred slightly. "What was it you said about Canada just now?" he asked, glancing at Nathan.

There was something there, just out of reach, but his thoughts kept slipping away. He fought the pull of sleep, forcing himself upright.

"Whoa, easy," Nathan said, reaching out, but Rocky barely heard him.

What had he been thinking about before they'd come in? He blinked, trying to focus, then fumbled for the tablet. Sarah Bouchard's face filled the screen, the paused broadcast frozen mid-sentence. Canada. The thought snapped back, hazy but urgent. The drug crisis. What if there was more to it? His pulse quickened. Yes. That was it. Something about all of this didn't feel right. He'd just proven himself a capable tactical leader, but whatever Canada was up against needed more than small unit tactics.

"We're at war," Rocky managed, his voice barely more than a breath.

Nathan pulled the chair closer and sat down, taking Rocky's hand in his own. "What are you talking about?" he asked softly.

Rocky returned the grip, trying to hold on a few more seconds. His eyes locked onto Nathan's. "There is something you can do for me..." he began, but the words faded, swallowed by the weight of the drugs and exhaustion pulling him under.

"Anything," Nathan said. "Name it."

Rocky's eyes flashed open briefly. "Lion. Find Matt Lion," he managed, before his eyes shut, overtaken by sleep.

Dear Reader,

Thank you for choosing to spend your time with *The Quiet War: Canadian Front*. Readers like you are the reason authors do what we do. Without you, the stories wouldn't matter. Your support makes it possible for me to keep publishing stories that look at global conflict from a Canadian and greater allied lens. And that matters a great deal to me.

If you have a moment, I'd be grateful if you'd consider leaving an honest review on Amazon, Goodreads, or whichever vendor you purchased your copy from. Whether it's just a sentence or a longer reflection, your feedback helps other readers decide in *The Quiet War: Canadian Front* is a story they want to take a chance on, and it also helps me understand what resonates as I continue building out *The Quiet War* series.

If you'd like to get in touch, you can reach me through my website or on Facebook. I always enjoy hearing from readers, whether you have questions, thoughts about the story, or just want to say hello. I'd love to hear what you think of *The Quiet War: Canadian Front* and where the series goes from here.

– Michael J. Lalonde

READ THE REST OF THE STORY

Thank you for reading *The Quiet War: Canadian Front.*

The battle in Belize is over, but The Quiet War has only just begun. Al-Najm's master plan is succeeding, and Canada is buckling under the weight of a crisis it cannot see.

The last desperate order given by Rocky was clear: "Find Matt Lion."

The Quiet War Series explodes in 2026 with the gripping sequel, *Alpha One*, the story of the legend himself, Captain Matt Lion. But what if the legend is no longer the man he once was? As Al-Najm's plan escalates and Canada fractures, one question remains: Will Alpha One rise again or will the legend die and take the best hope of stopping The Quiet War with him?

Sign up for my newsletter at www.michaeljlalonde.com to stay up to date on the launch of *Alpha One* and bear witness to the story of JTF2's greatest warrior.

Thank you for your support.

– Michael J. Lalonde

ABOUT THE QUIET WAR SERIES

Beneath the surface of global politics, a shadowy cabal emerges, led by the elusive Al-Najm al-Saghir, The Little Star. Backed by powerful generals from Russia, China, Iran, North Korea, and Venezuela, they seek to dismantle the Western world through a ruthless fusion of traditional warfare, terrorism, and subversion.

This war isn't just fought with bombs and bullets. The cabal wields transnational crime networks, cyberwarfare, and a propaganda machine engineered to manipulate social media, radicalize Western youth, and erode public trust. Misinformation floods the internet while coordinated attacks destabilize nations. Their goal? Total Western collapse.

Canada is the first target, but it's only the beginning.

With high-stakes action and chilling political intrigue, *The Quiet War Series* delves into the terrifying power of modern terrorism and the fragility of global stability. Each book delivers military precision, ruthless deception, and a conspiracy that threatens to bring the world to its knees.

This gripping thriller series, where the battlefield extends far beyond the front lines and into the digital, political, and psychological arenas of modern warfare, will captivate fans of Tom Clancy and Vince Flynn.

ACKNOWLEDGEMENTS

I learned quickly that writing a book is a solitary endeavour—something I'm not exactly accustomed to after a long career in the military and a brief stint in politics. Other authors often say the process is full of stops and starts. In my case, I found it closer to running a marathon that never seems to end. Every so often, I'd fall flat on my face, patch myself up, then soldier on. But this journey wouldn't have been possible without the help, feedback, and encouragement I received along the way.

First, I want to thank fellow Canadian military-fiction author R.A. Flannagan, creator of the *CANZUK at War* series. When I first started sketching out *The Quiet War* back in the fall of 2024, I combed through his website blog, where he'd posted advice for new authors. I reached out, not expecting a reply, and to my surprise he wrote back. We've become friends since, and his support has been invaluable.

I'm also grateful to Cole Chase, the heist-thriller author behind *The Valiant Thrillogy.* He generously read some early chapters and provided feedback that made a tangible difference.

A huge thank you goes to Adam Hay, who designed the cover art for this book and the rest of the series. He went out of his way to guide me through the process, sat through several Zoom calls, and humoured me through an impressive number of tiny revisions—something most designers would have told me to take a hike over.

My editor, Amanda Clarke, deserves special recognition. The first manuscript I handed her was a 250,000-word monstrosity. She gently informed me that this was *slightly* too long for a debut novel. She then followed it up with fifty pages of detailed, incredibly valuable feedback. Her guidance and her willingness to help me meet the December 9th deadline I had naively committed myself to was instrumental in shaping this book. Her input has made me a far better writer.

Speaking of writing, I also want to acknowledge fellow Canadian author Ann Y.K. Choi, my instructor at the University of Toronto's creative writing program. She went above and beyond, spending extra hours discussing the manuscript with me. There were moments when I genuinely felt she was more enthusiastic about my project than I was. Her energy came at just the right moment, particularly when I was running out of steam.

My thanks as well to Timur Saiful, Laura Finnagan, and Peter Morel, who volunteered their time to read the entire manuscript from start to finish, offering helpful insights from a reader's perspective.

I also want to thank Adam Hay, narrator of *The Quiet War: Canadian Front* audiobook edition. He has bent over backwards to bring this story to life on short notice, delivering an incredible performance and showing endless patience as I threw several last-minute edits his way.

My gratitude extends to the Book Whisperer team for helping bring this book into the world. There's the old saying: If a tree falls in the forest and no one hears it, does it make a sound? Writing a book works much the same way. If no one knows it exists, it might as well not. When I first spoke with Shaun Loftus, the owner, she told me they needed at least two months to prepare for a launch. As a new, self-published author, I had taken what I believed was the most direct route from point A to point B—which is to say, I tumbled down a mountain, collided with every piece of debris, ditch, and tree trunk along the way, and somehow crashed over the finish line. It was certainly not a masterclass in how to organize a project effectively. I asked, "How about two weeks?" I'm deeply grateful to her and her team for jumping aboard late in the game.

I would also like to thank Randy Turner, former JTF2 operator, for his insight and feedback. As a busy entrepreneur running a successful YouTube podcast and Direct Action Combat Performance, training both law enforcement and military personnel, he still made the time to help a fellow veteran.

Likewise, Gordon "Gordo" Hurley, former CSOR operator and passionate advocate for alternative treatments for veterans with PTSD, also took time to offer valuable input.

And last, but certainly not least, Olena. I've often said it's every soldier's God-given right to complain about anything and everything—a habit I've yet to completely shake. From start to finish, she has been there through it all: listening patiently, shutting me up when necessary, and providing an unwavering supply of encouragement. Without her support, I would never have completed this project. In fact, without her suggestion after my first round of edits, this book might never have existed. Amanda had advised cutting the Belize arc, which I resisted like any stubborn first-time author. Olena was the one who said, "Why not turn it into its own novel and release it on December 9th?" That idea became *The Quiet War: Canadian Front*—the book you've just read.

Thank you, Olena, for your love, your support, and that game-changing idea.

ABOUT THE AUTHOR

Michael J. Lalonde is a former Canadian Armed Forces intelligence officer turned military thriller author. Drawing directly from his experience in military intelligence and national security, he brings uncompromising realism to his fiction, blending covert operations, battlefield tactics, and political intrigue. With *The Quiet War*, he has launched a bold new series that puts Canada at the centre of a geopolitical conflict. His work offers a gritty, authentic look at what Canada's elite warriors can do when the stakes are highest. When he's not writing, he can be found scuba diving in the depths of the St. Lawrence River.

Made in United States
North Haven, CT
30 December 2025